DEATH'S LONG SHADOW

DEATH'S LONG SHADOW

Judith Cutler

**SEVERN
HOUSE**

First world edition published in Great Britain and the USA in 2021
by Severn House, an imprint of Canongate Books Ltd,
14 High Street, Edinburgh EH1 1TE.

Trade paperback edition first published in Great Britain and the USA in 2022
by Severn House, an imprint of Canongate Books Ltd.

severnhouse.com

British Library Cataloguing-in-Publication Data
A CIP catalogue record for this title is available from the British Library.

ISBN-13: 978-0-7278-5024-9 (cased)
ISBN-13: 978-1-78029-823-8 (trade paper)
ISBN-13: 978-1-4483-0561-2 (e-book)

All Severn House titles are printed on acid-free paper

MIX
Paper from
responsible sources
FSC
www.fsc.org   FSC® C013056

Typeset by Palimpsest Book Production Ltd.,
Falkirk, Stirlingshire, Scotland.
Printed and bound in Great Britain by
TJ Books, Padstow, Cornwall.

For Keith, with all my love

ACKNOWLEDGEMENTS

For their expertise in vital areas of this book, I have as usual turned to *The Rise and Fall of the Victorian Servant* by Pamela Horn; *Keeping Their Place* by Pamela Sambrook; *The Victorian Kitchen* by Jennifer Davies; *Domestic Life in England* by Norah Lofts. As always I turn to my patient friend John Marshall for ecclesiastical information, mostly imparted over delightful lunches.

ONE

Matthew

'One funeral in this weather and there'll be six mourners dead of pneumonia within the week,' Marty Baines, the innkeeper, observed, sotto voce, huddling into his greatcoat. 'You mark my words.'

'Not if I have anything to do with it,' Dr Page whispered firmly, hunching his shoulders and holding tightly on to his hat. 'And for once even Mr Pounceman seems to be using his common sense.'

The rector, wearing a clerical cloak as if it was an archiepiscopal cope, was indeed rattling through the graveside service as if he was late for an appointment at another great house on the far side of Shropshire. He had, it must be said, a small congregation. This was hardly surprising: before her last illness and slow death, the dowager Lady Croft had been living in seclusion for many months. During her most recent years she had made, it was rumoured, more enemies than friends, even among her social circle, of whom there were notably few present. As for those from the estate and in the village, I suspected that many had presented themselves here not out of love but out of fear of some vague reprisal – and also for the most basic of reasons, that the estate was paying for the winter-weight mourning clothes of those prepared to brave the arctic winds which sliced through their thinner garments. Those who had not attended the service had stopped along the roadside, hatless and heads bowed, as the cortege had wound its way to the church. When they got home, they could all congratulate themselves on having done the decent thing.

I glanced at her only son, a man just turned thirty but not in good health. Was it wise to let his lordship appear at such a public event? Dr Page had dosed him as liberally as he dared to prevent any outbursts; a casual observer might think the young man was simply too grief-stricken to speak. Prompted by Hargreaves, once his valet and now his devoted nurse, he scattered earth on to the coffin. Then, apparently overcome by emotion, he staggered on Dr Page's arm to the waiting carriage, and was returned to Thorncroft House.

In the absence of a close family heir, his lordship's illness precluding marriage, it fell to me as his lordship's land agent, to accept the handshakes of condolence that he would in better times have dealt with. Since I also dealt with everything else concerning the estate and those living and working on it, I had taken it upon myself to invite back to Thorncroft House all those who would expect to receive refreshments there. Many, however, had used the winter weather as a reason to decline, knowing of course that they would not be supporting the grieving son, but merely accepting hospitality from his trustees. We were, after all, not the sort of people with whom most county people, let alone the aristocracy, would wish to mix: lawyers, servants and innkeepers were useful in their place, but their place was not at the top table, one might say. Perhaps Tertius Newcombe, a wealthy farmer, dressing more like a gentleman each day, aspired to it: he was already summoning his own equipage. At last, I ushered the rest of those who wished to attend into the waiting carriages, pulled, as far as possible, by black horses. Our friend Sir Francis Palmer had travelled by railway from his estate near Oxford, having, in fact, brought enough luggage to suggest he might fear being trapped for a long period by the snow which had already delayed his journey. The Family's lawyer, Montgomery Wilson, swiftly engaged him in conversation, thus – possibly coincidentally – taking a place in the first carriage to depart, an honour he extended to Francis' colleague, a very handsome professor of mathematics who gloried in the name of Hudson Fulke-Grosse. They did not seek to accommodate a fourth guest, but bowled off briskly to the House. I saw the remaining mourners into their vehicles and despatched them, till I was left with no one but the rector.

'I hope that you will be joining us too,' I said, as he appeared in two minds about his next move. 'I know the ladies have been making extensive preparations for this gathering, and they would appreciate knowing that you were present in the company.'

Mr Pounceman bowed graciously, taking his place and making room for me. I for one was grateful for the sheepskin rugs which the stable hands had provided, along with hot bricks, even though we had a journey of not much more than a mile. Was he going to disdain comfort? But no one would have seen his self-sacrifice, so he too accepted the warmth on offer.

We had never been – and perhaps would never be – friends or even close allies, but at least these days we maintained a polite front. While his clerical concern for the sick usually confined itself to more affluent parishioners, he had recently condescended to visit the patients in what we in the House still referred to as the Family wing, though these days it was chiefly estate workers and their dependants who occupied the wards it now comprised. These were supervised by Dr Ellis Page and run with considerable efficiency and kindness by a nurse trained by Miss Nightingale herself. One of the patients was the former butler, Samuel Bowman. He had suffered a terrible injury in the autumn, and though the outward signs of damage had now almost disappeared, his memory had become intermittent, and at times he suffered such distressing headaches that he had to be tended like the child I feared he was fast becoming. On good days, however, it gave him great pleasure to return to his old room and polish the family silver, giving the younger servants orders they humoured him by obeying, ostensibly at least. He often shared the servants' midday meal, but rarely joined the senior staff in the Room for dinner, preferring to return to the Family wing and the comfort of his bed there.

One of us had better break the silence. 'It is a great shame that Mr Bowman was unable to attend the funeral,' I observed. 'The last of her loyal retainers, having served her even before my wife became her housekeeper. And a shame too that custom doesn't allow women to be mourners – Harriet would have liked to say her farewells.'

'Can you imagine one of the weaker sex at a graveside?

No, Rowsley, a lady's constitution is not designed for such events.' Before I could object that my dear Harriet was as capable of controlling her emotions as most men, Pounceman leaned forward. 'I must say that Mrs Rowsley's position is very awkward. A housekeeper is directly employed by the lady of the house, is she not? Does it mean that as Lady Croft has died, your wife no longer has a post?'

It was a situation that had given rise to some discussions – I do not like to use the word *arguments* – between us. But these were private matters so I did not answer directly. 'Can you imagine a place like Thorncroft House without a house-keeper as loyal as Harriet? Even though our last attempt to find his lordship's heir was unsuccessful, the House and indeed the entire estate must be maintained, must it not, to the very highest standard. It is my dear wife and her team of house-maids who are the first to notice and report items and fabric in need of repair – indeed, it was one of the youngest maids who noticed the crack in one of the Elizabethan chimneys! Imagine if it had widened and the whole structure collapsed in last week's gales!'

'Ah! I had observed the scaffolding. Dear me, Rowsley, I must admit that when I see men toiling so high I give thanks that I do not have to be one of them!'

'As do I!' We shared a brief laugh; rarely had I heard him make such a revelation.

'But to return to Mrs Rowsley's position – surely you would prefer it if your wife did not have to work – it is scarcely fitting for a man in your position.'

I noticed that he did not use the word *gentleman*.

'Which should take precedence? Her duty or social conven-tion?' I asked. *Or,* I might have added, *her inclination.* I could hardly tell him it was none of his business – as one of the trustees he would be consulted on the issue at the meeting that Mr Wilson had convened for the morrow. 'Dear me, I believe that is a snowflake – the first of many, I fear.'

However much they might or might not be grieving, Harriet and the housemaids had burnished and polished every public part of the House as if half the peers of the realm were expected to be paying their respects. I was sure that Bea Arden and her team in the kitchen would have been making equally impressive preparations – though probably on a more cautious scale. After all, a treatment of beeswax and elbow grease would last for months, but the funeral baked meats would not keep for long – unless, as Harriet pointed out, an o'er hasty wedding could be arranged for someone. I feared that even more food would be left over than she anticipated: only twenty-five mourners were accepting sherry in the huge state drawing room, a room I had never known to be used in the year I had worked here. Their voices, apparently honed on the hunting field, swelled to fill it, however; not a single gentleman seemed to be speaking quietly, although they were in a house in mourning. It was as if they were relieved to be freed from the polite conventions that having their ladies with them would impose. The footmen behaved as if the raucous gathering was an everyday occurrence, discreetly refilling an empty glass here, adjusting a seat there. Their usual rather garish red and gold livery had not been simply muted with black bands but entirely replaced with black coats and grey waistcoats. Dick Thatcher, who still styled himself as the acting butler, even though it was clear that his promotion was permanent, had taken, as he put it, the liberty of suggesting a style more in keeping with his own dark suit, though with frogging and a smattering of silver buttons. The maids were now all in black, of course, but Harriet had insisted the mourning warehouse supplied styles a young woman might be pleased to wear, as fashionable as anything in the latest ladies' magazines. She had also dispensed with the deeply unflattering caps her ladyship had insisted on, replacing them with kinder designs. Their aprons, too, were prettier, to be replaced with sensible pinafores when dirtier tasks were involved. Some might say she was usurping the role of lady of the House. Perhaps she was. But she was also ensuring that the staff were as happy as they could be with their strange life while the House was in limbo.

For all that the household depended on her, however, she would not appear till the last guest had gone. Could not, as a woman or as an employee. I looked at and listened to the men about me. How must it be for her when some idiot who knew nothing brayed his foolish opinions to the world because he was a baronet's son and went to Eton and must therefore know everything? Even I had to button my lip and bow as I burned to correct him.

Montgomery Wilson appeared beside me. 'This is a most curious situation, is it not? Normally I would expect the Family to gather for the reading of the Will. But we have no Family! I do however feel that the contents should be disclosed in a fairly formal way. What would be your advice, Matthew?'

'We have the trustees' meeting tomorrow. Would not that be an appropriate opportunity?'

He pursed his lips. 'Perhaps I should reveal its contents to you and Harriet first. No, let us do this as you suggest. At the trustees' meeting.'

Was it his tone or his words that worried me? 'But there is something else I wish to discuss with you – in absolute private. Perhaps in your office?'

'If it involves the House, then Harriet must be present too.'

He raised an eyebrow, but then nodded. 'As soon as the last mourner has departed then. In total confidence. Perhaps you should not arrive together. Could you simply despatch a note – a sealed note?'

I bowed my acquiescence. Montgomery Wilson was a man for games, and it was simpler to indulge him.

It was almost impossible for a woman wearing even a bombazine skirt over a layer of petticoats to go anywhere in complete silence, but Harriet slipped into my office like a black ghost, curtsying to Wilson before she took a seat. Her eyes asked questions that did not reach her lips.

For once, Wilson's preamble was brief. 'I am the first to confess that when we admitted Mr Timpson, "the putative heir",' he added, with a smile at Harriet, who had coined the phrase, 'I did not check his bona fides adequately. I have no doubt that our more extensive enquiries will flush out others falsely claiming to be Lord Croft's heir. To offer them accommodation here is natural – but it comes with risks, since there are so few people, servants or even fellow visitors, to keep an eye on them. You, Matthew, have duties that take you away from the building – and your position, assuming you continue as housekeeper, Harriet, carries too many domestic responsibilities for you to be able to prowl round the House in the hope of catching someone red-handed.'

'"Assuming you continue"? Forgive me if I interrupt, Mr Wilson, but is there doubt about my role here?'

'Only in that you formerly answered directly to her ladyship. In theory, at least. Personally, I would imagine the authority would now transfer smoothly to the trustees – but of course, you might not wish this. You might not even wish to remain in your post.' He shot an unreadable look at me, not her.

Her bow was as inscrutable as his glance. She made a tiny gesture, as if inviting him to continue, which accordingly he did. 'What I would like to do is introduce more servants to be my eyes and ears, to keep an eye on any and every guest.'

I believe Harriet and I sighed simultaneously. 'The man you recommended at Christmas only lasted five minutes,' she said flatly. 'He really did not like it here – too quiet all round, he said. And of course, he had no one to watch. We had no visitors at all.'

He swallowed. 'Do you think he might have watched anyone else? His fellow members of staff?'

'Perhaps one. But you will understand that I will make no vague insinuations.'

'Of course. And I honour you for it. However, now there are people here like Sir Francis' professor friend. And you mentioned calling in other experts to assess the House's contents. There is much here to tempt such a man. Do I have your agreement in principle at least to repeat the experiment?'

I looked at Harriet; this was more her area than mine.

'Of course. But as I said before, a man would be able to watch on only half the House. One of these experts might bring a wife, so I think a detecting maidservant would be useful. A maid has access to places a footman would have no reason, no pretext, to go. I would suggest that if we repeat the experiment I am seen to interview them – in the case of the manservant, with the butler. So they will need convincing experience and have the right demeanour, which Perkins assuredly did not. And any footman must be tall and presentable. That is de rigueur.'

He gave his rare smile. 'I had not thought of that. Thank you.' He closed his file. As far as he was concerned, the meeting was over.

Harriet smiled too. 'You will forgive me asking, Mr Wilson, but the staff are wondering when the Will is to be read. For all her late eccentricities, her ladyship could be generous to those who saw to her needs.'

He bridled. 'And what might they be expecting?'

'Small legacies, perhaps. Keepsakes. Mourning rings. Their expectations are not high, but when you have very little, anything extra is welcome. Think of her coachman, for instance. Out in all weathers, subject to all her whims. I would go so far as to suggest that if people like him are left nothing, then the trustees should offer some . . . some kindness.'

He bowed. 'All will be revealed tomorrow, at the trustees' meeting.'

And with that we had to be content.

TWO

Harriet

'So,' Matthew was saying, scrabbling on the bedchamber floor for the collar stud he had dropped, 'we have to wait till tomorrow to hear something I felt we should learn today.'

I spread my hands. 'Why on earth should he waft those hints before our noses – my role here! – and then change his mind? Mr Wilson is a reasonable man – but this does not feel reasonable at all. But then,' I reflected, 'he likes to make mischief, does he not? Think of the way he introduced us all to the man he believed was his lordship's heir. And think, too, of his dealings with Bea. Is he malicious or simply unable to imagine the full effect on others of what he does?'

'I like to think he genuinely changed his mind today. My love, this damned thing seems to have a mind of its own . . .'

I took the offending stud and dealt with it, though not deftly. Sometimes I wondered why simple matters such as getting dressed should involve so much effort.

He asked, twisting and making my task harder, 'What do you really think of this notion of more spies in our midst?'

'I wish that they were in place now, to be honest. And doing some work, proper work, while they are detecting. But they would have to be good at it, as well as being good spies.'

'You don't think the servants suspected something was amiss with Perkins?'

'Possibly. Which is why his successors must be my choice.'

'And not just Wilson's.' Tetchily he tweaked one of the ribbons on my cap. 'Black. Some sort of mourning for a whole year. And your skin and your hair and your eyes cry out for blues and greens.' He kissed me. 'Promise me you'll start to wear grey and lavender the very instant etiquette permits!'

'Most respectable housekeepers stick to black the whole

time, on the basis that they ought probably to be in mourning for someone or other!' I observed. But most, for all they styled themselves as 'Mrs', were single women without a loving and much loved husband to please.

He grinned. 'Now, imagine if Lady Croft has decided to sell the House over his lordship's head and give the proceeds to a home for fallen women. We could be free!'

'Could we? No house in the grounds? No income? You really want that sort of freedom?'

'There are other great houses, my love. And I hear of a duke in Derbyshire who would pay a hundred guineas a year more than this estate pays.'

As he dealt with the myriad buttons on the back of my gown, silk for evening, I reflected on the Will. All I could do was pray that its contents would not deepen the tiny shadow of disagreement between us. Though he did not openly say so, I sensed that Matthew would have liked me to leave the House to become his full-time wife, retreating to our own home and doing whatever ladies of leisure did. I would be a copy of all his friends' wives. But much as I loved the idea of living in the delightful house that came with his post, I did not know what I could do there. I could do none of the things with which polite ladies occupied their time. I was not brought up to have accomplishments. I could not sing or play the piano. I had never held a paintbrush in all my life, or a pencil except to write notes. My needle had never been used to sew for decoration but only for practical use – and even Matthew might admit there was a limit on the number of shirts he could use. Yes, I loved to read: books had been my passion, my lifeline in harder times, and I was never happier than when we read aloud to each other or, with Francis and Mr Timpson in residence, acted roles in Shakespeare. Oh, how I would have loved to be an actress, giving voice to those wonderful words! But that was even further than my current employment from Matthew's tacit ambitions for me.

Of course, I could do charitable work amongst the villagers, as I did already. But my budget would be considerably less: Matthew's income was beyond my imagination, but not as great as that at my disposal as her ladyship's representative.

Once the school in Stammerton had been built and was full of ragged children, I could swan in and hear them chorus their reading – but how much more wonderful to see one of the young household staff smiling at the revelation that those black shapes represented the sounds they used every day. I felt like a Mother Goose that had seen its goslings take triumphantly to the water.

Matthew kissed the back of my neck. 'Whatever you wear, you are always beautiful.' He turned me round, pulling me into his arms. 'And whatever the wretched Will contains, nothing will change us. We are one, are we not?'

'We are indeed.' I kissed him, but eventually pulled away with an ironic smile. 'And as one we must act as hosts again. It has been a long day for everyone: I know Bea and her team were hard at work before it was truly light.'

'Really? Then I hope no one will want to linger over the meal. Will she manage to re-use all the leftover food?'

'If she does, we will never recognize it.'

We had been in the drawing room only two minutes when our new guest, Professor Fulke-Grosse, was announced. He had arrived with his valet, as had Francis, who had brought Parker on this occasion. Francis, of course, knew that our staff numbers were declining and it would be hard to find anyone with time to spare to dedicate themselves almost exclusively to a single guest. Ambitious young footmen wanted posts where they would be noticed by potential employers with deeper pockets – and at the very least would be supplementing their incomes with tips from visitors. So perhaps he had warned his friend to bring his own man, Hodge, too. Their presence might enrich the servants' hall but it also reminded the remaining men and women that there was a world out there ready to welcome them.

Professor Fulke-Grosse was not an artist himself, Francis stressed, but an authority on art. He had apparently been inspired by his study of Leonardo's scientific work on proportion to explore Renaissance art as a whole, and then spread his scope even wider. Thus he would be able to advise us on the value of some of the many paintings in the House, only

a small proportion of which were on display. In the two days
he had been here he had already declared himself quite horrified that so many were stored in the attics, subject to changes
of temperature and humidity. They must, he declared, be
removed to a better place immediately. Perhaps Oxford
academics did not have to trouble themselves over the logistics
of such a manoeuvre, or the cost of the galleries he wanted
created and heated.

Now, having accepted sherry from Thatcher, he did not sit
down, but sauntered over to a portrait of a long-dead and
never beautiful Lady Croft. Producing a lorgnette, which he
held with his little finger uncomfortably but elegantly extended,
he shuddered as he gazed.

'Are all the family as ugly as this?' he asked.

'Surely Lely always painted his women with long noses and
double chins!' Matthew laughed. 'So there must be ugly families
across the land.'

'And on the throne! Heavens, our own dear queen is hardly
an example of feminine pulchritude. And although she considers
Albert to be beautiful, there cannot be many in the country
who share her perception. Indeed, last time I saw him I thought
he looked positively liverish. No, no! I must say no more lest
I be accused of lèse-majesté! The sad thing is that their children
seem to have acquired the worst of both parents' features, not
the best.'

I hardly knew how to deal with such forthright comments.
I could see that Matthew was struggling too, but in his case
not to laugh. Fortunately at that point Francis was announced,
smiling at Thatcher as he took a glass.

'Dear me, Hudson! You will have our friends wondering if
you plan to erect a guillotine over here for our aristocracy!'

'Only for the ugly ones, I assure you!' Looking in the mirror
over the fireplace, Mr Fulke-Grosse smoothed his own thick
fair hair away from his forehead. I suspected he spent a lot of
time before mirrors checking for imperfections. He would have
found none in his dress this evening, though he dashed away
an invisible mote of dust from his beautifully cut smoking
jacket. Perhaps he was disappointed by the comparative informality of all the gentlemen wearing smoking jackets; he would

have looked very fine indeed in evening wear. Clearly he knew
he looked good as he was; like us, he was wearing black, which
we would all wear for at least three months. But the subtle
silver embroidery quite denied any notion of mourning. In
everyday wear, he must be a real peacock.

Thatcher, as deadpan as could be after overhearing the
professor's comment, offered sherry to our next arrival.

Mr Wilson showed less discretion, catching my eye and
raising an ironic eyebrow as he kissed my hand. He spoke as
if we had not met earlier. 'Might I ask you, Mrs Rowsley, to
congratulate all who were involved in this afternoon's events?
I do believe, my dear lady, that the trustees should authorize
a small vail for them all, visible and invisible.' Only Mr Wilson
would use such an old-fashioned term for a tip. 'Would you
and Thatcher take responsibility for distributing it?' He took
the glass that the young man proffered.

Thatcher bowed deeply but silently. Dear Samuel Bowman
was not a man for effusive thanks, and neither would his protégé
be. After a moment, however, and perhaps prompted by a tiny
nod from me, he said, 'The servants were all pleased to mark
her ladyship's passing as she would have wanted it, Mr Wilson.
But they will be grateful for your kind words and for your
generosity.' Another deep bow. He stepped back, almost
cannoning into Mr Timpson, whom he accordingly announced.

Mr Fulke-Grosse turned with animation. 'Ah! My dear
fellow, where have you been hiding yourself? It is to you, after
all, that I owe my invitation here!'

Mr Timpson, who had a face that might have been designed
to express modesty, shook his head. 'Hardly, sir. I merely
observed to the trustees that there was so much in the House
that merited an expert's eye, books and documents particularly.
I am no more than a clerk, sir – and it is as a clerk that I have
been working since your arrival.'

Matthew nodded. 'He worked extraordinary hours to make
sure the funeral went well. Thank you, Timpson.'

It was not quite true that Mr Timpson was no more than
a clerk. He was a clerk who had masqueraded as the family
heir. But now, as Matthew observed, he was doing invaluable
work as his secretary, and as such would remain with us until

he found another post. It was true that a comparatively lowly employee was not a traditional dinner guest, and he had chosen to eat at his desk since Francis and the professor's arrival. But where else might he fit in? Not in the servants' hall, where he was still regarded with suspicion. And there was no governess, no tutor, who might be his equal in social standing.

I was pleased to see that after his frank admission, Mr Timpson forgot all about his status, and was expatiating at some length about the manuscripts he had uncovered in the attics during his free time. Although it was hard to catalogue items which he could hardly decipher, let alone translate, he had set up what her ladyship would probably have called a muniment room, in fact a sub-library, adjoining the library itself.

'One of the men I worked with when I had the honour of being one of Mr Brunel's employees put me in touch with a professor at Cambridge,' Mr Timpson was saying. 'He and I have been in correspondence ever since. He was kind enough to tell me how vellum pages and scrolls were best stored, and Mr Rowsley and the trustees have enabled me to act on his advice.'

It was good to see him so animated. I hoped that Francis had said nothing of how he had come into the household; certainly the peacock professor was absorbed by every word he uttered, even though he tutted in disapproval at the mention of Cambridge, as if it was clearly a lesser institution.

Mr Wilson slipped across to sit next to me, but the arrival of Bea brought him to his feet again. They exchanged polite greetings, neither betraying any suggestion of the emotions that might arise after a failed proposal of marriage. Bea's arrival was a tacit declaration that all was well in the kitchen and I expected Thatcher to announce that dinner was served. However, she shook her head minutely, leaning towards me.

'Harriet, Dr Page has arrived to check that his lordship suffered no ill-effects this afternoon. We are a strange number at table – would it be appropriate to invite him to join us?'

It was, of course, but I suspected she had an ulterior motive – not one I disapproved of, as it happened. I nodded, looking up to catch Thatcher's eye. 'If Dr Page accepts our invitation, show him down here and have another place laid. Bea and I at either end of the table, and the gentlemen can sort themselves out!' We exchanged a smile; I should imagine the servants' hall was abuzz with speculation on how soon the good doctor would declare himself. He bowed, and made a silent exit.

THREE

Matthew

The party broke up early, soon after nine, Ellis Page declaring that if he lingered after the dessert he would never get back home through the still heavy snow. No one else had such a problem, of course, but once Bea had been caught out stifling an understandable yawn, the rest of the party braved the icy corridors safe in the knowledge that the staff had kept the fires going in each of their chambers. I ventured to suggest to Timpson and Francis, whom I knew best, that since they were strong and healthy they might for the rest of the evening keep the grates topped up with coal themselves; all the servants had been heavily engaged for the last few days and were entitled to their rest too. The other men offered to do the same, Fulke-Grosse with some fastidious reluctance. Perhaps Thatcher felt he should protest; instead he would convey the good news to the servants' hall.

'You were right: if Bea used any of the funeral baked meats for dinner tonight, I for one could not detect them,' I said, suiting my deed to my earlier words as I made up the fire in our bedchamber.

Harriet smiled. 'I would have been amazed if you had. She really is wasted here, you know, and could walk into another position tomorrow.' She looked at me sideways. 'Why do you think she stays?'

'To see if she can bring Ellis Page up to scratch?'

'You put it so elegantly! They would make an ideal couple.'

'Of course they would. But I am not sure that Page is looking for a wife, any more than Francis is.'

'But Ellis is a widower, not a confirmed bachelor. And gives every appearance of enjoying Bea's company.' She bit her lip. 'Perhaps because he always leaves here warm and dry and well-fed,' she added ruefully.

'Cupboard love? All the more reason to marry her!'

She pondered. 'It's not unknown for a gentleman to marry his cook, is it – but to marry someone else's cook? Would he do that?'

'I married someone else's housekeeper,' I pointed out. 'The most exceptional woman . . .'

Our long embrace was interrupted by a loud pealing.

'The front door? At this time of night?' She pulled away. 'My love, we must continue this – discussion – later, must we not?' She turned, straightening her hair, so that I could fasten her dress. I threw a shawl over her shoulders to conceal the inadequacy of my rebuttoning efforts. There! But for her heightened colour and the brilliancy of her eyes, she was transformed into the calm professional that everyone but me assumed was all she ever was.

'Wait – I will come with you!'

'My love, that is Thatcher's job.' One more kiss and she was gone.

Thatcher's job it might be, but what man would let his wife roam a building the size of this on the mere assumption that Thatcher was not only awake but ready to deal with whatever was going on?

I had forgotten, of course, that Thatcher and Luke, his deputy, had been trained by the formidable combination of Harriet and Samuel Bowman. She might have been in the entrance hall first, but they were only a few yards behind. As I came down the staircase, they glanced at each other and at her. Then Luke opened the door. He staggered back, driven by the wind, the snow piled up against it and a female figure who collapsed at Harriet's feet.

As Harriet helped her up, Thatcher and Luke ran outside. I took the last flight of stairs two at a time, and ran after them. I was in time to help them lift a motionless figure, heavy under the weight of snow plastered over his coat, from the steps. He seemed to have fallen from the rear of the coach. Struggling to hold him was another woman. Somehow we got both of them inside.

Then Luke dashed out again. He was scrabbling up beside the coachman, pointing to our stables. Soon the equipage was on its ponderous way. Thank God Luke had the sense to slide back down and fight his way back up the steps.

I seized his arm. There. Safe. Between us we shut the door. More footmen were running towards us.

Harriet turned away from the women. 'Job, Henry – help Mr Thatcher carry this poor man straight to the Family wing, and summon Nurse Webb. Of course strip his coat from him if it makes it easier to carry him. Just leave it there. Go. Now!'

From somewhere the woman – little more than a girl – who had been trying to lift him found enough energy to haul herself up and stagger after them, ignoring her mistress's calls.

Harriet was not one to ignore. 'Luke. You're already cold and wet – find a coat and go and rouse John Coachman. Put him in charge of the vehicle and horses, because her coachman must be brought straight into the House: he must be half dead too. Put a greatcoat on! Remember! And make sure everyone else does too before they try and unload the carriage!' She smiled. 'And then go and change every stitch of your clothing before you do anything else. Good lad.'

He sped off.

I gathered up the discarded livery myself, my mourning garb making me almost indistinguishable from the menservants, one of whom was quick to relieve me of it. I was happy to remain anonymous – my wife needed to give all her attention to the matter in hand, which must now be to soothe a clearly distressed guest who was dabbing her eyes with a lace handkerchief. At least she managed, in response to Harriet's repeated question, to reveal that she was Lady Stanton.

Harriet bobbed a curtsy, saying, with a smile, 'Your ladyship, welcome to Thorncroft House. We will do everything we can for your servants. But you too must be in need of rest and refreshment. May I suggest you adjourn to a warm room? Meg – her ladyship's cloak, please. And her bonnet!' They were carefully removed, and taken away to dry – not that much snow had fallen on them.

Her ladyship turned as if by instinct to one of the Venetian mirrors gracing the hall and smoothed her golden hair. I suspect she caught me watching her – she gave an extra twirl to one of the ringlets, lifting her hand almost flirtatiously, even at such a time. All this in front of a man she must have believed was a servant!

Was that what prompted a quick but quiet order from Harriet? 'Thomas: will you mend the fire in the yellow drawing room? I will escort her ladyship there. Grace – her ladyship will need accommodation, as will her ladyship's maid, of course.'

The servants moved quietly and easily about their tasks.

'I am Mrs Rowsley, the housekeeper, your ladyship.' Harriet curtsied again. 'You will notice that the House is in mourning, your ladyship. Perhaps you are unaware that Lady Croft was interred this afternoon.'

Refraining from any comment at all, Lady Stanton smiled graciously and indicated that Harriet was to lead the way. I suspect she flicked a glance at me over her shoulder, but at this point I turned to Thatcher as he returned to the hall. 'Frozen nigh to death, Nurse Webb says, the poor bastard,' he said grimly. 'But she fears, sir, that the weather's too bad to send for Dr Page.'

'Thank you, Dick. I'll discuss that with her myself. Meanwhile, I fancy you are needed in the yellow drawing room.' I wished I might be there too to support Harriet. But how could I appear without upsetting the balance between servant and hostess she was trying to strike? She and her protégés must do their jobs, while I must do one new to me. Run errands.

'You are bathing him!' I said incredulously, staring at the hip bath in front of a roaring fire. Kettles sang on the hob.

'I couldn't think of another way to warm him up,' Nurse Webb admitted. 'We keep raising the temperature of the water, just a little at a time. I don't know what else to do. And I honestly don't think even Dr Page could do more. And to send for him would be to risk the messenger's life and the good doctor's.'

My voice was very solemn. 'Do you want me to try to reach him?'

'Heavens, no, sir! You're no longer young, and the estate needs you too much. You and Mrs Rowsley. And I can't imagine she could live if she lost you.'

I might argue that I was not yet forty, but could not dispute her other points.

'No,' she continued, 'if anyone goes, it must be a big, tough lump of a lad.' She bent to take the young man's wrist. 'Thank God! I fancy his pulse might be stronger. What was the woman doing, letting him stay outside the coach like that? Heavens, could she not have had her coachman pull over at an inn – any inn! – to take shelter? Even an ordinary private house, for goodness' sake!'

'I fancy our guest might have standards she wishes to maintain,' I said dryly. 'There was a servant in hysterics,' I added. 'Where is she?'

'Poor child, she was in no state to help as she wished. Not that it would have accorded with my notions of decency. One of my nurses is with her in the women's ward.'

'Good.'

She had no more time for me. 'Hurry up with that kettle!'

Down in the kitchen, all the staff were up and dressed going efficiently about tasks I did not even know about, the well-trained team that they were. A stranger, the coachman presumably, was sitting before the fire, swathed in blankets under which he sported a vivid dressing gown long since discarded by his lordship. Someone was pouring hot water into a footbath which smelt strongly of mustard.

'Get him up to the care of Nurse Webb!' I snapped at two footmen. 'Heavens, I wish we could ask Ellis Page to come – but Nurse Webb doesn't want anyone risking their neck to fetch him. Or, of course, Dr Page risking his own neck.'

Her face unguarded for a second, Bea said quietly, fervently, 'I hope he got home safely.' She straightened her shoulders. 'Who is this Lady Stanton, whoever she is when she's at home? And is it just her and the three servants?'

'I presume so.'

She shot a look at me. 'You've not been there helping?'

'Would it be help or interference? Ah! Luke! Warm and

dry, I hope?' We exchanged a smile. 'Good lad. A bad business this, Luke. Have you any idea what's been going on?'

'No more than you, I'd say, sir. John Coachman and a couple of stable lads are seeing to the horses. Oh, and they've unloaded the luggage. Where shall I get it stowed?'

Bea said, 'Polly's got a fire started in the Japanese chamber; there's room for a truckle bed for her maid there if her mistress insists. Put the luggage in the dressing room.'

I took a moment or two to return to our room to bank up the fire and ensure that I was as presentable as I could be, as his lordship's de facto representative. With as much gravitas as if I had been his lordship in person, Thatcher announced me as I entered the yellow drawing room. On the sofa, her ladyship was as poised a lady of fashion as one might imagine. Perhaps she had been aided by the champagne that Luke had produced and some of Bea's delicate creations to nibble. Harriet, still standing, took a step forward. 'Lady Stanton, may I introduce to you his lordship's estate manager, Mr Rowsley?' A step backward.

Lady Stanton smiled up at me, graciously extending her hand, which I duly kissed. Something told me she recognized me as the man who had watched her preen before the mirror. Why had Harriet not introduced me as her husband?

'May I add my voice to the welcome you have already received from my wife, your ladyship?' I smiled swiftly at Harriet. 'I am sure that if there is anything else you need, we will do our best to provide it.' Of course, Harriet would already have said all these things – why was I echoing them? 'Have you travelled far?'

'Too far!' she laughed. 'And now I fear I am dropping with fatigue, though the champagne has done much to revive me.'

Thatcher took the hint, topping up her glass. He looked enquiringly at Harriet, though he must have known that she would touch nothing while she was on duty.

'And tomorrow I am to travel again,' she added, when she had taken a sip she managed to make almost flirtatious. She smiled at me, indicating I should sit beside her.

Like Harriet, I remained standing. 'Tomorrow? Your

ladyship, I'm afraid my colleagues report that the roads now are completely impassable.'

She put her hands to her face in what seemed genuine dismay. 'But I am to travel to Chester.'

'I think it unlikely, ma'am.'

'I have taken the liberty of having a room prepared for you, ma'am,' Harriet said.

'Good. Send my maid up, will you?' Then she turned to me, holding out her hand. Clearly I was expected to escort her.

I caught Thatcher's eye. 'The Japanese room, I understand, Thatcher. Meanwhile, ma'am, I am afraid your maid is unwell. Do you care to visit her?'

'The poor girl's probably asleep already. I will see her in the morning. Oh – the driver and groom. They must have got cold. How are they?'

'In a worse state than your maid, ma'am, I'm afraid.'

'They are all in the hands of our very capable head nurse,' Harriet assured her. 'Meanwhile, Florrie, a very able young woman once the late Lady Croft's maid, will be waiting in your room to assist you.'

She earned a charming but oddly dismissive smile, as again Lady Stanton held out her hand to me.

I withdrew to Harriet's side. As one, we bowed.

We went up to the Family wing together, to find Nurse Webb still with her patient. He was now propped up in bed, in a room as hot as a succession house. But he was still breathing.

'So far, so good,' she said, mopping her brow and pushing back tendrils of hair sticking to it. 'I fear he will succumb to inflammation of the lungs, of course – but perhaps tomorrow Dr Page will be able to reach us, by sleigh if not by trap. I will sit with him for another hour, and then Mr Martin, the orderly, will take over. You did well to have the poor coachman brought up. He is now in there.' She nodded towards the adjoining ward. 'He is not as ill as Davies here, but I wanted to keep an eye on him. Nurse Richards is putting Olwen, the lady's maid, to bed in the women's ward, to sleep off the laudanum drops we had to give her.'

'Has any of them been well enough to say where they had

come from? Or anything about Lady Stanton? I don't ask to gossip,' Harriet assured her, 'but we simply know nothing about our guests. Absolutely nothing.' She gave a warm if apologetic smile. 'I presume she comes from the sort of circles in which your family moved.'

The other woman smiled in return. 'She might well do. But she wouldn't have numbered an eccentric blue-stocking like me among her friends. How strange, though, simply to turn up out of the blue. I'll keep my eyes and ears open.'

'Thank you.'

She gave a weary smile, but her face became deadly serious. 'What of the villagers, Mrs Rowsley? How will they manage?'

'The farmers have a well-tried system, from Mr Newcombe to the meanest smallholder,' Harriet said. 'The draught horses pull snowploughs. And the labourers go out in teams to dig out every cottage. At last this year we are lucky enough to have you and your colleagues to nurse those in need. You will be very busy, I fear. But we will do all in our power to help you.'

'One last visit to the servants' hall?' I asked as we left the hospital area.

'Bea will have seen to everything – but yes, if anyone is still around, we must send them to bed.'

It was after midnight when we adjourned to our room, warm from the fire, mercifully still alight. I added more coal from the scuttle someone had refilled – without having been asked, of course, just as someone would have refilled all the other coal scuttles. Someone – the most junior tweeny, possibly young Mary – would be getting up at five in the morning so that she could clean out grates and start new fires. Another would boil kettles, so we could all have hot water when we, in our now warm rooms, got up. Out there, under the snow, other families would sleep huddled together for warmth. Some would die. And without Harriet's intervention – handing out food, fuel and blankets to everyone who needed them – more would have suffered. Her charity: yet another thing tying her to the House.

I said as much to Harriet, kissing her neck as I started to undo all those buttons.

I felt, as well as heard, her deep sigh.

At last she spoke, turning to face me, her face troubled. 'Whatever we gave to Stammerton wasn't enough, was it? Even when the new model village is built and they are safe inside their new cottages, there won't be quite enough. And still people like Lady Stanton's coachman and groom will . . .' She spread her hands. Then her voice changed. 'It seems a strange thing to do, doesn't it, to set out in such cold weather. And heavens, why did she not take a train? Not that the railways won't be disrupted too, of course.'

'It rather depends where she was coming from!'

'Of course . . . Davies, Olwen . . . They sound like Welsh names, don't they? Not so many railways in Wales. Not that her accent is Welsh – it's pure aristocratic English, isn't it? But to press on in such appalling conditions – why on earth would any sensible person take such a risk?'

'Is she the sort of person you can ask?'

She wrinkled her nose. 'I don't think *I* can. I tried a couple of times and got firmly put in my place for my pains.'

I nodded. 'And she was delightfully evasive when I asked. She seemed concerned for her maid, didn't she? But not enough to go and see her . . .'

'Well, perhaps so late at night . . . I hope she will tomorrow. Today! Even her late ladyship – before her illness made her too weak – always visited even a scullery maid if she was ill. Meanwhile, I hope Lady Stanton behaves well to Florrie. You could ask. She definitely seemed taken with you!'

Alarmed by the unease in her voice, I said, with absolute truth, 'There is only one beautiful woman in the world for me.'

'Ah! So you noticed she was beautiful!' She pouted.

It was late. So I had to stop an argument, serious or not, in the most appropriate way.

FOUR

Harriet

Although Matthew fell asleep almost immediately, my mind became a treadmill of foolish anxiety. Lady Stanton: where had she sprung from and why? All I knew of her was that although she was flirtatious, she was not as young as she appeared to be. I had noticed the lines on her face that must have troubled her as she looked in every mirror available. And secondly, that she wanted to get to Chester. She had given no explanation at all of her reasons for stopping at this precise place – and she must have passed any number of possible places of refuge. At least she might explain herself to someone she perceived as her social equal, so I could ask Francis to cross-question her, his charm matching hers. Yes! But dragging my thoughts away from her, I started to worry about other matters. I reminded myself that the House had dealt with snow before, and had on one occasion survived with a whole houseful of guests and their servants for some three weeks without the guests noticing any shortcomings. Today we had the same provisions to draw on and a mere handful to consume them. The staff were their usual professional selves; they could be proud of the way they had responded to the night's crisis, on top of all the extra work for the funeral.

And then, perhaps inevitably since it was a situation completely new to me, my mind circled back to the problem of Lady Stanton. Trawl through my memory as I might, I could not recall ever having read about her in any of the newspapers and periodicals that came my way. Which meant nothing, of course. But the addition of any lady, whose views on the informality we practised in social matters could not yet be known, might complicate life for us all. She might be charmed by the situation – but equally might expect to be chaperoned. Who might do that? There was also the

considerably more important matter of her sick groom. If
he survived the night, at some point an attempt must be
made to ask Ellis Page to examine and treat him, using one
of the estate's sleighs if necessary, always punctiliously maintained by our John Coachman. If the groom – and her
coachman, of course, now also very ill – did survive, how
long would it be before they might work again? And if they
did not, if they died here in the House, how might she
obtain replacements and go on her way? It wasn't pure self-
ishness that made me wish that all might soon be well. The
presence of extra horses and the coach itself would render
more difficult the half-finished scheme to turn the laundry
into a communal area for villagers whose cottages had no
boilers; they would also benefit when half the stable block
was turned into male and female bathhouses. How would
these families survive?

And how would I survive if it was no longer my job to
worry about them? That was what was really causing my mind
to spin. Technically I was not one of the servants under
Matthew's authority. I had been employed by her ladyship in
person, and was answerable to her. However much Matthew
wanted me to leave service, I now knew quite emphatically
that I did not. And yet that might well be the consequence
of her Will.

What if the trustees could not all get through the snow to
the House to meet? What then? Would Mr Wilson decline
to read the Will? And would any delay make my life better
or worse?

My unease must have reached Matthew. He rolled over and
gathered me in his arms. At least there was one thing not to
worry about, our love for each other.

When the duty maid woke us by knocking on our door, I
was still deeply asleep. Soon she would come back to bring
us our hot water, and to make up the fire. Matthew, already
alert it seemed, threw open the curtains to reveal the strange
light of the snow. He was soon on his knees before the fire
and, satisfied with its progress, was ready to take the hot water
as soon as it was delivered.

'This out-dated system!' he said. 'What a waste of effort! As soon as the thaw comes I shall bring in a team to start plumbing the house. We have the trustees' authority already. What is to stop us?'

'Visitors in the House?' I suggested dryly, making my way to the window. Yes, the snow was still there. It had drifted in the driving wind, leaving patches of the parkland almost bare while others were so thickly covered it was impossible to tell what lay beneath – the familiar hedges, statues, bushes were all invisible.

He came up behind me and kissed my neck. 'If the snow goes, the visitors can go. And those that won't leave will simply have to put up with any noise and mess. Heavens, we have enough rooms for everyone to be moved as far from the activity as necessary.' He waited for me to turn and laugh. 'Harriet, you're usually so ready, indeed eager, for action. What's troubling you? Tell me.'

It was hard to say it out loud. 'One thing is her ladyship's Will.'

'How can the Will possibly worry you?'

'She never seemed the sort of employer who would want to pour posthumous largesse on to a servant's lap – anyone's lap, come to think of it. But that does not mean she would not want her influence felt beyond the grave.' I turned to the window, to lean my brow against the cold glass – selfish, of course, since it would be little Mary's job to clean it later this morning. 'She may leave . . . difficult . . . instructions. And I am afraid – yes, I am, Matthew! – of what will happen to the House if I have to leave. For all her faults, Lady Croft trusted me. You know that. She gave me free rein. I suspect the late Lord Croft might have encouraged her.'

I nodded. Everyone agreed that he was a decent, kind man.

'I can't tell you how much he taught me! Even more than my dear mentors when I was a child. He loved books, Matthew. Loved them.'

'As you do.'

'Even more than I do. I love the contents of books: he loved their very fabric! And you know that I was the only one allowed to dust those in the library. I can see him now: when my work was done he would open the wonderful tomes – a Book of Hours here, a first edition there. And he would show me some magical page. What if someone else who cares not a jot takes responsibility for them?'

'Talk to Wilson – he'd not let that happen. Are you worried about this Fulke-Grosse? Because I am, deep down. In some ways it might have made sense for him to travel with Francis when he came for the funeral, but it seems . . . an intrusion.'

'It does indeed. But he came to be useful and perhaps useful he can be.'

'I remember,' I said slowly, 'how shocked I was when you wouldn't let even Francis inspect those books unless you were there. You won't be handing over the keys to Fulke-Grosse, I take it?'

I shuddered. 'The very thought! But if I have to chaperone Lady Stanton – she may require it! – how can I do my regular work and guard the precious books he needs to see?'

He took my hands and clasped them in his. 'Lady Stanton is a guest, true – but she has her own maid, and if the maid is not well enough to sit with her, it behoves Lady Stanton to sit with her maid, does it not? Oh, I know we were disappointed in her last night, but now she is rested I'm sure she will do her duty, and with luck behave with a little more courtesy. But back to the books: would you feel able to let Francis supervise his colleague?'

I looked him in the eye. 'No, I would not. You, yes. But not Francis and not even John Timpson, though I believe he loves them as much as I do and those early documents far more. If the director of the British Museum himself wants to inspect them, I would still want one of us to be there.'

'And if the British Museum wanted them? On loan?'

'That would be a matter for the trustees, wouldn't it?' I smiled. 'Thank you. I feel better for having said things aloud.'

'So now they can stop chasing each other round your head. Don't tell me they weren't last night! But now,' he said, catching sight of the clock, 'I really must shave!'

And, once dressed, there was something I really had to do myself. I slipped down to the library, feeling uncomfortably furtive, though in fact there was nowhere on earth I felt more comfortable. *Debrett's* was where it should be, of course – an edition some five years old. Now let me find out about our guest. But I had got no further than finding that she was the granddaughter of an admiral ennobled after Trafalgar, now a landowner in Yorkshire, when there was a tap on the door. It was the professor, eager to start work. I closed the book, ready to take it down to Matthew's office.

'Forgive me, dear lady – I interrupt you.'

'And I am afraid I will interrupt you in turn, professor. A new guest arrived last night, and I am asking all you gentlemen to join her at breakfast, which will be served at nine thirty. I will be sending a note to the others, but now you have a face-to-face invitation.' I allowed my dimples to show as I curtsied.

He responded with a courtly bow. 'Which I have the honour of accepting.'

'Thank you. I fear, however,' I lied, 'that I have just discovered indisputable evidence of mice in this most precious of rooms. Imagine if they start eating the leather bindings! So I am forced to ask you to leave. I need to lock up while my colleagues put down poison – and then dispose of the poor corpses. I am so sorry. I realize how much this will inconvenience you.'

He started. 'Lock up! My dear Mrs Rowsley!'

'The poison,' I murmured, pulling a face.

'Ah! Indeed!' And off he scuttled.

My idea was that our guests would not only meet Lady Stanton, but also take it upon themselves to entertain her, so limiting their ability to lurk in different rooms would perhaps encourage them. I had other plans, too. Meanwhile, I had already told Florrie, detailed to wait on Lady Stanton, to try to have her up and dressed, and to escort her downstairs. I would have liked to talk much longer to the girl, but not when her ladyship might be waiting for her services.

That done, I went to check on Lady Stanton's coachman. Although the doors to the Family wing had been guarded for months to prevent his lordship trying – yes – to escape, I still found it strange to have to identify myself, especially as the guards were all former estate workers no longer capable of the hard physical labour they had done all their lives. But for safety's sake, I always obeyed the rule, waiting for them to make a painstaking cross against my name, which, alas, they could not read for themselves. Only then did they talk to me about their families and their health. Sometimes getting in was a long business.

Understandably Nurse Webb looked very tired, but greeted me as always with a smile. 'Our patients live. Lady Stanton's groom, Thomas Davies, and her coachman, William. Despite the laudanum we gave her, Olwen, her maid, woke early this morning, and has glued herself to Thomas's bedside. I don't believe the poor girl has stopped crying. But in my opinion she should rejoin her mistress – it will be good for her to have her mind occupied by something other than Thomas's illness. And, to be frank, she is in the way.' She frowned. 'I really would like Dr Page's advice. Is it possible to send for him now it is light?'

'Not yet. Even if we could get a message to him, he would never be able to get here. But Farmer Twiss will soon be trying to plough a way through the huge drifts. Rest assured, as soon as it's safe I will despatch an outdoor man. Meanwhile, if you have kept both men alive, you must be doing the right thing, surely?'

'I am only a nurse.'

Arms akimbo, I repeated, 'Only a nurse? Our dear Miss Nightingale was only a nurse – but one who knew more about health than all the doctors in the Crimea! Please do not sell yourself short. That Thomas still lives is solely because of your efforts! You are not *only* anything.'

She laughed. 'Is this how you speak to your staff, Mrs Rowsley? Because you will be setting them all on the path to women's equality. You may stare: my father is a friend of Mr Mill, who is already saying openly that men and women should be treated equally.'

My eyes rounded. 'That is Mr John Stuart Mill? Dear me, Miss Webb, I should dearly love to hear you speak of him when we both have time. But now – you have your patients and I have a houseful of quite disparate people to organize.'

Exchanging smiles, we both went about our business.

* * *

Luke appeared with the news that all the guests except her
ladyship were in the breakfast room. I despatched him to
her ladyship's bedchamber to alert Florrie, to have him return
with the information that appear she would not. After the
alarums and excursions of the previous evening she would take
breakfast in bed, where she might well stay all day. If only her
own maid were there. She needed Olwen. Luke conveyed this
information, his face as deadpan as I am sure Florrie's was
when she regaled him with the news.

Though Matthew, John, Bea and I, with our daily work to
do, usually ate before and separately from the gentlemen staying
with us, this morning we had thought it best to join them,
with me supporting Lady Stanton. Even though there were
no introductions to be made, we kept to our plan, helping
ourselves to coffee and cold meat, crumpets and scones.
Eventually, since it was I who had summoned everyone, I
explained why – and why they had put themselves out in
vain.

'I think in the circumstances we might forgive her,' Mr
Wilson said dryly.

'Of course! The poor lady! What a dreadful experience for
her! All alone in that dreadful snow!' Professor Fulke-Grosse
cried. 'Dear me! If only there was something one might do!
Ah! Mrs Rowsley, can you not bid a gardener to find flowers
for her in one of your hothouses?'

It did not seem necessary to tell him that with one exception the hothouses were now reserved for more prosaic uses
such as bringing on seedlings for the vegetable garden. 'I am
afraid, sir, that all our outdoor staff are engaged in more
essential work, like heaving coal and clearing snow. I cannot
ask them to break off. Not,' I added, 'when it is vital that the
drive to the village is cleared – the lives of her ladyship's
groom and coachman hang in the balance and Nurse Webb
is adamant that Dr Page must be summoned.' I forced myself
not so much as to glance at Bea. 'But I will ask Olwen, her
ladyship's maid, to convey our good wishes when she is deemed
well enough to return to her service. In the meantime, Florrie,
one of our senior maids, will do everything she can to make
her comfortable.'

The professor still seemed inclined to flutter in anxiety. 'Surely this doctor must treat the poor lady too!'

But Francis, who had known me longer than anyone present, winked at me. 'You are acquainted with Lady Stanton, Hudson? Is she very beautiful?'

'Every lady is touched by the hand of Beauty,' he declared. 'And we must all want to cherish and protect each one!'

'Of course. Even your washerwoman?' Francis asked, as if on my behalf.

The professor declared, without so much as a blush, that he would lay down his cloak for her to protect her from a puddle. Mr Wilson swallowed his coffee the wrong way.

Sadly the professor would be unlikely to have occasion to extend any of his courtly gestures to Bea and me as we withdrew to implement the House's strategy for dealing with snowfalls like this.

'All this fuss and palaver about this Lady Stanton,' Bea chuntered as we headed down the corridor. 'Flowers in this weather? I don't know how you kept a straight face. Not bothering to get up, indeed . . .'

'Quite. Indeed, Bea, it's never ceased to astound me that gentlemen should be trumped so easily by the Little Lady card.'

FIVE

Matthew

Perhaps, as I came into the House via the servants' entrance, after checking, quite unnecessarily, that Farmer Twiss had everything under control, I expected Harriet and Bea to be wringing their hands and tearing their hair as they faced the prospect of feeding extra mouths with limited supplies. As it was, I found them drinking coffee and laughing.

'Remember to leave your boots outside!' Bea called, over her shoulder. 'I don't want any more snow on my nice clean floors.'

'Of course! And I've hung up my coat too,' I called back. The coffee smelt good so I padded in in my stocking feet.

A mere child of a maid produced another cup and saucer; another plate of biscuits materialized. Then she disappeared up the backstairs. She was back, before I could even stir my coffee, with a pair of my shoes on – of all things – a cushion, which she laid carefully on Bea's clean floor.

If I felt uncomfortably like Cinderella, I had to applaud her initiative. 'But why the cushion, do you think?' I asked softly when she was out of earshot.

'Mary knows footmen put things on silver salvers,' Harriet suggested. 'And she knows silver salvers are not appropriate for shoes. Full marks, I'd say, wouldn't you?'

I smiled. 'Full marks indeed. Now, we are well on the way to having a path cut through the main drive, so young Harry can have another shot at reaching Ellis Page. The track to the station is still completely blocked, and it wouldn't surprise me if the railway line itself is too. All the roads round here are probably in the same state as the drive – half almost clear, half under six-foot drifts. Ten foot in places. How far this stretches I have no idea – just Shropshire? The whole of the country?'

'Whichever it is, we may have our visitors for some time,' Harriet said unenthusiastically. 'All of them. An interesting mix.'

'And probably more patients from the village for Nurse Webb,' Bea added, with something like a note of hope, I suspected.

'But surely you can't take more people in – think of the coal and food!' I said.

They laughed. 'You've not been studying the accounts as thoroughly as you ought,' Harriet said mock-seriously. 'You should have noticed that every winter, we increase our coal stocks, for instance. And our wood. Throughout the year Bea and her team are preserving and drying – me too, when I have the chance. Look in the still room: you will see the shelves of jam and pickles, the cakes sealed in tins. There is flour aplenty. The only things we worry about are fresh eggs, which are always a bit short in the winter anyway, and milk – but Farmer Twiss rarely lets us down. This morning's delivery was a little late, but we have enough for Lady Stanton to bathe in, should the mood take her.'

I glanced at her. 'I know I said she was beautiful, but she's no Cleopatra! Or was that asses' milk? I thought it was very bad form of her, by the way, not coming down for breakfast. A bad day she might have had, but you and your team worked all hours yesterday, Bea – and you managed to get up in time to cook our breakfast.'

Arms akimbo, she demanded, 'Would you have expected me to do otherwise, Matthew?'

'The day you do, the heavens will fall.' I put my arms round both of them. 'Your value is beyond rubies. Thank you. Her ladyship would be so proud of you both.' This comment managed to reduce them both to tears.

It was clearly time to escape to my office.

I had only just reached it when there was a tap on the door. 'Mr Wilson, sir,' Thatcher announced with something of a flourish. In the past he had made a little too much of a habit of waiting around as if to eavesdrop on what were meant to be private conversations, but as butler he was both too grand and too busy, even with only a handful of visitors, to have time. Perhaps he had introduced Luke into the ways of benign espionage, but he was nowhere to be seen. Could he be watching Timpson? When working as my clerk, not as an amateur bibliophile when he was in the muniment room, Timpson had an office next to mine, formerly the gun room as it happens. His lordship's illness had required us to find somewhere more secure and less obvious for any weaponry; Bea locked away the kitchen knives when they were not in use.

Wilson stared at the pile of paperwork on my desk, remarking, with a sympathetic smile, that it resembled his own. 'The more people there are in the House, the more the servants are running round after them, the more chance for anyone to make something disappear. This Fulke-Grosse, for instance, what do you make of him? Not to mention her invisible ladyship.'

'You're the best judge of character I know. I only met Lady Stanton briefly, so I couldn't comment on her.'

'Yes, you could. And I'm sure Harriet could. I would trust her judgement above my own, incidentally.'

'So would I,' I said, ambiguously.

'And?' he prompted me.

'Fashionably dressed. Assured.' I bit my lip. 'I hesitate to say this, but I do believe she was inclined to flirt with me. Harriet behaved like the highly professional housekeeper she is, not attempting to behave with any familiarity. She stood, as far as I know, the whole time Lady Stanton was sitting.'

'As you would expect of her. But was she not invited to be seated?'

'I don't know. She was on her feet when I entered the drawing room. Her ladyship gave me her hand to kiss. She didn't quite answer when I asked where she had come from. We discussed the state of the roads. Then she expected me to escort her to her bedchamber. I delegated the honour to Thatcher. And that is the sum of my acquaintance with her. I don't think her failure to visit her servants, however briefly, endeared her to any of the staff, from Harriet down. Harriet was somewhat put out by her refusal to quit her bed to meet her fellow guests this morning. Remember, though, that Harriet is—'

'Enough, Matthew.' He stood, raising a hand. 'I infer that you are going to explain away Harriet's attitude, which is in fact one which I personally share. I have known your wife for many years, though never well, of course, till his lordship's illness brought us together as his trustees. She was always the quiet woman in the background on whom every member of the household absolutely relied. I have seen her work when other people would have taken to their bed with illness. Equally I heard that she once removed a child's broken tooth before the child realized it had gone, the mother having hysterics the while. I believe she is entitled to have any opinion she likes, with far more basis than most of us have for ours.' He sat down again. 'I trust I have made myself clear?'

No one had spoken to me like that since I was a boy – my headmaster? My father? Either I punched him in the teeth or swallowed my pride and acknowledged I was in the wrong. 'You have indeed, sir.' A deep breath. 'And I thank you for it. I was going to apologize for her and say she should not underestimate a lady's sensibilities. In fact, on reflection, I suspect her ladyship's behaviour would have been considered rude in anyone except a pretty young woman.' We shook hands.

'I'm glad we understand each other, Matthew. I was here to ask you whether you thought we should press on with the trustees' meeting tonight, assuming the road to the village is clear enough for the three from the village to get through. But you will now understand why I think we should ask your wife's opinion too.'

'Of course.' Would her word carry more weight than mine?

'Mrs Arden makes the most wonderful biscuits and her coffee is unsurpassed. And she, of course, is a trustee with a view of her own. Should we adjourn to the kitchen or invite them both here?'

'On this occasion, Wilson, I suspect you would recommend that Mohammed should offer to go to the mountain. And it will be warmer in the kitchen, will it not?'

As we walked along the corridor, which was of course as cold as all the other corridors, he said, 'Are you forced to ration coal?'

'Wilson, this is a staff corridor. A servants' corridor. And I am sure that Mr Darwin might one day discover that servants are biologically inured to temperatures that would make their employers suffer. In their dormitories and bedchambers too. But for once Harriet might not listen to the great man. Recalling that at more than one establishment she used to have to break the ice on the water with which she was supposed to wash, she sees to it that here the servants' rooms have fires. One of the footmen patrols the nearby corridors to ensure that the fires stay in their grates: we want warmth, not stray sparks setting fire to the place.'

The coffee was as excellent as the biscuits, and the fire in the Room was bright. Like Bea's sitting room, it had just been redecorated and refurbished, with new curtains and a carpet retrieved from an unoccupied upper room. Harriet had even replaced the dismal foxed prints with brighter paintings, also from unoccupied rooms. The two viciously uncomfortable armchairs had found a home on a bonfire, but the dining chairs had simply been re-upholstered and the table repolished. It was a room to be proud of, if now more an office than a parlour. Traditionally Harriet had hosted Bea and the other senior servants for supper each night; I had been happy to join them. But things had changed when Samuel Bowman, the butler, was taken ill. Thatcher took his place quite admirably, but when he himself had been unwell, it was clear that Luke was uncomfortable with being singled out from his fellows. Then there was the issue of Wilson and Sir Francis. They welcomed our company, Bea's too, so dinner for the upper servants in the Room was almost a thing of the past.

A certain rivalry had developed between Sir Francis and Wilson, the latter offering Bea marriage, but Sir Francis merely wanting her services in his kitchen. The company had also included John Timpson when he appeared to be his lordship's heir. To their credit, they still treated him like an equal. The arrival of the professor and now Lady Stanton would complicate things once more. Should all the guests dine together, without the benefit of a hostess to support her ladyship? Or should we continue with our informal gatherings mixing above and below stairs?

I did what Wilson – always Wilson, never his first name, perhaps because it was so polysyllabic – would probably have advised. I raised the topic with Bea and Harriet before we discussed the problem of the trustees' meeting.

'Funny,' Bea said. 'We've just been discussing the same thing. Harriet suspects her ladyship might not like us lower orders sitting down to eat with her. Even you are a paid employee, Matthew, despite your ancestors.'

'And I am no more than middle-class,' Wilson pointed out with a smile. 'John Timpson is lucky he's not in gaol. But how might a lady feel about dining unchaperoned with two strange gentlemen? Is that proper?'

Bea looked at Harriet. 'Why not ask her?'

Harriet smiled back. 'That's hard while she keeps to her room. I would suggest a fait accompli. She is welcome to join us and if she makes a fuss we can deal with the problem then. Meanwhile, we have been wondering about tonight's trustees' meeting. It's thawing slightly now, but if we have a frost tonight it will be lethal for horse and rider alike.'

Wilson glanced briefly at me. 'What would you suggest?' he asked her.

Bea jumped in: 'A daytime meeting, so at least visitors can see when they're going to fall flat on their faces. Perhaps a luncheon tomorrow for the participants and a meeting after that. Those not involved can surely entertain themselves for an hour or so.'

'Can the gentlemen involved be informed?'

'One of the lads would think it a real treat to be sent slipping and sliding to the village,' Bea assured him.

What could we do but acquiesce?

And why did Harriet's face look even more troubled?

'Beg pardon, sir, but might I have a word in private?' Thatcher said, breathing rather than uttering the words.

I gestured: in my office. At least it was warmer than in the corridor, though the fireplace was small for the size of room. While he made up the fire, which had burnt low, I lit the lamps, for warmth as much as light.

I sat; after some hesitation he did the same.

'I'm glad you wanted to speak to me,' I said quietly, 'because I wanted to speak to you – to thank you for all your excellent work yesterday and last night in particular. Will you pass my thanks to your colleagues, Dick? I'm sure Mrs Rowsley has already thanked the maids.' I waited. It seemed that he could not speak. 'We're all in a very strange situation, aren't we? And I'm afraid Lady Stanton's arrival will make it more complicated. What would make it easier for the staff?'

'We can cope, sir. Whatever we have to do. You can rely on us.'

'I know that. But there's something I don't know. Which is what is troubling you enough to want to talk to me and then be reluctant to.'

He shifted uncomfortably. I wished he'd approached Harriet rather than me – she'd have got him to confide more readily. After all, running the House was more her area than mine.

'It's about her ladyship's Will, sir. There's a rumour that Mrs Rowsley will come in for a lot of money, sir, and will want to give up working here. And we don't know how we'd manage without her – and you, of course, sir,' he added quickly, after an embarrassing pause.

I would never be surprised by servants' gossip, but I confess that I was shocked by the direction it had taken. I said repressively, 'I can tell you truthfully that I have no idea what is in the Will. It was supposed to be read to all the trustees tonight. But there is talk of postponing it, perhaps to tomorrow afternoon.' I hoped I didn't sound as irritated as I felt. I also hoped none of them took it on themselves to mention their feelings to Harriet. It was going to be hard enough without their moral blackmail to persuade her to give up her daily toil for a fulfilling period of rest. Travel too, perhaps. Duty sat on her shoulders like the heavy shawl she wore today. I allowed myself a glance at the clock. I registered for the first time just how ugly it was.

Thatcher got to his feet. 'Thank you, sir.' His bow was unwontedly dispirited.

'I wish I could reassure you,' I said. To divert him, I asked, 'Harriet apart, you must know the contents of the House better than anyone. You don't know anywhere we could find a better clock than this dreadful specimen, do you?'

His impish smile reminded me how young he was to wear the butler's mantle. 'As it happens, sir, I can think of several. I take it you would prefer something from one of the unused rooms?'

'It would be altogether wiser, would it not, and more tactful, perhaps. May I suggest we go and look for a replacement clock, assuming you have no more immediate duties to fulfil?'

'I believe I should tell Luke, if it's all the same to you, sir, so there is someone at hand to answer my bell. I will be back in a trice, sir.'

He was. We set off like two schoolboys granted an unexpected half-holiday, chattering about the forthcoming cricket season – which seemed all too far away on a day like this. I was trying to explain how I had changed my grip on the ball when I bowled, only to be nonplussed; it seemed Harriet was teaching him what she had taught me. Of course she was. He was twenty-five, twenty-six at most, and had far more years of cricket before him than I did.

He conscientiously locked each room after we had regarded the timepiece within; some occasioned gusts of laughter, others puzzled frowns – how could anyone ever have considered them attractive or impressive enough actually to buy. And then he exclaimed, 'Sir, this door is unlocked!' He added anxiously, 'And I am sure I checked it last time I was in this area.' He opened the door and strode in. I followed. It was a bedchamber. The blinds were down, but he strode across to wind them up.

'There. Now the dog can see the rabbit,' he said with satisfaction. 'If we leave them up, the sun rots the curtain fabric, you see.' He stroked what looked and felt like silk. 'Lovely. And the tester hangings are probably the same under all those dustsheets. Fancy sleeping in a room like this, sir.'

'You know what my wife would say: fancy being the person

bringing coal up all those extra stairs every morning, and taking away the chamber pots.'

He nodded. 'But we need some work, sir – and what we do is not in our hands, is it? My little brother – I think you might have seen him at cricket practice, skinny with red hair – he says he hears there's work that pays better in the towns and cities, so he's going to move to my auntie's in Dudley as soon as he can. Not that it's very nice, working in factories, is it? Still doing work that's not in our hands.'

'If you could choose, Dick, what would you do? Just between ourselves.'

'I don't know, and that's the truth. Because I was tall, my mother always said I should go into service, not on to the land. And I've been lucky, sir, getting to be butler at my age. I just wish it hadn't had to be at Mr Bowman's expense.'

'They say you still go and read to him.'

'Aye. And he still corrects me – some of those long names in the Old Testament, sir . . .' He straightened his shoulders, and looked around, almost as if he was a dog sniffing the air. 'I can't see anything amiss, can you, sir? All nice and clean and tidy, just as you'd expect.' He checked the service door in the panelling. 'Hmm. That's unlocked too. I don't like that. I'll mention it to Mrs Rowsley, sir.'

I knew better than to offer: the correct protocols must be observed. He tweaked a picture frame, covered, like all the pictures, in heavy cloth, tutting under his breath. 'I think some maids leave them skew-whiff just to prove they've dusted, sir.'

'They have to dust them even when they're covered up!' I was appalled.

'No. I suppose not. So why is this . . .' He looked more closely, finally removing the picture from the wall. 'There's something wrong, sir, and for the life of me I don't know what it is.'

He passed it to me. It was a portrait of an old man, the paint so clouded with age that only his skin was visible, his clothes and hat merging into the dark background. It was probably a foot by eighteen inches, in a gilt frame which had fared much better, still bright, especially in the strange white

snow-fuelled light. The glass had not a speck of dust on it –
but then, it would have been dusted before it was draped,
wouldn't it?

'It's strange to put what looks like a very old picture into
such a new frame, isn't it, sir? No, it's just very clean, not
new at all. It's just like some of the others we have. But look
– even the back is clean.'

'It is indeed. You know what, Dick, I have a yen to have
this picture in my office.'

He shook his head, pointing at the wall. 'You can see
where it's been, sir – we'd need to replace it with something
else. Trouble is, all the storerooms and the attics are kept
locked these days – we can't just sneak up and get one. Ah!'
He eyed the keys I was jangling. 'The quickest way is up
the backstairs, sir.'

It was so cold in the attics I headed for the first stack of
pictures I could see, lifting the dustsheet and grabbing any oil
painting that was much the size of the one I was borrowing.
It was a still life, which would have to do. I tucked the
remainder up again before locking up carefully and running
back downstairs. 'There! It looks quite good there!' I dusted
it with my handkerchief and flung the shroud back over it.
Over in the corner was a dressing table, on which congregated
all the room's ornaments under one sheet. I burrowed underneath it. 'And you know what, this clock will do nicely for
my office. Let's move those vases a little to cover up the
space.'

Grinning, he obliged, carefully covering them again. 'Just
as if they grew there, sir. Now, shall I carry the picture or you,
sir? I'd best just lock up, too.'

'You, if you don't mind. I don't want to drop the clock.'

'Very handsome, sir. If you'll permit me, just another inch to
the right? It's a really nice picture, isn't it? Sir, do you know
about art?'

'I know more about fields. Maybe Professor Fulke-Grosse
will be able to tell us about it.'

He turned quickly.

'Go on, Dick – say what you were going to say.'

He shifted.

'No? Then I'll say it for you. Perhaps I shouldn't ask the professor or anyone else just yet. And perhaps I'll keep this door locked.'

'Just in case, sir.'

We exchanged a grin; Harriet's phrase had become something of a watchword in the House.

SIX

Harriet

Luncheon was served in our new relaxed way, with a mixture of staff and guests. Bea excused herself. I gathered that something vital had been spilt in the kitchen requiring her skills and experience to rescue the situation. Lady Stanton neither put in an appearance nor sent her apologies. Her absence continued to cause speculation, which I did my best to avoid. I ought, perhaps, to have been more assiduous in attending to her needs. Admittedly I had had a busy morning, dealing amongst other things with a parlour maid who was in hysterics after tearing one of the curtains that her late ladyship had intended to replace last spring, until she became too ill to make decisions and too fratchy to listen to the suggestions she asked for. Poor lady: she had not had a kind death. Though I had had to run the House without the benefit of her advice or even consent for nearly a year, I had a sudden pang of grief stronger than any I had felt since her death. If I left the table it would, however, disturb everyone. Francis, Mr Wilson and Matthew were bickering amiably, John Timpson was laughing with an amusement he rarely showed, and the professor was looking piqued – as if he felt he was being excluded. Someone noticed my distress, however. Luke, the footman on duty, refilled my glass without being asked, bending close to my ear to ask if I needed an urgent message from the kitchen. This was the House code for an excuse for removing oneself from an unpleasant situation. No one had ever had cause to offer it to me. Ever. Luke's kindness brought me even nearer to tears. I managed to shake my head and smile my thanks. What a good, kind, young man he was becoming – and observant too. I would miss him when inevitably he went off to another, more promising establishment.

I shook myself. Someone must engage the professor in conversation. I doubted if he would object to giving me the benefit of his knowledge. I floated our honeymoon visit to the Uffizi. Almost rubbing his hands with glee, he embarked on a learned disquisition about the contents. I shocked him by saying I thought Botticelli was my favourite artist there, with *Primavera* the loveliest painting I had ever seen. He changed the subject abruptly as if he thought such subjects were unsuitable for ladies. Why? How? But out of politeness – and a recollection that he was a stranger, not a friend like Francis with whom an intellectual tussle was more than acceptable – I held my tongue.

Then Luke rescued me with a genuine and very welcome message: Dr Page had managed to reach the House and was with his new patients now. If I would care to meet him in the Room in about fifteen minutes' time, he would be able to give me his assessment. I could excuse myself and leave the gathering.

Ellis's news was not good. Despite all Nurse Webb's efforts, the groom was fighting for his life, and the coachman not much better: both had inflammation of the lungs. 'As for the maid – what's her name? Olwen? – she is in desperate straits. She is with child, I suspect, and the groom is the father. If her sweetheart dies, I fear she will lose the baby. I can understand her wishing to be beside the young man, but to my mind she would be better off engaged in some useful pastime.' He frowned. 'You disagree?'

'I am no doctor, Ellis, but I know if Matthew were ever near to death, I would want to be at his bedside, holding his hand and speaking to him. I would want to hear his last words.' I straightened. 'Unless you thought that I was hindering his cure, of course. Hysterical tears will do no one any good, of course.'

'I cannot imagine your succumbing to hysterics whatever the circumstances – either of you,' he added, taking the cup of tea that Bea proffered. 'Thank you.'

'Would she not be better off with her mistress?' Bea asked.

'A mistress who has not even been to see how she does?' I

asked coolly. I glanced at the clock. 'Heavens, I really should go and speak to her ladyship. She might be genuinely unwell and need your assistance, Ellis.'

'For an invalid, her appetite's remarkably good,' Bea said flatly. 'She asked for a very light luncheon – but ate pretty well the same as you and the gentlemen.'

Knowing what she'd like to add, I said it for her. 'I am sure there is still good food aplenty, Ellis, if you have time to eat. And there is a fire in the Room.' I mimed rolling my sleeves up and straightening my shoulders. 'Time to do my duty!'

'You look ready for battle,' Bea laughed. 'You really didn't take to her, did you? Do you have to go?'

'There's no one else to do it,' I pointed out, 'take to her or not.' And then I had an idea. 'Ellis, some people only hear what men say – if necessary, might you explain how ill her staff are?'

I thought perhaps that a more formal visit might impress her. So I invited Dick Thatcher to escort me up through the main, not the staff, corridor and announce me, assuming, of course, that her maid – our Florrie – was allowed to admit a visitor. It seemed she was. But she dutifully retired to the dressing room when I entered.

Lady Stanton, wearing a most exquisite negligee, reclined on the day bed. She greeted me with a languid smile, but one that discouraged familiarity.

My curtsy acknowledged our social distance. 'I am here to enquire whether all is to your liking, your ladyship.'

'Such a bore, is it not?' She gestured in the direction of the window. 'Flossie, or whatever her name is, tells me that they have managed to plough a way through the snow so perhaps I can be on my way soon.'

'I fear it is unlikely, ma'am. Neither your groom nor your coachman is well—'

'A chill, I gather. And Olwen throwing hysterical attacks.'

'She is understandably upset to see her swe— her colleague on what may well be his deathbed.' I cursed my slip of the tongue, which had not gone unnoticed.

'Sweetheart? I do not know what the rule is in this house,

Mrs Roe, but in mine servants are not allowed to walk out with each other. Or with anyone else.'

I bowed, suppressing the observation that the poor groom might never walk anywhere again, but be carried out from here feet first.

'Would you care for one of my colleagues to arrange rail travel to Chester for you as soon as the trains can run again? The estate has its own railway station,' I added.

'I always travel in my own coach,' she said, as if bemused by my suggestion.

'I suspect the rail tracks will be cleared before the roads,' I said carefully.

'I can wait.'

My curtsy was meant to be non-committal, but she might have thought it acquiescent. 'Now, his lordship's physician is in the House at the moment. Do you feel you should consult him yourself? You must have endured a very unpleasant journey last night, and one can never be too sure, can one?' Let Dr Page have the experience of a conversation where neither contributor actually responded to what the other was saying – in my case, I simply did not dare react because I would lose control of my temper if I did. In hers – because I suspected she only ever listened to herself and her needs.

'Indeed. And I have been all too aware of my palpitations today. Thank you, Mrs Roe.'

Curtsying, I withdrew in response to words that were far more of a dismissal than an expression of gratitude.

Dr Page was mopping his forehead when he returned. 'Heavens, one might grow tomatoes in such heat. I hope you're not short of fuel, Harriet.' Absentmindedly he sipped from the tea cup that had mysteriously appeared in front of him.

'Not yet. When do you think that she will be fit to depart? Even if we have to supply her means of transport.'

'You'd not send John Coachman out in this!' he exploded. 'His rheumatism—'

'The railway. If she needed to leave for some reason . . . a problem in the House, perhaps . . .'

He threw back his head and laughed. 'You begin to persuade

me that you are an accomplished liar! I lie about Samuel
Bowman's whereabouts, I discover a quite fictitious outbreak
of measles in the House – with what disease do you want me
to scare her off?'

I smiled sweetly.

Bea topped up Ellis's tea, before looking at me specula-
tively. 'You're not jealous, are you, Harriet? Luke says her
ladyship was all over Matthew like a rash, but surely you're
not anxious?'

Ellis stirred his cup. 'I suspect, Bea, that her ladyship's
manner is not one to endear her to anyone she does not want
to please. I fear I could not discover that her pulse was
tumultuous or that her palpitations were a cause for concern.
After that she became pettish, and lamented that no one
understood her constitution like her dear Dr Marchbanks.'
He produced a grin I could only describe as malevolent. 'I
suspect I trained with her physician; we knew him – not
altogether affectionately – as Dr Mountebank. Anyway, I
discovered she could pout as well as she could smile. And
yet, and yet . . . I wonder if I should write to him about
something I found.' He sighed. 'As for her servants, I almost
wish Mr Pounceman was here to pray for them. Perhaps he
might after tomorrow afternoon's meeting. But now I fear I
must leave you. I promised to look in at Mrs Mayle before
sunset. She has the migraine again, and I think she might
benefit from some tincture of feverfew.' We walked with him
into the passageway where he had left his outdoor clothes
and boots. 'I have left Nurse Webb complete instructions,
because I fear I would not want to turn out again tonight
– and if I did, I could do no more than she. But I will visit
the patients tomorrow morning before luncheon. All of them.
And then we have the trustees' meeting – I wonder how long
that will last,' he added gloomily.

'Ellis, if you wish to bring an overnight bag, you will find
a room prepared for you. We might just manage enough coal
to heat it,' I said, mockingly. 'And Bea's catering is always
generous enough for us to be able to make room at the dining
table for another guest. Indeed, you may find it graced by
Lady Stanton.'

'The prospect is tempting indeed.' He kissed our hands, and was gone.

'He'll stay,' I said, with a smile. 'You mark my words.'

'And her ladyship?'

'We need Florrie to speak glowing words about the professor. I fancy she is a woman who prefers the company of gentlemen to that of ladies. Not, of course,' I added dryly, 'that we are ladies.'

'And why would you want to be, Harriet? Answer me that!'

'Do you want a truthful answer? Because I'm not sure I can give you one. I don't mind being invisible, Bea – because that shows how efficient and useful we're being. When her ladyship summoned me, she did so because she needed my advice and my help to make the House run smoothly. She didn't have to like me or dislike me. We had a good working relationship. Just as you did.'

'Of course. Even though she didn't take much interest in the day's menus, she knew it was as much her duty to approve them as it was mine to cook them.'

'Exactly. We knew where we were in the hierarchy, didn't we? But now, while you and I are actually vital – the House literally couldn't run without us, could it? – I am treated like the carpet by a woman, a lady, who is, to be brutal, using the House like an inn, though I made it clear when she arrived that we were in mourning. Oh, before you say it, I acknowledge that she can do little else physically, but her attitude . . . How Dick and Luke and the others who are in regular contact with visitors manage to hold their tongues I do not know.' I smiled, before adding seriously, 'These last six months have spoiled me. Our friendships with Francis and Ellis and Mr Wilson have spoiled me. I feel as if I have been let out of a box and do not wish to be put back in.'

'There's a lot to be said for knowing your place, isn't there? Because you can't repine for something you've never had. And, like you say, once you've tasted something else, you don't want to give it up.' She sat down, elbows on table, leaning towards me. 'How does Matthew feel?'

'About his position or about mine? His position is trickier in many ways, coming from a family as good as any in the

county and beyond, but accepting money for what he does.'
I shook my head. 'Socially he's come down in the world,
while financially he's probably gone up. What strange times
we live in.'

SEVEN

Matthew

Lady Stanton fluttered down the main stairs just as the trustees' meeting was about to start in the splendours of the red dining room, luncheon having been served in the warmer and less formal breakfast room. The men not attending the meeting had intended to adjourn to the billiards room, but now wavered, as did we all.

Harriet stepped forward, catching Dick Thatcher's eye. He must deal with the practicalities of what she had to offer. 'Good afternoon, your ladyship.' She performed brief introductions – Mr Baines, Mr Newcombe, Mr Wilson, Mr Timpson, Mrs Arden, Professor Fulke-Grosse, Sir Francis Palmer – from left to right, with no distinction of rank.

Her ladyship, however, picked out the three most likely to be gentlemen. Then, to my delight and amazement, Samuel Bowman appeared, leaning heavily on a stick and supported the other side by one of the male orderlies. Clearly he needed to take his seat as soon as he could, and until we had rid ourselves of her ladyship that was impossible. Perhaps Harriet's voice was curt as she spoke to her again. 'Might we offer you luncheon, your ladyship? My colleagues will make the arrangements and will endeavour to satisfy your every need.'

Thatcher, swiftly taking in the situation, bowed. 'I believe there is a good fire in the yellow drawing room, your ladyship. If your ladyship will step this way?'

Ignoring him, she waved a charming hand. 'So many of you – are you all stranded here too? What fun we will have!'

'I am afraid most of us are here for an important meeting, your ladyship,' I said, giving Harriet a chance to have a whispered conversation with Thatcher and Luke. 'Both Mrs Rowsley and I have to attend it too.'

'Can't you put it off?' She pouted. The lines on her face

suggested that she was less of a girl than her demeanour suggested.

'I am afraid not, your ladyship. But most of us will meet again for sherry before dinner.'

She laid her hand on my arm. 'I shall keep you to that. And you can tell me all about it!'

I bowed, stepping back out of range.

There was a dry cough. 'Sadly, madam, that will not be possible,' Wilson intervened. 'The matters are entirely confidential.' He looked ostentatiously at his pocket watch. 'If you will excuse us, we must leave you. Mr Bowman should not be standing like this. Moreover, some of the trustees need to leave before it gets dark and freezes over again.'

'But what am I to do?' she wailed.

In her place I would not have trusted Francis' limpid smile as he offered to entertain her – but she could not have known that as Harriet's utterly devoted friend, he would let nothing cause her distress, not even a one-sided flirtation with her husband. Neither could she have seen the wink he gave Harriet. It promised that though he was not the marrying sort, he would behave like the most eligible of bachelors delighted to have met a beautiful, titled woman. Possibly he would encourage his friend Hudson Fulke-Grosse to join in the game, though I was fairly sure that the professor found his own personal beauty more interesting than that of any woman. John Timpson would not be party to it, not yet at least. He would be minuting our meeting.

Her eyes found another target. 'Dr Page! Your visit did me so much good yesterday or I am sure I would not have been able to come down now. Are you to feel my wrist again?' She held out her hand to receive his kiss of homage.

He bowed. 'I fear I have another pulse to worry about – that of our forthcoming meeting.'

As she swanned off, Pounceman arrived. She did not turn as he was announced, however; presumably a clergyman was not of any interest. Soon he was leading his flock from what he might well come to regard as a she-wolf in lamb's clothing.

*   *   *

Once we had stood while Mr Pounceman prayed for his lordship and the rest of the diminished household, Wilson took charge. He surveyed the table, immaculate with carafes of water, crystal tumblers, jotters and pencils. 'Since its contents might be germane to later items on the agenda, I humbly propose that I read Lady Croft's Will first. I accept that this is unusual, but I crave your indulgence.'

There was a murmur of assent. I knew that Harriet was deeply anxious, but not sure why exactly. We seemed to have had no time to talk about her fears and I could not reach for her hand and hold it. Did I hope that Lady Croft had included a personal bequest to her, so enabling her to step away from the shackles of her job? Did she or did she fear it? She was white to the lips. It was Samuel who took her hand – though perhaps he sought comfort as much as he wanted to give it.

Montgomery Wilson was not a man to dispense with formalities or preliminaries.

At long last, he came to Lady Croft's legacies. 'You will excuse me if I . . . er . . . translate into English as I go. I always took her ladyship to be a woman wholeheartedly devoted to idleness, perhaps, with hindsight, excusable by her illness. But petty though she could be, waspish, even, she had a fair idea of what went on in her house. To that end, she has made a number of bequests to her staff, including Mademoiselle Hortense, who served her until – do I remember aright? – her ladyship injured her quite seriously. One hopes that Mrs Rowsley and her team will be able to run her to earth.' Having raised expectations, he coughed saying that perhaps he should deal with items in order so that he did not omit anything by mistake.

There was the mildest trickle of laughter around the table. It must be clear even to him that he was irritating us, particularly Farmer Newcombe, finely dressed as usual, and Marty Baines, landlord of the village's only inn, to both of whom time was money. But given his delight in manipulating people, this could well have been intentional.

At last!

There was a pleasant surprise for me: the sum of eight hundred pounds to build a school large enough to serve both

Thorncroft and Stammerton, on condition that it bear her name. In another setting there would have been a round of applause. Hortense was indeed to receive a hundred pounds, with a gift of a further fifty on her marriage. For John Dobbs ('John Coachman,' Harriet explained in a whisper), fifty pounds, and twenty-five a year when he retired. He was also to be found a permanent rent-free cottage on the estate. In addition to a gold watch, Samuel Bowman would receive a hundred and fifty pounds, and when he retired fifty pounds a year and a cottage on the estate. Did he understand? Perhaps he did. He pressed a handkerchief to his lips, and shook his head, but said nothing. Since Ellis Page was watching him, I said nothing. Neither did Bea, who somehow contrived to ignore his presence.

Wilson pressed on. All the male and female servants were to receive the sum of twenty-five pounds to buy mourning rings or lockets. Harriet was writing on her jotter. If I knew her she would pay for a bulk purchase, so the staff could spend their bequests on something they really wanted. In addition to a gold watch, Bea was to receive a hundred and fifty pounds and, if she chose to remain in his lordship's employment, a pension of fifty pounds and a cottage. If she chose to leave, both the pension and the cottage would be forfeited. It was impossible to tell from her face what she thought of the last clause. Interestingly the Will did not specify what would happen if she were dismissed.

'"To my loyal and dedicated housekeeper, Harriet Rowsley, in addition to a gold watch, the sum of two hundred pounds."' Wilson quelled the gasp with a swift glance. 'There is a codicil.' He read the text in front of him. '"I do not approve on principle of women working after marriage, but in this instance, Mrs Rowsley's loyalty to the Croft family has been exemplary. If she agrees to remain in the post until the marriage or death of Lord Croft, or the birth of her own child, for a maximum of five years, then this sum will be doubled. I also bequeath to her for her use until the marriage of my son my personal jewellery. Should my son remain unmarried and predecease her, then they are hers to keep for her life-time. They will return to the Croft family on her own death.

Furthermore, it was my dear husband's wish that she retain control as long as she was able over the library, particularly the precious books that gave them both so much pleasure. He suggested that for this duty she should receive the additional emolument of—"'

There was another gasp. Harriet had fainted.

Bea was first to respond. Taking one of the carafes of water, she dashed the contents on to Harriet's face.

Ellis was on his feet. 'Bea, that is a treatment for hysteria!'

'And, it seems, fainting!' As Bea gently dabbed the water from her face, Harriet spluttered and opened her eyes. Bea took her hand. 'Gentlemen, could you give us a few minutes? You too, Matthew. Though I could do with your handkerchief first, please.'

I paced, distraught, in the corridor, hearing the hubbub around me, seeing Page easing Samuel into a chair, but making no sense of anything. Did Harriet's terrifying reaction mean the legacy was a triumph or a disaster for her? After a few minutes, I could bear it no longer. To my own surprise, I tapped before I opened the door. Bea opened it the merest crack. 'I'll leave you to it,' she said.

The colour was returning to Harriet's face. 'The library! It is safe!' she said. And burst into tears.

There was a knock at the door. Trying not to peer into the room, Thatcher passed me a salver supporting two balloons and a decanter of brandy. 'His late lordship's finest, sir.' He withdrew, closing the door firmly.

'So it may be,' Harriet declared, 'but I always did loathe the stuff. You have some: you're as white as your shirt.'

I obeyed.

She took my hand. 'Better? My love, we have so much to talk about, but let us get this wretched meeting over and done with so we can do it in the comfort of our bedchamber.'

It was clear that the conversation in the corridor had been vigorous, but, after an interrogatory smile, Wilson resumed his seat and his place in the Will as if Harriet had had no more than a bout of hiccups.

'"Looking after the library will entail an additional emolument of a hundred and twenty pounds per annum.

"Rumours abound that my son, the eighteenth Lord Croft, begat a living child. It is my earnest desire that this child should be located and her education secured, all expenses to be borne by the estate."'

Wilson peeled off his spectacles and looked around the table. 'Ladies and gentlemen, there is much here for us to digest, but I suggest that as soon as we may we begin our meeting proper, conscientiously following the agenda so that we may conclude in a timely manner.'

We applied ourselves steadily, eyes on Samuel, pale and shaking, the clock and the sky outside. At last we reached the item dealing with Harriet's future now that her ladyship was dead. Who would be her legal employer?

Marty Baines was the first to speak, his Manchester accent much in evidence. 'Surely – if she wishes to continue to work here – Mrs Rowsley should be answerable to the trustees.'

'Indeed no,' came Mr Pounceman's contribution. 'She should be answerable to her husband, in her work here as in all other things.'

Harriet raised a hand. 'Might I speak, Mr Chairman? Despite her ladyship's great generosity. I have not yet decided if I wish to continue to work here.' There was a shocked gasp. 'I am more than happy to be answerable to the trustees in the interim, but perhaps we might adjourn a full discussion of my future employment here until the next meeting.'

EIGHT

Harriet

T he sun was just setting when the meeting concluded so there was a rapid exodus, led by Mr Pounceman who was in too much of a hurry to go and pray with Nurse Webb's patients. Only Dr Page accepted our invitation to dine. Having kept me back in the dining room to establish that I had recovered from my fainting fit – 'It was genuine, this time, I think, Harriet? You did not fake it as you did on that famous occasion in church?' – he made his way straight up to the Family wing to check on Samuel, promising to join us later for sherry. He clearly did not feel that Lady Stanton merited a second personal consultation. Matthew had obviously spoken to Thatcher, who said quietly, 'I understood that you might need tea in your bedchamber, Mrs Rowsley. You will find it there. I have just made up the fire. I can assure you that Luke and I will do all that is needful for our guests.' He bowed. 'Permit me to say that the household could not be happier to hear the news about Mr Bowman and you.' Suddenly his discreet mask slipped. 'You deserve it, you really do – ma'am,' he concluded hurriedly.

I found I could not speak. I hoped my smile showed him how moved I was.

Matthew gave me his arm with a flourish as we headed up the main, rather than the backstairs. 'All will be well, Harriet. I promise you.'

'Are you saying that to reassure me or to reassure yourself? You're still as pale as I feel,' I observed.

'I am more concerned about you. Half of me wants to urge you to walk away from the post instantly. But the other half knows that despite what you said you simply cannot.'

I stopped as we reached the first landing. 'If you found another post, where would that leave the new model village we both desire so much? And the Roman site which Francis could not excavate without the landlord's co-operation? Despite what I said, I can't go yet, can I? And where would it leave me?'

'So that was a tactical salvo? Well done.'

As we passed a grandfather clock, its case gleaming in the lamplight, as if on cue it struck four thirty. Matthew did something then that he never did in public. Taking my face between his hands he kissed me on the lips.

I sank into a chair, bending to unlace my boots. At last I asked, 'Could you bear another five years here?'

There was a tap at the door. Swearing under his breath, Matthew strode over to open it, meaning, I suspect, to snarl at whatever chambermaid had chosen to interrupt.

'Sorry, sir. Sorry, ma'am,' Thatcher panted. 'I thought you'd want to know that Mr Pounceman has taken a tumble. A bad one. Just as he was getting into his barouche. One of the lads ran upstairs for Dr Page. They're carrying Mr Pounceman up to the Family wing now.'

'Thank you, Thatcher. You'll let us know what we can do, won't you? Yes, we'll come down to the Room.'

What else could Matthew have said? Sighing, I laced up my boots again. Not even five minutes to ruminate on my fortune, specifically to work out whether it was good or bad.

Matthew cursed, pulling a comical face. 'I had planned a little celebration,' he said, disappearing into the dressing room. He returned with an ice-bucket from which emerged the neck of a champagne bottle. 'Not to toast the golden shackles of the bequest but to raise a glass to the future of the library. And now we have to go and worry about the wretched Pounceman! Typical of the bloody man!' He covered his mouth with an apologetic hand. 'I'm sorry, my love.'

'Why? It *is* typical of the bloody man. Do we have time to drink a cup of that tea, Matthew, before we go? No, it'll be lukewarm.'

It was. But it gave us a moment to breathe.

'If I stay on,' I said, because I had to, 'there must be changes. If we can't live in our own home, we need to have part of this house that is ours and ours alone. Time in each day that is ours and ours alone. I have never worked anything other than hard, but I have always had private hours with which no one would interfere. You are not employed to run errands – don't think I didn't see how many tasks you undertook last night! – but to run the estate.'

He smiled, helping me up. 'We will work out how to set limits. If, for instance, you are expected to be the hostess, you cannot be troubling yourself with checking unused rooms for dust.'

'Sometimes I check for more than that, you know. And I was alarmed to find a clock missing from the Willow Room turning up in your office. And a strange picture on your wall.'

'I will tell you more about that picture as we walk down. Backstairs or the main ones?'

I raised my chin. 'As hostess for the evening, the main staircase, without a doubt. If you will give me your arm, Matthew?'

'Only if I may give you my arm when we return to dress for dinner.'

'He will have a scar, I'm afraid, where he hit his forehead on the steps. And a terrible headache. But worse is his ankle – I think he sprained it as he fell. There may even be a break. Whatever it is, it will take a long time to heal. May I ask if he may remain here under Nurse Webb's care for a few days? Though I am afraid he will make a difficult patient. He is already demanding that his valet be summoned.' Ellis drained his cup, looking over my head at the clock on the Room's mantelpiece. 'What an interesting day this is turning out to be, Harriet. Will it be even more interesting yet? Will Lady Stanton be joining us for dinner?'

'To my shame, I have given her plans very little thought. So I will despatch Luke to find out. Perhaps her afternoon with the gentlemen may have proved too exhausting. Or she may have enjoyed herself so much she has forgotten to be ill.'

'Let us hope so. May I say, before I adjourn to the bedchamber you were kind enough to have prepared for me, that I applaud your courage this afternoon. I cannot imagine the House without you, but you surely cannot continue to be both Lady of the House to your guests and responsible for the day-to-day running of the establishment.'

I smiled as if we had not just had the same conversation ourselves.

'And now you are to be librarian in chief!'

Matthew nodded. 'The last role is in fact the one you value most, Harriet? So, if you will excuse us, Page, we will go and celebrate it.'

I put my hand on his arm. 'Unless we should visit Mr Pounceman first?'

Ellis laughed. 'I have allowed him a little laudanum, Harriet. I would say it is your positive duty to let him sleep. And I will offer on his behalf his apologies for not joining you at the dinner table tonight.' He bowed. 'Ah! One question. How much of this legacy is known in the House?'

Suddenly tired and sick of my boots, I said, 'I should imagine every last detail is already being discussed. I am not happy at being treated differently from Bea – not for anything would I want to jeopardize our friendship.'

'It is not you but Lady Croft who made the legacies. And I do not believe that Bea, who regards you as her dearest friend, has a shred of resentment in her being.'

'Thank you.' I squeezed Matthew's arm. It was time to depart.

I was, I must confess, almost giggling like a maidservant as we mounted the stairs. 'My love, have you any idea how ambiguous your suggestion was that we should celebrate?'

'Not until you pointed it out. Let us go – and be ambiguous!'

Even as Matthew poured our champagne, there was a knock on our door. Tempted as I was to ignore it, all those years of training made me abandon the battle with my boot laces and open it. Mr Wilson greeted me with a bow. 'My dear, nothing can give me more pleasure than to bring this to you.' He handed over her ladyship's jewellery cabinet. 'I understand from Thatcher that the finest pieces are already in the safe, which two of you have to be present to open. But perhaps they would not be suitable for a gathering like this evening's.'

At this point Matthew made a terrible mistake. He emerged from the dressing room with two glasses. Was I surprised that Mr Wilson assumed one was for him? And would wish to talk about my plans? And make me sign for each individual item? And run to earth one missing earring? And concede that although the sapphires might have been designed for me, only jet was possible in the current situation. 'After all, there will be every opportunity to wear the other items: they are yours for your lifetime, are they not?'

I smiled my agreement. But even as I put them back on their velvet pads, I realized the danger of beautiful things, even if they were not absolute treasures. Suddenly I was afraid that someone might steal them.

NINE

Matthew

'What we really need is a room with a large round table,' Bea observed as I led her in to dinner.

I could not argue. What with the uneven number of diners, and Lady Stanton's late decision to grace us with her presence, the seating arrangement at the conventional long dining table became very complicated. Harriet and I, actually the hosts, were of course considerably her ladyship's inferiors in social status. It had never mattered to Francis, who might well have trumped her, but it assuredly did to her ladyship. In the end a hurried conference between Thatcher and Harriet put Francis at the head, with her ladyship as the honoured guest beside him. Honoured guest she might be, but Francis was detailed to discover as much as he could about her. That settled, the rest of us must take our chance with the seating. Wilson materialized at the foot of the table, insisting that Harriet sit to his right. Bea looked relieved that she could find a place between John Timpson and Ellis Page. I almost wished that Pounceman had been well enough to make the numbers more manageable. But at least we were spared his protracted grace. Wilson's was short and to the point.

If dinner was socially awkward, the hour afterwards was decidedly uncomfortable. Perceiving the piano, Lady Stanton kindly offered to play – but then tried to insist that I sing with her, or at the very least turn her pages. It would be ungallant to decline – yet I could not rid myself of a strange notion that the invitation was in fact a means of snubbing Harriet.

Perhaps Francis had the same idea. Flashing a sharp glance at me, he leapt to his feet. 'My dear ma'am, pray do not overlook me. I was born to sing alongside you. Our voices will blend in true harmony, will they not?'

Was she flattered or piqued? She surely could not be so

rag-mannered as to argue. There was a terrible pause. 'Surely you, Mrs Rolly, can support me in my request? Would not such a handsome man have a wonderful voice?'

'I fear not – not if it's the one I hear while he is taking a bath, ma'am. I am afraid I cannot vouch one way or another for any of the other gentlemen's musicality.' Harriet's chuckle sounded genuine, not like the tinkly confection that greeted her riposte.

Jumping into a somewhat shocked silence, Francis said, 'Hudson – you have a very fine baritone. Shall we attempt the Figaro and Almaviva duet? Lady Stanton, would you accompany us?' Heaven knows where Francis had found the score, but he laid it on the piano with an aplomb I envied.

It turned out that both Wilson and Page could sing too. Much as I wished to join in, I sensed I must not. Those who could perform were sharply separated from those who could not. Bea sat barely paying attention except to Page, and Timpson was reading some periodical. Harriet was listening intently, as one might trying to understand a conversation in a foreign tongue. Some pieces clearly caught her imagination. Others seemed to leave her cold. I felt a sudden surge of anger at her lack of education in this most wonderful of the arts. At least I could help others like her: when the school to which her ladyship wished to give her name was built, music must be on the curriculum. Yet even as I hoped, I despaired. These children would be confined to the most basic of lessons. Few would even want to maintain their education, as Harriet had clearly done. My urge to entertain the gathering with a Beethoven bagatelle faded abruptly.

There was an awkward hiatus. We could not tell our guests to retire to bed, but I for one wished devoutly we might. The clock ticked on; without a pause to encourage conversation, her ladyship remorsely attacked the keyboard, possibly the better to cover her often uncertain voice. What might I do? At last I caught Page's eye. At the end of the next song he was on his feet.

'My dear lady, I fear as your acting physician I must call a halt to the proceedings. After such exposure to cold and distress, your vocal chords are dreadfully vulnerable. Pray, allow yourself to be selfish, and deny us any further treats.

No, you must not even speak your goodnights: I insist on absolute rest for your generous throat.' He took her hand and felt her wrist. 'Yes, as I feared, your pulse is quite tumultuous. To your bedchamber with you, your ladyship, or I fear we will not hear your voice for a week!'

Francis was not to be outdone in chivalry: he put her wrap about her shoulders, and offered a gallant arm.

'What was all that about?' I asked Harriet as arm in arm we went upstairs. 'Why the wilful mispronunciation of your name, but not mine? It is as if she is deliberately needling you.'

'She succeeded, did she not? I was so ashamed of myself for reacting. I have spent thirty-odd years controlling my temper, and never had a terrible lapse like tonight's. Vulgar.' Head down, she bit her lip.

I lifted her chin, kissing her lightly. 'But so very enjoyable.' Taking her hand, I ran up the stairs and along the corridor. But our laughter died as soon as we entered our bedchamber. Yes – everything was still in its place. Almost. The fire still burned, but was very low. The scuttle was full, but a black handprint on the service door suggested that someone had started, at least, to make up the fire. The door was locked, as the main one had been. But from the outside – the key must still be in the lock as I could not use mine. Grabbing a lamp I dashed to the unoccupied chamber next door, let myself in and flung open the service door. Harriet was not far behind me, and was now lighting all the candles she could lay hands on. Despite all my efforts, the backstairs were very gloomy – especially when someone had extinguished all the lamps.

I picked my way carefully down. And stopped. Halfway down the stairs, blocking my way was a small black-clad figure, the neck at an unnatural angle. It was the child who had brought my shoes on a cushion. Mary. And though I hoped against hope, touching the still-warm neck in the forlorn hope of finding a pulse, I knew she was dead.

'Poor child. Dead within the last half hour,' Ellis Page said. 'Even if you'd come across her the moment she landed, you could not have kept her alive.' He snapped his fingers, in a horrible and probably unconscious mimicry of the crack of her neck. 'It's quite possible she simply tripped.' The ineffable sadness in his voice was at odds with the spectacular crimson-lapelled dressing gown he sported. The lapels were the only colour in the scene. 'Trying to scamper too fast, perhaps – you know what youngsters are like.'

'In the dark? For some reason none of the lamps were alight when I came down.'

'And she had left a tiny handprint on the doorframe – oh, and here's another on the skirting board,' Harriet added. Her voice almost broke. So far she had been almost unnaturally calm. Tears would have been healthier, surely. 'Not like Mary at all. She would never have left any mark anywhere. And someone had jammed a key in the service door – not the one to the door, as it happens. Mary would never have done that. But the stairs wouldn't be used by anyone except servants at this time of night.' She shook her head as if to rattle her thoughts into a cohesive whole. 'And no one would hear – despite all the commotion now, no one has come to see what's going on.'

'Shall we move her?' Ellis asked me quietly.

Harriet hesitated. 'Francis is a photographer. I believe he has his equipment . . .' She took a ragged breath. 'I would like to ask him to – just in case . . .'

'You're serious, aren't you?' Ellis asked in what sounded like disbelief.

I didn't bother to ask. I went in search of him myself. I found myself praying that I would find him in his own bedchamber, not someone else's. I did. Alone.

His dressing gown vied with Ellis's for attention, but he was as professional behind his tripod as Ellis had been with his new-fangled stethoscope, clearing us all to a discreet distance so that he might concentrate.

'It is the saddest work I have ever done,' he declared at last. 'I often photograph the Roman dead, some of whom have clearly met violent ends. But this . . .' He wept as he gathered up his equipment. Then he asked the question no one else had been able to. 'Where can we move her to? Her bedchamber?'

Harriet shook her head. 'She shares – shared – one with two other girls. It must be somewhere . . . cold, must it not? But not . . . it must not be inappropriate.'

Francis asked, very quietly, 'Might she – could she have wanted to end . . .?'

Ellis's nostrils flared. 'My dear man, if I infer correctly what you imply, she is hardly more than a child! But since the coroner must be informed—'

Harriet completed his sentence quietly, 'There must be a post-mortem examination.'

'I know it will pain you, Harriet, but yes. You are right. And it must be performed with great respect. Would you like me—?'

I could see the effort it took her even to move her lips. But her brain was still working. 'If that is legal, yes please.'

'And we must tell young Constable Pritchard, as soon as we can,' I added. 'But God knows when he will be able to summon his sergeant. Meanwhile, of course, no one must leave the House. No one at all,' I said, wishing almost as much as Harriet probably did that I could see the back of Lady Stanton at least. 'Harriet, where shall we let her rest?' Surely not the dairy or the meat room, which would be the coldest places, attics apart.

'The flower room, I think. She used to love cleaning up in there when I had finished the arrangements for the hall and the library. The long zinc-covered table would support her. Let me fetch some sheets first.' She turned to leave, but swung back swiftly. 'If we wish to find out – we have to find out – if someone did this deliberately, this might mean checking who is in their room now. Who is not. Can we? Privately? And – dear God – it should be now!'

I stared. 'You mean, go and wake people up and interrogate them?'

She shook her head. 'I mean creep up these stairs and peer through the keyholes in the service doors. All should be darkness – but if anyone is still up, then they must be questioned, if not now then in the morning. Don't look at me like that. I know the very notion is distasteful. And – yes – we must check the servants' rooms too.'

'My dear Harriet,' Page remonstrated, 'that is spying, to put no too fine a point upon it! On a lady and on gentlemen.'

'And on servants who have always been perfectly trust-worthy,' I said, more supporting Harriet's suggestion than agreeing with Page. 'If we were heard, we would say we had heard a scream, something like that, or someone calling out. And truly, there are very few chambers to check. If Harriet will deal with those occupied by women, I will undertake to check the men's.'

'And the . . . and the body?' Francis asked, in a hoarse whisper.

'Let you and me remain here with her,' Page said. 'Though I hate to agree with such . . . snooping . . . I believe it is on order here. One thing: you should do your rounds, if not make your inspections, together. One death is one too many. And I – I am going to do something strange myself. The oil lamps. I would love to know if they have been extinguished recently or if the poor child crept up the stairs in darkness.'

'She should not have done. House rules,' Harriet said almost wildly. 'No! She was the most obedient child.'

'I'll help you check. But won't you two need lamps for your prowl? Better than guttering candles. And altogether less Gothic,' Francis added with a grim smile as he reached for one. 'Hm. Not icy cold, but not warm either, Page.'

Page shook his head. 'Sadly, I doubt if we can deduce anything. But we might try the others . . .' Lifting his candle, he led the way.

Shaking with something like an ague, Harriet managed to take my hand, and we set off together.

All was quiet. Had there really been an assailant, a killer, as we now seemed tacitly to have agreed? If so, he or she was in a darkened room. Not knowing whether to be relieved or depressed in the absence of any clue, we returned via the linen room, carrying the promised sheets as if they were votive offerings.

At last Mary was laid in cold dignity, surrounded by candles; I had an idea that the Harriet who had denied Lady Stanton flowers might find some for this child, the lowliest of servants.

We took one last look at the clear innocent face, at the bruised arms crossed across her chest.

With utmost gentleness Page touched more bruises, these on her thin shoulders. 'She could not have inflicted these herself, I fear. We all understand the implications.'

There was silence.

At last, as Harriet draped a sheet over her, I offered a prayer. But then we had to consider our own health, and Ellis herded us to the kitchen, requiring cocoa and brandy for us all, which Harriet prepared while Francis admitted their examination of the lamps had been entirely inconclusive. We sipped, clutching the mugs for warmth and comfort, because, fearing I might wake Bea, who slept nearby, I was reluctant to poke the fire into life. But even when we had completed our strange Communion, all of us speaking in the hushed tones we had used since we found the little body, we had raised no one. I should have been pleased – but there was no doubt that the vastness of the House and the silences weighing on the empty spaces would make it very hard indeed to run Mary's killer to earth.

TEN

Harriet

All the meals in the servants' hall were taken without conversation, but today's silence had a different quality. Pain. Since it was clear the young women in particular needed to comfort each other, I relaxed the rule for once, going round to each in turn to answer any questions that they might have. Bea, her face puffed with tears, dispensed porridge which congealed uneaten in many dishes.

'I don't want anyone else having an accident like Mary's,' I reminded them at the end of the meal. 'Make sure all the lamps are lit before venturing down the stairs. If they're not, use the main stairs. Don't carry so much that you can't see your feet. Tell each other where you are going so that we find you if you are delayed. Please, please, however much you want to say goodbye, do not disturb Mary where she lies in the flower room. I am afraid that is not so much a request as a direct instruction. Remember too that Mr Pounceman injured himself in a bad fall on the ice – take extra care. And if in your free time you must throw snowballs, do it where you can do no harm and no one can be offended.' My smile was watery, but some of the lads looked as if I'd lifted a weight from them. They were young and alive and had all the deep feelings of colts let loose in a meadow.

Bea and I retired to the Room.

'All that going on and I heard nothing!' she exclaimed, leaning on the back of a chair. 'Nothing! Why didn't I hear her cry out? What was I doing?'

'You were probably in the drawing room with the rest of us,' I said. 'And I should imagine you fell asleep the moment your head hit the pillow. I don't know how we all kept our eyes open – you especially, after the last few days. It was only because it was clear there was something strange and out of place in our room that we were so alert and curious about the locked door. Oh, Bea, the poor, poor child. I had hoped for so much for her − she was bright and willing far beyond her station . . .'

'The poor mite. A workhouse orphan. Dying alone in the dark. No family to mourn her . . .' Suddenly Bea pulled her shoulders straight. 'But we'll do our best for her, Harriet. There won't be the posh canapés that we had for her late ladyship's wake, but we'll do her proud. Even if we have to wait until this lot thaws.' She jerked her thumb disdainfully in the direction of the window. 'And if our guests don't like us servants being off duty for an hour or two, they must lump it.'

'If they're still here.'

'Oh, once she knows there's an extra man in the house, a bachelor to boot, Lady Stanton will stick like glue.'

We giggled like a pair of tweenies. 'To be fair, she can't travel now, and her journey depends on her groom and coachman, doesn't it?'

'From what I gather from young Olwen, she might have to manage without them altogether. If she loses her sweetheart, Olwen'll want a job here, you mark my words. She's already sniffing round, in a manner of speaking.'

'Sniffing? About what?' I asked more sharply than was necessary.

Bea raised an eyebrow. 'She's ill, Harriet, with her baby's father dying!'

I couldn't quite back down. 'All the same, if she's well enough to sniff for a job, she should be well enough to tell us where she's come from. According to Francis, who says he used every scrap of charm he could summon, all her ladyship would reveal was that she had been visiting friends in the Borders. She parried his questions with questions of her own − and really interrogated him about his ruins.'

'I have done better than that. But not much. Some Welsh village. That's all. I couldn't make sense of the long name Olwen gave me, and she can't read or write.' At last she sat, leaning forward on her elbows. 'What do you make of the woman, apart from being so secretive? I'm not expecting an impartial answer, don't worry.'

'I looked her up in *Debrett's*,' I said. 'Nothing wrong on the face of it. Though we've all treated her like an innocent debutante, she's longer in the tooth than she would have us believe. Why doesn't she mention her family or the friends she wants to reach in Chester? Do you smell a rat?'

'Not in my kitchen!' she laughed. 'But I'll talk to young Olwen again. And again. Meanwhile, you need to have a conversation with Matthew about That Woman. The way she treats you! Atrocious! Tell me, is she someone from Matthew's past? No! There's no call to look like that, Harriet. I was joking.'

I pulled myself together. 'I'm sorry. Of course a man of his age must have a past. He's mentioned . . . flirtations. Not to make me jealous, just to be honest. But I hate it when she throws herself at him – she did within an hour of arriving in the House. And he's too much of a gentleman to be straight with her.'

'So you did it for him. I nearly cheered. There, you've nearly got your colour back now, that's better. Just keep talking to him, Harriet, so he knows how you feel. Mind you, Francis doesn't need telling, does he?'

'That's what friends are for.' I took a deep breath. 'But, even more than Francis, you are my friend, Bea, my best friend, and I have to ask you: the Will – how do you feel?'

She looked me in the eye. 'I was inclined to be jealous, truth to tell. But the old lady's tied you up good and proper, hasn't she, one way and another? I should be sad to give up my legacy, but it won't stop me leaving – should circumstances change.'

I said carefully, 'I know that if you leave of your own accord you lose it – but perhaps not if the trustees see fit to dismiss you, for whatever reason. And I'm sure we could find one – such as the indisputable fact that a cook of your talent and experience is wasted here. Anyway – we're still friends.'

'Of course we are.' She gave me a quick hug, as if embarrassed to show affection. Then she looked at her watch. 'And I've got the guest breakfast to think about. Will you be there today?'

'Yes. I cannot expect Francis not to mention the events of

the night, so Matthew and I will make a formal announcement at breakfast to those present.'

'Really? Can you expect people to be interested in the death of someone's most junior servant?'

'Not really. But their routines may be disrupted when Constable Pritchard arrives. A young man as conscientious as he may wish to speak to the guests as well as the household. And then I will visit our sick.'

She pulled a face. 'What about the sick villagers?'

'The usual routine: we'll start packing baskets of supplies so that they can be distributed as soon as it is safe.'

As Bea had predicted, the news of Mary's death hardly interrupted the buttering of toast. Francis was already all too aware of the situation, of course, but simply nodded, as if it were news to him too. I had not expected Lady Stanton to be present, nor was she. As soon as I could, I excused myself and went about my business.

Mr Pounceman was better, but did not want to receive visitors.

'And I can't say I blame him,' Nurse Webb said cheerfully. 'He's not the prettiest of sights. Otherwise I'd say he could be moved to a room more suited to his elevated status,' she added dryly. I had forgotten that she was far from being an admirer of his sermons – what she would have said about them before he had been persuaded to moderate his judgemental language, I could only imagine. 'In a couple of days he should be able to hobble about on crutches, so you might look out for a convenient bedchamber for him.'

'I might prefer to look for a convenient way to get him back to the rectory,' I said, thinking of the number of footmen it would take to wait on him to his satisfaction. 'After all, there are a dozen servants there to make his life bearable.'

'It would make for a happier household here,' she agreed. 'He is a . . . demanding patient and, in my experience, as people convalesce they become crabbier.'

'What of your other patients? Thomas and William? How do they fare?'

'I think William may live. But though Thomas is so much younger and fitter, I fear . . . But I do not want to be overheard, Mrs Rowsley. Olwen . . .' She dropped her voice. 'I cannot persuade her to leave him, and I fear for her reason if he dies.'

I was about to retort that I had never known anyone die of a broken heart, when I remembered Maggie, the gatekeeper's daughter abandoned by his lordship, who drowned herself. It was for her child that her late ladyship wanted us to search. Yes, hearts might not break, but spirits could – and did. 'Could Mr Pounceman be persuaded to pray for the sick men? That might comfort her?'

'What? Does Mr Pounceman work miracles?'

'Maybe not, but the One he serves can.'

She nodded silently as if to accept my gentle reproof. 'Very well. I will ask him. Or perhaps suggest Olwen does. Her tears will be stronger than any words of mine.'

Although Ellis would have told me if Samuel were unwell after yesterday's extraordinary events, I wanted to talk to him myself. In particular, I had to be the one to give him the awful news about Mary.

Fully dressed and freshly shaved, he was sitting beside a good fire. He smiled in distinct recognition as I took his hand and sat beside him.

'It was a big day for us both yesterday, was it not?' I began.

'It was indeed.' His face clouded. 'I should be grateful, I know I should, but I am not. Not yet. The thought of a cottage on my own!'

'You do not have to think about it yet, Samuel. Your place is here in the House.'

'But what's that about money and a cottage if it's not a way of getting rid of me?'

'They are there for when – for if! – you want to leave the House. And I promise you, Samuel, that there will be a place here as long as you want it. Dick Thatcher is doing very well, but he still needs your advice, doesn't he? And he's not moved into your room – neither does he want to.'

He nodded. 'It'll need a lick of paint before he does. As for me, Harriet, I'm best off here for a bit. I don't know why, but my brain and my legs don't always seem to talk to each other!'

'You had a dreadful bang on the head, remember. Now, I have some very sad news for you. One of our girls has had an accident. Little Mary. You may not recall her.'

'Of course I remember the girl!' he said. 'Tall? Red hair? No . . . Do you know, I don't think . . . Oh, dear – should I?'

I squeezed his hand. 'She'd only been here a few days when you were attacked. But the poor child . . .' I strove for control. 'I am afraid she's had a bad fall. Very bad indeed.'

'Is she the reason everyone's tiptoeing round? No, that'll be these newcomers. Turning up late at night like that – a rackety thing to do, Mrs . . . Mrs . . .'

'Could you use my first name, Samuel? You always called me that until we both became so important. Harriet?'

He smiled with relief. 'Harriet. That was it. You're sure I don't have to go to this cottage now?'

'Certain. It's not just Dick Thatcher who needs your advice: I do too . . .' I explained about the problems Lady Stanton was causing me.

He listened intently, a frown deepening. 'Dine with the guests, Harriet? That cannot be right. On the other hand, the lady visitor cannot be unchaperoned. Cannot. And you cannot ask her to eat in her room all the time. As a guest she must have the best treatment. I fear – yes, I am a little muddled. I may need a little time to think.'

I bent to kiss his forehead. 'You shall have all the time in the world. God bless you, my dear friend.'

I left the Family wing and walked down the main staircase, deep in reflection. Much as I wanted to comfort Olwen – perhaps even offer her refuge, as Bea suggested – I still felt that the person who should be speaking to her was her employer. I had only seen a bad side of her ladyship, but if anyone could make her show a better one it must be the maid who knew all her intimate secrets.

Was I the person to suggest that Lady Stanton might visit her in the Family wing? I could imagine her amazed disdain if I approached her. Or should I turn to Matthew to do it? Every feeling revolted! Ashamed as I was of my resentment – my jealousy – of her, I found I could not ask him to approach her, cap in hand as it were. But I could certainly ask Francis, who was giving a very good impression of a man interested in what the professor would call the Fair Sex. He might even escort her up to the Family wing himself. And what if—?

'What a strange house this is, Mrs Rolly. In mine, servants keep to the backstairs!'

I almost missed a stair I was so surprised. Belatedly I managed a curtsy and a polite smile as I stepped aside to let her continue upwards. 'Good morning, your ladyship. I'm sorry if one of my colleagues has offended you in any way. I'm afraid that all our routines have been upset: one of the young maids died suddenly last night. A lovely child. We will miss her.' It was only as I spoke that I realized that her criticism was directed at me. But this morning I would not bite, whatever the provocation. Would not. I waited in vain for any words of condolence. 'I have just been to what we still call the Family wing, ma'am, to see how our patients go on. Would you care for me to show you the way so that you can visit Olwen?' When she did not respond, I added, 'I fear that the news about your groom is not good at all, and Olwen is naturally very upset.'

'I believe I have told you that in my house we do not have followers.'

'You have indeed, ma'am. But you do have loyal employees who would surely benefit from your presence, however brief a visit it might be. I believe even our rector, badly injured in an accident last night, may well try to rise from his sick bed to pray for them.' I turned, managing to fall into step with her as she continued on her way. 'Such a handsome man: I do hope he is not scarred for life,' I added, perhaps a little generous with the truth. However, young and eligible Mr Pounceman was, and though an air of mutual loathing had marred our early acquaintance, we could at least now be polite to each other in company – and indeed in private.

She inclined her head. 'Very well.' She stared as I tapped on the locked door, and identified us to the retired gamekeeper on duty today. I showed her into Nurse Webb's office. 'Lady Stanton, may I present Nurse Webb, who is in charge here?' As Nurse Webb offered her usual shallow bob of a curtsy, I continued, 'Her ladyship naturally wishes to see her staff: is that possible, if only for a few moments? Excellent.' I turned back to Lady Stanton. 'Nurse Webb will ring as soon as you wish to conclude your visit, and one of my colleagues will escort you wherever you wish to go.' I offered my professional smile and a curtsy not much lower than Nurse Webb's.

It was only as I was about to leave the wing and was asking Jem Blade about his family and his rheumatics, that I started to wonder what her ladyship had been doing in this part of the House. Her bedchamber was in the guest wing, where all the principal rooms in which she might be interested were also located. I had never yet met house guests who thought they were entitled to explore every corner of their hosts' home. If I had run into one in a private corridor, he or she would usually ask me for help finding a particular picture or curio, if not a room of interest.

It was something I would mention to Mr Wilson when I saw him.

Unasked, my feet took me to my new area of responsibility – the library. Mine for life, in effect, just as her ladyship's jewellery now was. It was unoccupied, so I locked it. And then I flew upstairs. The jewellery was supposed to be safe in my care – with the horror of poor Mary's death it had completely gone from my mind. All I had to hope was that it had not completely gone from our room.

ELEVEN

Matthew

'It had been moved but not opened? What a relief!' Wilson declared, sitting down hard on one of the chairs at the far side of my desk. Harriet shifted her skirt slightly to give him more space; how on earth did ladies manage with such voluminous clothing? 'I cannot believe that you did not notice – but perhaps in all the upset caused by that poor girl's death . . . And the keys?' He quickly returned to his usual tone.

'Still where you saw us put them: one on Harriet's chatelaine, and one on my key ring. But though neither of us is ever knowingly parted from them, the best thing, we felt, was to move the jewellery to the House safe. It has protected all the Family silver for the last fifty years, and we would be happier to keep it there.'

'Except for the jet,' Harriet added. 'I believe her ladyship would have wanted me to wear it. So Matthew will keep it in his office safe, retrieving it every evening.'

Wilson nodded. For some reason his smile reminded me of a tortoise. 'How far was the cabinet moved?'

'From the far end of the dressing room to the end nearest the service door.'

He frowned. 'So this young servant might have moved it and been scared when she heard you coming?'

'That would require a combination of strength, knowledge and guile I do not believe Mary possesses. Possessed.' Harriet swallowed before continuing, 'I believe that she came to make up the fire, but interrupted some intruder. She was pushed and put her dirty hand on the door jamb to try to avoid falling. Obviously . . .' Another hard swallow. 'And the stairs were in complete darkness, the lamps having been extinguished.'

Wilson nodded his appreciation of her theory, but raised an index finger. 'But who was the intruder and how would he or she know where the cabinet was kept? That, indeed, it was even in your room, not her late ladyship's? Or even, to take one step further back, that it existed at all?'

She held her head up, her chin slightly raised. 'I have no idea. But I intend, with Matthew's help and that of all the good men and women here, to find out.'

Did Wilson notice that she omitted to name him alongside me? Surely she did not mistrust him? Or perhaps on principle she was cautious of everyone except me. I declared, 'A child who brings my shoes on a cushion must receive justice.' More circumspectly, I continued, 'But I have no idea how to bring it about. Have you, Wilson?'

He sucked his teeth. 'I know I have said this before, but how I regret that that detective chose to leave. Strangers in the House! Oh, I know that that peacock of a professor is a friend of Sir Francis.'

'He is, indeed, and Francis vouches for him.'

'But what of his valet? And Sir Francis' own man? And, in a house this size, where do these valets and other servants go when they are not actively waiting on their principals?'

'The servants' hall,' Harriet said, biting back, I suspected, an impulse to point out that the professor arrived with Wilson's positive encouragement and we could hardly have predicted Lady Stanton's precipitate arrival. 'As for Lady Stanton, she would never make me her confidante, so perhaps one of you gentlemen . . .'

She did not look at me but did not need to. 'Lady Stanton has made it her business to embarrass me and humiliate Harriet. I would not be in the same room as her by choice, and certainly not alone and indulging in a conversation I fear would embarrass me further.' To my ears I sounded priggish, but at least sincere, I hoped.

'Very well. I will do that. But you will understand that as a man of the professions and no more, I simply do not understand fully the implications of what someone from the Upper Ten Thousand might say.'

Harriet smiled. 'You are a lawyer, Montgomery, and you

know the value of truth. If you engage her in conversation – as one might a chance acquaintance in a railway carriage – you should be able to find out a great deal about her without her realizing she is giving you information.'

He shook his head. 'I was sadly mistaken when I took Mr Timpson's tale on trust. But I will endeavour to be more alert this time. I will speak, oh, so casually, to our guest. Be as charming as Sir Francis, in fact. He has achieved nothing from his whispered interrogations, I collect? But in all honesty, I cannot see the professor or her ladyship entering someone else's room in person: it would look too particular. So my original question stands: where are their servants? Who keeps an eye on them?'

'Thatcher, as butler, is responsible for the conduct of our manservants and would always want to know the where-abouts of the valets lest their masters rang for them,' Harriet said. 'Similarly I know in theory where all maidservants are – there is a chart on the wall of the Room showing each one's duties by the hour. But if one finished a task early – who knows? We rely so much on trust and personal loyalty, as if we were a family. I would hope that if any of our people found cause to distrust a colleague, or a visitor's valet, they would speak to me or to Thatcher.'

I nodded. 'But if someone in the servants' hall said, "I have to be on duty when my master returns to his room," and simply leaves, people might not think twice about it. Of course, they might expect them to be summoned by their bell, but they would not argue.'

'At least we don't have her ladyship's maid to worry about as long as she is glued to her sweetheart's side. Oh, the poor child – although I took her mistress to see her this morning, I cannot feel the visit will have cheered her much. Heavens! How could it have slipped my mind? I found Lady Stanton on the staircase leading to the Family wing this morning.'

'Ah! And did you challenge her?'

'On the contrary, Montgomery, she challenged me!'

'I beg your pardon?'

'In her household mere servants do not use the main stair-cases and corridors. I thought at first she had found a tweeny crossing the entrance hall with a chamber pot in her hands. Then I realized it was me she was criticizing.'

'And your response was—?'

'Belated! And rather sanctimonious, to be honest. But I was provoked. Matthew already knows that I am embarrassed by my tart riposte last night, so at least I retained my manners and my dignity. And my curiosity. What was she doing there?'

'I suppose the laws of hospitality would prevent you asking her outright, even if you were on good terms,' Wilson reflected. 'But equally, surely one does not expect one's guests to wander round on their own. Especially if the guest is essentially uninvited and unknown. What does *Debrett's* tell us about her, Matthew?'

Harriet coughed gently. 'I looked her up just before breakfast yesterday morning. The granddaughter of one of Nelson's admirals, whose seat is in Yorkshire. Malton.'

The response to her flat announcement was some amazement. 'We are,' Wilson observed with a slight cough, 'a considerable distance from there – assuming that is where she still lives. We know she is trying to reach Chester. And that she came from an unpronounceable part of Wales. But where was she before that? My dear friends, it seems we know even less about her than we knew about the egregious Mr Timpson. And she apparently has the run of a place full of treasures!'

'Not quite,' Harriet said. 'I confess that I have used my new authority to lock the library. Now the poor gentlemen have nothing to do except entertain her ladyship. Oh, a trifling excuse – mice, I think I said. We needed to poison them before they ate the leather bindings. Which we would, if we had mice.' Whenever she smiled like that, my heart turned over in my breast. That such a creature should have condescended to become my wife!

'You don't?'

'Not if I can help it. Beetles aplenty, in the kitchen. We now have a resident hedgehog, who worked very industriously consuming them after dark. Sadly for Bea, however, the beetles have returned. Apparently hedgehogs hibernate. We have rats, of course, so we hold terrier days, when they are flushed out. You can imagine rats wreak havoc amongst the hens. And,' she mused, 'we certainly do not want them in the House.' She looked him straight in the eye. 'Can you be our terrier, Montgomery?'

Did his heart turn too? Or had she gone too far?

'I will see what I can do. But I still need to contrive a reason to speak at length with her.' He pressed his index finger against his lips to show how hard he was thinking. But clearly inspiration did not visit him, for he got up slowly and heavily, shaking his head. 'Very well. I must think of some plausible reason. Leave it with me.' He was at the door when he turned back to Harriet. 'I remember your leading a group of us visitors around the House once – pointing out paintings, china, even furniture of note. Would that provide an occasion for her ladyship and me to fall into conversation?'

'It would indeed. But would you wish me to point out to a visiting vixen the plumpest fowl in the hen house? I fear I would be attaching "Steal me!" labels to our Oliver and Hilliard miniatures, to our Rembrandt self-portrait, or our Reynolds family group.' Though she spoke quietly she spoke with passion.

'In the absence of servant-detectives, Wilson,' I added, 'I cannot see how we can keep a constant patrol with so many yards of corridors and so many inviting doors – even two more dedicated staff would still amount to little more than a gesture. Somehow we must contrive to keep our visitors herded together under discreet surveillance.'

'Fewer fires,' Harriet said suddenly. 'No fires in bedchambers till the early evening when they go to change for dinner. It was a technique one of my early employers used. Very effective at getting rid of unwanted guests it was too.'

'Except we can't get rid of her ladyship if she cannot use her coach,' Wilson said dryly. 'And I should imagine there will be no trains for a while. Unless you send your own coachman and groom instead of hers – and then how would they get back?'

'John Coachman should have retired years ago, and even if we asked him to go, Dr Page would veto the plan,' I said. 'But I will send a couple of lads over to the railway station to see what the situation is – at the very least, they'll enjoy an opportunity to lark about a bit.' I looked at the clock I had acquired. 'I know that we have not resolved all our problems, indeed, any of them, but I think we deserve some coffee. Shall we have it here, or all adjourn to the Room, Harriet?'

TWELVE

Harriet

'Dick, just close the door and sit down, please,' I said, gesturing to a seat opposite mine at the table in the Room. 'Thank you. I know you're the butler, but you're young enough to talk to your junior colleagues, aren't you?' He looked about to bridle – butlers needed to be above the common herd. When it came to imposing silence at mealtimes, he was even more conscientious than I was. I corrected myself: 'To keep in touch with them? To know the general mood? Can you tell me what everyone thinks about poor Mary's death? Now I have to eat with our guests, to act as chaperon to her ladyship, I miss the little hints about things, the stifled whispers . . .'

'We don't know how it could have happened, Mrs Rowsley, and that's the truth. As you know, at night Luke and I see that one of us goes all round the House making sure everything is as it should be. These days we check that the doors of the unoccupied rooms are locked too. It's all very well Mr Rowsley taking a fancy to a clock and a picture, but we don't want anyone else doing it, do we? Is there any news of that picture, by the way?'

I shook my head. 'We've been worrying about other things, as you can imagine. I want to take you into my confidence, Dick. And you know me well enough to know that when I ask you to keep it completely between us it's important.'

He coloured. 'Mrs Rowsley, ma'am – can you doubt me?'

'Of course I don't. I trust you as if you were my own nephew. But I'm going to ask you to do something quite unpleasant, something a butler is never expected to do. I want you to spy on someone.'

He knew he should look shocked, but could not keep a gleam of excitement from his eyes. 'Ma'am?'

'The trouble is I'm not quite sure who. Dick, someone got
into the bedchamber Mr Rowsley and I use. The main door
was locked, so whoever got in must have used the service door.
Got in, moved something, and probably pushed Mary to her
death.'

'Ma'am, might I ask what was moved?'

'The cabinet we locked in the safe this morning. The cabinet
containing her late ladyship's jewels.'

'Good God! Beg pardon, ma'am – but the very notion!
How on earth did anyone know it was there?'

'Exactly! I suppose if someone saw Mr Wilson carrying it
along the corridor they might have made an intelligent guess.
And there would have been servants around then.'

'Most of us – most of the footmen – use the backstairs,
don't they? But the valets don't. Or the guests, of course,' he
added with what I felt was a little emphasis.

I cocked my head in what Matthew had once referred to
as my intelligent sparrow mode.

'That professor, ma'am – he wanders all over the place
peering around like a hen after corn. No, a cockerel, he's so
glossy and full of himself. And suddenly – peck! – he's as close
to a picture or a pot as he can get. That Lady Stanton – her
too.'

'Really? You see, you clearly know things I don't! Do you
get the impression that they might know each other?' I asked,
surprising myself.

He stared. 'Not really. It's your friend Sir Francis who's
dancing attendance on her, isn't it? But I could ask his valet.
A nice chatty gentleman is Mr Parker. Not like the professor's man, Mr Hodge – an oyster's nothing compared with
him.'

'And how do they get on in the servants' hall?'

'Well enough. It's as if they're wrapped in some sort of
invisible mist – they're there but not there. But that's sometimes
the way of it with visiting servants, isn't it? Do you remember
that friend of her late ladyship's who brought the snootiest
lady's maid—?'

The butler's bell rang. He got up automatically, but by the
door he paused, as if looking at something a long way away.

'Ma'am – I keep on imagining it's my little sister lying on that table in the flower room.'

Mary was leaving the House with dignity – more than had accompanied her ragged, terrified arrival from the workhouse, certainly. There was logic behind my decision to have her carried through the great entrance hall and the wide main doors: those carrying her body would have no awkward corners to negotiate. But even as I asked all the staff, from Thatcher to the meanest scullery maid, to gather there to bid her a silent farewell, I knew I was going to cause surprise and perhaps offence. By their own request, Matthew and Thatcher were to carry her on a makeshift stretcher. And I would further defy convention by walking behind them carrying some white geraniums the gardeners had overwintered in a succession house.

There! She was laid on the black-draped sleigh. John Coachman had taken the bells off the matching harness and chosen two staid black horses. He refused to let anyone else drive her but at least he was swathed in the sheepskin rugs her ladyship once used. The three of us watched from the broad steps as he drove gently away.

Ellis, muffled to the ears, materialized behind me. 'You have made my task ten times harder, Harriet. I prefer not to think of the bodies I examine as people, and nothing brought home that child's human state more than the tiny bier carried by two strong men.'

I smiled sadly. 'At one point Dick Thatcher wanted to carry her in his arms, as if she were a baby. But I did not think any of us could have endured that.'

'A wise decision.' He touched my hand. 'Just bear in mind that death by a broken neck is very quick. Now, I will leave you and go and record the . . . the evidence . . . the coroner will need.'

'There is something else – in my . . . I should have . . . I forgot to take the keys from her pocket. The House keys for all the rooms she was responsible for.'

'I will keep them safe.' A groom brought round the other sleigh. 'I wish I could have persuaded Sir Francis to have come

along with his camera: it would have been very useful to have
the child's injuries recorded.'

I looked him in the eye. 'Useful in a trial?'

He nodded.

'In that case, I will talk to him, with the privilege of an old
friend.'

'Will you? Thank you.'

'I hope you will forgive me but I knew you would have
. . . other matters . . . on your mind. And be very busy with
the new patients. I talked to Samuel about his legacy. I think
he grasped it. But tomorrow—'

'Who knows?' He smiled. He pointed to the sleigh. 'I must
go. Thank you for dealing with Samuel – the poor man is still
very confused, is he not? If I can, I will return to see my
patients here this evening, and I will bring news . . . news of
what I have found – meanwhile, you have another visitor,
Harriet. Constable Pritchard.' He broke into a disconcerting
smile. 'Does he qualify for the front door or shall I send him
round the back?'

'The front. After all, he will need to speak to everyone in
the House at the time, not just the staff.' Then – and I could
not stop myself – I asked, 'Is it . . . is it possible . . . that
someone . . . interfered with her?'

He looked at me with steady compassion. 'I dearly hope not.'

I shuddered. If she had been raped, I would have to kill the
man responsible.

'Talk in front of all the gentlefolk?' Elias Pritchard squeaked,
as Matthew and I greeted him on the steps. 'But I don't have
permission!'

Clapping him on the shoulder and sending a shower of snow
on to his feet, Matthew said, 'You don't need to ask permission
to bowl a lord out at cricket. Or to yell, "Howzat?" if you catch
one out.' He ushered him inside, allowing the footmen to close
the doors at last, to everyone's great relief. One of them relieved
Elias of his hat and cape. 'Well, imagine you want to catch one
of these out. In a manner of speaking, of course,' he added with
a grin, because though lacking in confidence, Elias was no fool.

'Permission from Sergeant Burrows, I mean, sir – Matthew,

I mean. Or in front of these people, Mr Rowsley is best, I think. Anyway, like I said, Sergeant Burrows is the one to give me permission.'

'Since we don't know when he can get through from Shrewsbury, I think you might have to act on your own initiative. I should imagine Mrs Arden has coffee and biscuits waiting in a nice warm kitchen, so let's all go in and talk our talk there while Thatcher gathers the guests. You've heard that he's been taking bowling lessons—'

'Not from you, ma'am – that grip on the ball?'

'The very same . . .'

'And no one has cleaned or dusted these stairs since the poor child died?' Elias asked, as, leaving Matthew to guest duty, I showed him up to the scene of Mary's death some fifteen minutes later.

'No. But because we have guests in the House, we have continued to use them. That,' I said, pointing at the soot mark where she had fallen, 'was where we found her. Later Sir Francis will show you how she lay – photographs,' I said, waiting for him to be impressed. 'Much as I wanted to clean that and the sooty smudge on our service door, I left them to show you and to learn what you deduced.'

He looked at me sideways. 'I'm guessing you have a theory of your own, Mrs Rowsley, ma'am.'

'Perhaps. But you are a policeman, Elias, and you know more about crime than I do. Ask me how to clean these stairs and I could tell you. But ask me about a poor child's death, and I would always defer to you.' This was not strictly true, of course – but the young man was looking apprehensive again and I wanted him to walk into the blue salon, where Matthew was herding our guests, with his chin high and his shoulders back. 'There is something else you should know. She will have keys about her . . .'

'Keys?'

'Keys to all the bedchambers and other rooms she was responsible for. I forgot to retrieve them. I've asked Ellis to . . . when he . . .' If I was not careful I would give way in the face of his earnest, calm kindness.

'If he forgets I'll ask him. I'll lock them in the evidence box.'

Before we went down together, I showed him our bedchamber, pointing to where the jewellery cabinet had been originally and where I found it.

'And now it's . . .?'

'Locked with her ladyship's state parure which was already in the butler's safe – which needs two of us to unlock.'

He grimaced. 'And a parure is what, ma'am?'

'I'm sorry. It's a set of pieces of jewellery meant to be worn together – in this case there's a tiara, necklace and bracelet. All set with diamonds. She wore it at Her Majesty's coronation.'

His eyebrows shot up. 'Does anyone else know about this? The parure and the cabinet being in the safe?'

'Matthew and Mr Wilson apart, only Dick Thatcher, as butler—'

'I thought Dick was just standing in for Mr Bowman.'

'He was. But though Mr Bowman is making an amazing recovery, thank God, it is not likely that he will ever work again – not as butler, at least.' And anything else would demean him, would it not?

He gave a sad smile. 'I remember the first time I met him properly. I was just a little nipper playing my first match and deserved to get his late lordship out. And Mr Bowman said quietly, "It was plumb leg before wicket, son, but not his lordship's leg."' The smile soon faded from his face as he looked around, taking in the handprint smudge. 'Strange having a front door and a back door for just one room.'

'Think for one moment about chamber pots,' I said. 'Guests do not like to meet them coming down the main stairs.'

He grinned. 'Just one thing, Mrs Rowsley. Could I see these jewels? To make sure they're safe and sound?'

More likely because he could never have seen such riches in his life before. 'Of course. I'll summon Thatcher. He should have rounded everyone up by now.'

Elias' eyes rounded as we opened first the safe and then the jewellery cabinet. 'The only thing not locked up here is the Whitby jet necklace and bracelet—'

'That's a parure?' he asked.

I smiled: I loved a quick learner. 'Nearly. But there's no matching tiara. The other items live in Matthew's office safe so I can wear them every evening in her ladyship's honour.' I looked at my watch. 'Perhaps we should lock up now, Dick, so we do not keep the guests waiting any longer. Then perhaps you'll gather all the servants together to listen to Elias?'

The constable shook his head. 'With all due respect, ma'am, I'd rather we just sprang it on them, so they don't have time to prepare their stories.'

'You're quite right,' I said. 'So neither of us will say anything yet. Now, Elias, as we go along to the blue salon, let me tell you something about our guests.' I set us in motion. 'First, let me warn you that we have a lady staying here. She simply arrived the night of the funeral.' I explained, watching his eyebrows rise further with each detail I gave. 'And we also have one of Sir Francis' friends – a professor who is advising the trustees on all the works of art in the House.'

'Really? But you say he's a friend of Sir Francis, so presumably he's . . . respectable?'

'Of course. Don't expect him to be another Sir Francis, however. And you know John Timpson.'

'Indeed I do.' And did not like him at all. 'What I'd like to do, ma'am, is tell them all what's going on and why I'm here, and then speak to them alone.'

'Excellent. If you want to do that immediately, you could use the antechamber, while we keep the rest penned in.' Of course my language was disrespectful – but I wanted to remind him that he could still giggle about people he had been taught from birth to consider a superior species. 'Now, as to her ladyship – it would really help me if you could keep her talking a reasonable length of time.'

He looked shocked. 'You're not planning to search her things, ma'am! That wouldn't be right!'

'Of course not. But I would like to talk to Florrie in a way that wouldn't be possible with her ladyship in the room.'

He looked at me steadily. 'Very well.'

'There – Matthew is waiting to introduce you,' I whispered, pointing to where he was standing beside a fine buhl table.

'Just pretend you're talking to that fat, ugly, old man in the picture at the back of the room.'

He nodded, but raised a finger. 'Just one second, ma'am.' He rubbed first one boot then the other on his trouser legs.

Matthew shook his hand as if welcoming him to the wicket in a friendly game of cricket, before addressing the guests. 'Constable Pritchard, ladies and gentlemen.' He stepped back.

Elias managed better than I expected. Francis leaned forward, as if willing him to do well, his professor friend leaned back in his chair, arms folded, as if judging a particularly weak student, Timpson took notes and Lady Stanton's face was a study in boredom. Actually, offensively studied boredom, involving the inspection of her nails. Matthew and I nodded encouragingly from our seats near the ugly portrait.

Fortunately Elias attempted no spurious jokes, and managed not to be overly obsequious. He explained what had happened, and then said he would have to question everyone in the House. 'Everyone,' he repeated. 'Begging your pardons, although obviously I shall be concentrating mainly on the people most likely to use the backstairs, I will need to speak to you – mostly about your servants' whereabouts.'

'In that case, young man, speak to us first. Then we can go about our preferred avocations,' Fulke-Grosse drawled.

Amazingly Elias did not appear to be cowed. 'Indeed and I will, sir. I understand the anteroom is ready for us now. If you are busy, sir, would you care to be first?'

THIRTEEN

Matthew

'The poor bumpkin,' Fulke-Grosse drawled, getting slowly to his feet. 'Stuttering and stumbling. One cannot have much faith in his abilities to solve this or indeed any alleged crime.' There was no doubt that his voice was meant to carry to Elias' ears.

I did not need to share Harriet's silent furious restraint. 'Not everyone has had the benefit of a public school debating society, professor. Or the Oxford Union, of course. And until we get policemen with the benefits of our education, we have to be grateful to decent, intelligent, hard-working men like Elias who do their best – which is sometimes a remarkably successful best, I must tell you. Indeed, I hold him in very high esteem.'

'So much is obvious,' he observed as he lounged towards the anteroom.

Francis rolled his eyes apologetically. 'At least he does not work in the Diplomatic Corps! I apologize on his behalf, Matthew, and will as always take care to treat the poor constable properly myself. Now what do I see? Harriet approaching her *bête noire*? But I fancy she would rather speak to her ladyship herself than watch you in conversation with her.'

'Which is why you are being so assiduous in your attentions to her ladyship?'

He dropped his voice. 'I love Harriet: she is the sister I never had. And though I know that you love her . . . No, I am phrasing it ill. Let me start again. Why should she be so nervous and anxious and prickly around her ladyship? Because she has never moved in circles where flirtation is a game. And, to be honest, because her ladyship probably enjoys seeding her jealousy. Look at her: everything about her is putting the most decent woman I know in her place.'

'Should I go—?'

'By no means. If she were a child being bullied, you would refrain because you would know that to leap to the victim's defence would lead to the offence being repeated with more venom. And in this situation, her ladyship would turn the full power of her undoubted attractions on you and thus make Harriet even more uneasy. Watch and wait: that is my advice.'

Smile and nod as I might at Francis' kindly meant words, I seethed with anger. How dare he try to intervene? But even as I fumed, Harriet caught my eye, offering the barest hint of a wink. And it dawned on me that her smiles to her ladyship had the quality of steely implacability, as if she were confronting an errant maid who was lying about a breakage. Her curtsy was perfunctory as she swept out.

'Ah! Harriet has quit the battlefield. I hope she won the skirmish.'

'Do you doubt her?' I said, able to return his smile.

'Never! You are aware that she asked me to go and take photographs of . . . dear God, I am to take photographs during the post-mortem examination! How can I bear it? How can I sit with that on my shoulders while Elias interviews me? I am to be transported by sleigh, that most festive means of transport! Pray God it's not the one that carried her . . .' He made a visible effort. 'Now, go and discuss something with poor Timpson, who is in a truly dreadful situation, come to think of it. And make sure that your handsome young butler prevents anyone from leaving: some people might try to sweep out, you know.'

Accordingly I drifted away. Should I make it my business to see how Elias was doing? No. That would be to undermine him. So I sat obediently beside Timpson.

Given his equivocal position in the household, I was surprised at the fervour with which he plunged into his theory about what might have happened. Since Elias had not mentioned the presence of the jewellery in our room, or indeed anything else about where Mary had been working and Thatcher would have his tongue torn out before betraying any family secret, I could not comment in any detail. But in essence we agreed: Mary had come upon someone doing something wrong and had been silenced – perhaps simply by being chased away and subsequently falling. Or, he added soberly, by being pushed. 'Which is why, no doubt, we're all being questioned. Tell me, sir, if you can, if all the priceless things in the House are safe? I cannot but notice that Mrs Rowsley has locked the Library.' Yes, it was clear he had used a capital letter. To him the library was not a mere room – it was a space as deserving of reverence as a church.

'Mice,' I said. 'We had to put down bait. Don't want anyone getting poisoned, do we?'

He blinked. 'Begging your pardon, sir, but if you had said rats I would have understood. And, if I might make so bold, I think you might need the same remedy in the document room. Or at least make sure it's locked when I'm not in there.' He bit his lip. 'I know you have every reason not to trust me, but . . .' He took a deep breath. 'There is no better worker than a poacher turned gamekeeper, is there, sir?'

'You never took anything, though, did you?'

He snorted softly. 'I could have taken everything, if circumstances had been different and I was about to be Lord Croft. But you know that I never cared for any of it. Becoming a lord, responsible for so much, must be hard enough if you're used to the life, knowing how to treat people great and small, but I felt I was in a strange dream – a nightmare, most of the time! I shudder to recall my behaviour at that time.'

So, in fact, did I, and anyone who witnessed it.

Now his eyes gleamed with passion. 'And then I handled those medieval documents in the attic. You know that they say new mothers have only to lay eyes on their babies, even really ugly ones, to love them. That was how I felt.' His face became rapt, his voice that of a lover. 'And one day when Mrs Rowsley had let Sir Francis see one of the books normally kept locked up, I was able to see it too, even to touch it. It was a book of hours, Matthew. So beautiful . . . And if I can do anything to keep it and all the others safe, I will.'

It was the first time he had ever dared to use my first name: that was how sincere he was. Or was it all a big confidence trick? If only Harriet had been party to the conversation. She would have known. As it was, Elias was hovering at the edge of the room, trying to catch my eye. 'Thank you, John. I believe you. And I will procure you a key for the document room. But now I see that it is my turn to speak to Constable Pritchard.' To my amazement I patted him reassuringly on the shoulder as I left him.

In fact, Elias did not want me to go over my story; he wanted me to protect him from Lady Stanton, though he did not put it in quite those words. Much as I would have preferred him to ask Harriet for help – where on earth had she gone, anyway? – I could not take away his fragile authority by suggesting it. Lest the lady be inclined to address me, I sat behind her, out of her eyeline unless she swung right round on the elegant gilded chair.

To my delight, Elias was a great deal blunter with her than any of us had dared to be.

'So, what brought you here to Thorncroft, ma'am?'

'I have already told the people here – have I not, Mr Rowsley?' Even though her head had to twist to an impossible angle, she fluttered her eyelashes.

'But you have not told me, ma'am, so that I can write it down, as I have to.' Elias licked the tip of his pencil. What on earth was he doing, behaving like a yokel? He waited, before asking again. 'So, what brought you here, ma'am?'

'I was visiting friends.'

'Lady Croft, would that be?'

'I did not know Lady Croft.'

'So who would your friend be? Poor Lord Croft? No? Sir Francis?' He lifted his pencil to write again.

'No. Sir Francis – I did not know him before, but . . .'

'But? But you are friends now? That's nice: a very clever man, Sir Francis. Clever with his photographic apparatus, I understand. Oh, I'm sure he'll tell you all about it. So which friend were you visiting?'

'Someone in Cheshire.'

He nodded, as if it made sense. 'So you decided to stop here. Now why would that be?'

'Did you not notice the snow, my man?'

He nodded. 'Oh, I did, ma'am. But why should you stop here, not at an inn? There must be inns on the way from – oh, now where did I write that down?' He made a show of running his finger down the notebook page.

My memory flickered: it was almost as if he were imitating a Shakespearean rude mechanical. Could he have been? No, his education would not have stretched to the Bard.

'No. So oblige me by telling me again, if you would be so kind.'

'Cwmbach Llechrhyd,' she said quickly, as if she wanted to make him ask her again.

Instead, he looked as if she had made him perfectly happy. 'Ah! Near Builth Wells. My great grandmamma lived there. But it is a very long way from here, your ladyship. And over poor roads too. No, you must have used the new railway – what a godsend that is. No? Oh, of course, you arrived by coach, didn't you? Where did you break your journey?' When she did not respond, he said, almost idly, 'So Cwmbach Llechrhyd is where you live, ma'am?'

'I do not believe I told you that.'

He pulled a face like an embarrassed schoolboy. Yes, even without the benefit of extensive reading, he was more than capable of acting, and of acting so well she did not realize it. In fact, the more stupid he appeared, the more Lady Stanton might give away.

'Beg pardon. I thought you did. So where do you live? To put it more simply, what is your address, your ladyship?'

'Malton Hall. The seat of the Stanton family.'

I was desperate to tell Elias that that was her grandfather's address. But I must not interrupt and damage his authority.

'Before you ask another stupid question, that's near Malton, Yorkshire, of course. Now, might I ask why I have been dragged in here to submit to your rambling interrogation?'

'Because everyone in a house where a sudden and unexplained death occurs has to make a statement,' he said, suddenly stern. 'Everyone. Now we have an address, your ladyship, perhaps you would also furnish me with your full name. I need to write more than Lady Stanton, you see.'

'Seraphina Ernestine Georgiana Stanton.' Gathering her skirts, she prepared to stand.

'Just a couple more questions, if you'd be so kind. First of all, let me get this straight. You live in Yorkshire but you were staying near Builth. From there you set out and drove to

Thorncroft, where you were given shelter and your servants treated for the effects of the cold. You have with you a considerable amount of luggage, as if you made a long stay in Wales and intend another long one in Cheshire.' Not surprisingly what little I could see of her face grew more and more thunderous at each stage of his recital. 'But you have vouchsafed none of this information to your kind hosts.'

Her eyes widened as if in disbelief at his stupidity. 'How could I? I have not met my hosts. Or rather, my host. Lord Croft has not so much as put in an appearance. It is terribly distressing.'

'Indeed. I believe I called him poor Lord Croft only a moment ago . . . Surely someone here has mentioned that his lordship is very ill, and does not receive visitors. Come to think of it, I am surprised that Florrie – your acting maid, ma'am – has not told you all about the Family's troubles.'

'I do not encourage servants' gossip. And since I understand that the person who died is a mere child, and actually the lowest servant of all, I am simply at a loss as to why you are questioning me.'

Elias remained stolidly straight-faced. 'I am obliged to bring her murderer to justice, ma'am. That is the Law, for the richest and the poorest. That's why. Now, I have explained to everyone the time and circumstances of her demise. Where were you when she died?'

She shrugged extravagantly. 'In the salon I should imagine, with Sir Francis and one or two others. Or in my bedchamber, attended by that country girl, who is all fingers and thumbs. I am told she once waited on Lady Croft – but how she could do so with such minimal accomplishments I do not know.'

'The time, ma'am?'

'Oh, how should I know? You are simply wasting my time, and I shall report you to your superior.' She stood, ready to sweep out.

'Just a couple more questions, your ladyship, if I may. Did you bring a jewellery box with you? A large one?' He gestured.

She froze. 'Why should you ask that?'

'All part of my enquiries, ma'am. Thank you very much.' He stood.

'No. That's not good enough. Why do you ask?' Her voice was very sharp.

'Because some people might think that with a miscreant on the loose leaving it unattended in a house with sixty or so rooms might be risky. Perhaps it might be more secure if it were locked in a safe. That's all.' He turned to me. 'I'm sure you'd be able to find somewhere to secure it, wouldn't you, Mr Rowsley?'

I bowed. 'If that is what Lady Stanton wishes, I'm sure it can be arranged,' I replied, as smoothly as if I knew what he was up to.

FOURTEEN

Harriet

'I don't know what to make of her ladyship and that's God's truth, ma'am,' Florrie declared, seated at the table in the Room, a cup of tea untouched before her. Was she as uneasy as I felt she was? It was true that not many maids ever entered the Room unless they were to be rebuked, but surely I had made it clear she was not in any trouble – rather the reverse. I had even held her shoulders and wiped her eyes as she sobbed for poor Mary. She was still pale, with dark circles under her eyes, and her hands fretted her apron, but ready, she insisted, to work as usual – as much to keep her mind off things as anything. 'I'm not sure she even knows my name yet. Speaks to me as if I'm not really there. But she keeps me busy doing things – re-doing her hair, for instance. She's so fussy about her ringlets that my fingers turn to thumbs when I try to get them as she wants them. And mending clothes – yet it's almost as if she's just undone hems or seams just so she can keep me occupied. I've offered to do something really useful, like unpack all her trunks – she's only let me open her valises – and press her clothes, but she doesn't want that. They have to stay piled up in the dressing room, still locked. If it was up to me I'd be back dusting and beating carpets tomorrow – but I know my duty, ma'am,' she added quickly. She managed a grimace. 'I'm not asking to change. All the same, I wouldn't want to be Olwen, no, not for all the tea in China. How is she, by the way, ma'am?'

'Physically I believe she is well. But she sits grieving at what is probably her young man's deathbed. And she won't talk. Not a word to anyone. And who can blame her?'

'I know her ladyship's seen her, but shouldn't she go and sit with her a bit? I know poor Lady Croft couldn't do much, not recently, but I remember once – before she was ill and her temper turned nasty – she found me crying with a splinter in my finger and she got it out herself. She wrapped the finger in one of her own handkerchiefs. She told me I might keep it – I have it still. Ma'am . . .' Her eyes filled and she bit her lip. It wasn't the first time – it was bleeding, as was the cuticle round her thumb nail.

'Yes, Florrie?'

'I wonder, ma'am,' she continued in quite a different tone of voice, one I couldn't identify, 'did you want me to – I don't know how to put it better – spy on her ladyship? Is that why you asked me down?'

I shook my head. 'I would never ask you to do anything either of us felt was wrong. I certainly wouldn't ask you to search her private things. But you are an intelligent girl, and if she says or does anything that worries or puzzles you, I would like to know. That's all.'

She nodded. 'I'm also wondering, ma'am, if you'd like me to go and talk to Olwen. One maid to another. I could say I don't know how Lady Stanton likes her laundry done, that sort of thing. Not just to find out, though I need to, don't I? If her sweetheart dies, Olwen'll need a shoulder, won't she?'

'And whose shoulder kinder than yours! That's a wonderful idea. But remember, you have been brought up well. You know right from wrong. And I will trust your judgement.' I looked at my watch. 'I should imagine Elias will finish speaking to her soon, and you must be back on duty. Just one thing: you say she likes you to be in her dressing room at all times. What on earth do you do, sewing apart?'

She patted her pocket. 'I'm supposed to be sitting quietly, aren't I? So sit quietly I do. With Mr Dickens for company. The book her ladyship gave me at Christmas, ma'am, God rest her soul.' Eyes filling, she drained her tea quickly, the cup rattling in the saucer as she replaced it.

'Amen,' I said. 'You were very fond of her.' To the best of my knowledge, however, her ladyship had had very little to do with her, apart from when she had injured her permanent maid in a wild attack and Florrie had braved her presence for a matter of a few minutes. It was time to be bracing, perhaps. 'Remember I am always ready to listen – and to try to find another maid for her if you really want me to.'

Another gnaw of her lip. 'Maybe it's best it's me.' She turned and left before I could ask what she meant. Should I call her back? Or should I let her grieve as she undoubtedly needed to do. A lot of faces in the servants' hall were still tearwashed – and everyone still had to endure Elias' questioning. I hoped he would be gentle.

In fact, he appeared a good deal more comfortable talking to the staff, who were sitting anxiously round the big table. He took care to give them the information he had given the gentry but in very straightforward words. It was clear to me that he thought they were the most likely to have seen anything untoward. Then he took the youngest servants into the Room in pairs, as if to reassure them. His notebook was less in evidence too, as I saw when I took through a plate of biscuits. Though as I left I closed the door behind me, those of us remaining in the servants' hall could hear occasional flutters of youthful laughter. And some sniffles too.

The last thing he would want was people he had interviewed telling the others what to expect, so as they emerged I despatched them quickly about their daily tasks.

Working through the older maids next, then the adult footmen, he left the visitors' valets till last. Both men, Hodge particularly, were decidedly restive by then, looking ostentatiously at watches and clocks in turn. Although they were unalike in appearance – Hodge, the professor's man, was stocky and starting to grey at the temples, though he was probably younger than the auburn-haired Parker, who I knew was in his later thirties – they both clearly considered themselves far too grand to mutter to each other.

Perhaps, however, it was my presence, as I sat at the far end of the big table from them, quietly checking the last month's accounts, that kept them quiet.

At long last – Elias was nothing if not thorough – Parker was summoned, smiling affably enough as he prepared to enter the Room. Hodge stared at the closed door as if it were a personal affront. But then, to my surprise, he spoke to me.

'It's so confoundedly quiet here! How do you bear it, Mrs Rowsley?'

'It used not to be like this. There was a constant bustle

about the place as you can imagine with the House full of guests and their valets and ladies' maids. Heavens, we used to refer to them by their employers' names.' No one gave it any thought. Perhaps it had taken Lady Stanton to remind me – if I had ever needed it – of the value of having your own name.

'They still do in some places, ma'am. Easier than learning twenty new names each week, I suppose. But this!' He spread his hands in something like despair. 'It's like living in a morgue.'

'The strange light . . . the snow killing the normal outdoor sounds . . . Yes, it's not altogether pleasant, is it? And you and Mr Parker are in a strange position, more or less forced together. Did you know each other before this visit, the professor and Sir Francis being friends?'

'No. Neither stays at the other's house, since they live so close, and this is the first time they have visited the same great house. And this is . . . this is enormous, is it not? Which makes me wonder if they have a chance of catching that poor maid's killer – all these corridors and stairs.' He shook his head in a mixture of doubt and sorrow. 'And all this damned snow! I beg pardon, ma'am.'

'If you and I were not the only ones in the room I would point out the swear box to you.' We shared a brief smile.

'Ma'am – I know some households discourage the practice, but I was wondering if anyone is walking out with Miss Florrie.'

'You'd have to ask her, Mr Hodge – it would be unlikely if a pretty girl like that didn't have a follower, but I haven't heard of it.'

'You wouldn't object?'

'Should I? Mr Hodge, you must know that I not only walked out with a gentleman while I was in service – I married him.'

He smiled. 'I just wondered if someone had broken her heart recently. When I arrived, she seemed very bright and chirpy. Now . . . Perhaps,' he said, striding to the window, 'she just hates this snow!'

'She was very attached to her ladyship. And she has lost a friend and colleague, has she not? But if you can take her mind off the poor girl's unhappiness, you have my gracious permission, if you need it, to try to cheer her up. But not to break her heart when Mr Fulke-Grosse leaves.'

'Or take her with me?' His grin was impish.

'In that case I would have to submit you to an inquisition. Ah! It seems you are spared: Mr Parker is emerging now.'

Hodge rose and, with a beautiful bow, went to join Elias.

Instead of scuttling off up the backstairs, Parker strolled airily towards me, bearing the almost empty biscuit plate, which he placed on the table between us. Then he sat down, legs crossed, arm over the chair next to him. 'And there I expected your Constable Pritchard to be a mere yokel! He's actually bang up to the mark, isn't he? I'm glad I didn't need to pull the wool over his eyes, I can tell you.' He offered me the biscuits. When I declined he helped himself to the last but one. And then the last.

I was disconcerted by his playfulness, which seemed out of place in a man of his years. But I could not imagine Francis employing a man like Hodge, whose demeanour had hitherto been so sober he might have been an undertaker.

So I decided to disconcert him if I could. 'Who might want to pull wool over the constable's eyes, Mr Parker? Hazard a guess!'

Gratifyingly he blinked sharply. Then he appeared happy to accept the question at face value. 'If they were not confined to what I believe you call the Family wing, the obvious suggestion would be Lady Stanton's people. But I understand that one at least may never rise from his bed again, another may take weeks to do so and the third is welded to the first man's side, so I feel we can discount them, don't you?' Sitting upright, he continued, 'What I cannot, cannot understand is how – not just why! – anyone would think it necessary to kill a mere child. None of us is perfect, ma'am, but to sink to such depths of turpitude . . . Let us say for a moment that I am a miscreant discovered in my crime. Of course my first instinct would be to lash out. But seeing my victim's age and sex, would I not instead issue such threats as to what I would do if she betrayed me as to make her blood curdle? Surely that would be enough?' He spread his hands. 'I was with Sir Francis when he returned from taking the photographs you suggested; perhaps he gave away, in his shock and distress, information he might prefer, on reflection, to have kept secret.'

I stared. 'Such as—?'

'The fact that all the oil lamps lighting the stairs had been extinguished. Now, was that done before or after the child fell? If it was before, it could mean her death was a simple accident, and if after, that someone did not want her body discovered. Or because that someone wanted her to trip.'

That someone had also locked our service door, though as I was more circumspect than Francis had been when he was so shocked and upset, I did not tell him about that. 'Sir Francis probably told you he tried to work out how long the lamps might have been out, but it was never going to be more than guesswork.'

'Of course. And he was disappointed that his attempts at detective work failed. And now he's gone off with his photographic equipment . . .' He shook his head in apparent disbelief. 'Ma'am, it is not impossible that we valets may see things that our masters do not; may we offer you our services if we may be of assistance?'

'Thank you. As you say, Mr Parker, a mere child . . .' I turned my face from him, as if once again overcome with emotion. In fact, I was thinking rapidly: why should he be offering to help me? Had he made the same offer to Elias Pritchard? Fortunately at this point the conscientious young constable emerged from the Room to ask to speak to me, so I was spared having to make any promises I feared he might want about our sharing information with him that Elias might prefer to keep secret.

I carried in with me a second tray of refreshments. Meditatively Elias stirred extra sugar into his coffee before reaching for a biscuit. 'I'm glad I'm not snowed up in here with you all,' he said with a grin, 'because Sergeant Burrows would expect me to solve the crime on my own – well, with your assistance and Matthew's. They say the railway line should be cleared by tomorrow evening – I daresay he'll come bustling in as soon as he can.'

'Are you allowed to tell me your suspicions?'

'It doesn't need me to tell you that Lady Stanton wouldn't know a straight answer if it bit her on the nose. She's a funny

one, and no mistake. But I tell you what, ma'am – I think
she's scared of something.'

'Scared? Of something here?'

'I didn't say that. But it does seem odd, doesn't it, coming
with all that luggage from the back of beyond – and seeming
quite content to want to hole up here. But I did worm out
of her the address of her friends in Cheshire.'

'And?' I stared at him hopefully.

'I think I should tell my Chester colleagues of her plans.
They might care to verify them for us.'

'Elias, I know you must not reveal information willy-nilly,
but what if we are nursing another viper in our bosom?'

He blinked. 'Like the dratted Timpson! But Lady Stanton
– well, she's a lady! A lady wouldn't do anything . . . anything
bad.' When I said nothing, he wriggled. 'I suppose her late
ladyship – when she was ill, of course, and not in her
right mind – she might have got a bit violent. Very violent.
But not trying to steal what wasn't hers and killing an innocent
young maid in the process. No, ma'am – that can't be right.
Can it?' he added as a desperate prompt. 'What do you make
of that Professor Whatsisname? He seems to think all this is a
minor inconvenience compared with his being denied access
to the library. Funnily enough, the one who seems to take it
most to heart is Mr Timpson. He's a funny bugger, isn't he,
ma'am – pardon my language. We could always get him to
help: set a thief to catch a thief, I suppose.' He did not sound
convinced. 'Sir Francis was ready to weep when he told me
about those photographs. What a good idea to have taken
them. And now to take more . . . They'll have to be shown
at the inquest.'

I coughed, delicately. 'Last time Sergeant Burrows should
have notified the coroner about a body, he didn't hurry. I hope
he doesn't dawdle this time.'

'To be fair, ma'am, that body was pretty old. Found amongst
Roman remains. He'll move more quickly on this case, I'm
sure. Specially as she's one of us here in the village and we
want to do the decent thing by her as soon as we can. I've
talked to the sexton, by the way – he says the ground is too
hard to dig a grave.' He dusted the biscuit crumbs from his

whiskers. 'Now, ma'am, just because Sergeant Burrows will ask, could you just tell me again exactly what happened before and after you found the little mite . . .'

It was hard not to weep myself as I told the story. 'And as you know,' I concluded, striving to be calm, 'I was so . . . overwhelmed I forgot to retrieve her keys.' I took a deep breath. 'Normally none of the rooms is locked, as you know. But at times the responsibility weighs heavy. This is not just a house entrusted to my care, Elias. It is a building full of things more precious than you or I could dream of owning. Think of what Mr Timpson could have taken had he been so minded. Think of what someone with a wide skirt and a capacious reticule might take and later conceal in a pile of luggage her acting maid is forbidden to touch.'

He looked truly offended. 'But ma'am . . .' He took a deep breath. 'Very well, I will talk to my Chester colleagues – or get Sergeant Burrows to. What if you're right and there is something fishy about her?'

My conscience gave a huge jolt. What if I was letting my prejudices overcome my sense of justice? 'I hope there isn't. I admit I don't like her, but that doesn't mean she's a criminal, does it? More important, maybe, is what you said about her seeming afraid. People who are afraid do things they'd rather not do. Or just keep others at arm's length.'

'I get the impression, ma'am, that she's done more than that to you. And I do wonder why a lady in her awkward position shouldn't want another lady as a friend.'

'Sadly that's the problem, isn't it, Elias? I'm not a lady.'

His chin went up. 'If a gentleman is as a gentleman does, isn't a lady as a lady does?' He scratched his head. 'Or do I mean it the other way round? If you behave like a lady, doesn't that make you one?'

'Not in the eyes of the world, Elias; you know that as well as I do.'

He laughed. We were both on our feet when he said, clearly serious, 'I may be about to do something quite terrible, ma'am. I want to talk to that poor servant girl of hers before I leave. And before Sergeant Burrows arrives.'

FIFTEEN

Matthew

Ellis Page was such a regular visitor to the household as a whole, I was surprised when late in the afternoon he sought me out in the privacy of my office. Still in his ulster, all he could do was sit with his head in his hands. I rang for Thatcher, intercepting him just outside the door, and asking him to bring tea.

As it was, Page fell on the tea as if it were nectar. 'You may need something more restorative,' he said. 'Francis will be down any moment, and I cannot imagine that tea will be enough to settle him. And yet at dinner I should imagine he will be as insouciant as ever. He's a braver man than you'd imagine.' He looked at the clock. 'He will not wish, I fancy, to hear me regale you with the details, so let me tell you what I found: there are bruises on her body, and on her shoulders. Distinct thumb marks, as if someone had grasped her – might I demonstrate on you?' His laugh was absolutely without amusement. 'Don't worry: I won't accidentally throttle you.'

He might have done deliberately if he'd cared to. His thumbs pressed between my shoulder blades and my neck; his fingers dug in near my clavicles.

'I doubt if I've bruised you, Rowsley, but whoever did that to little Mary meant to hurt her. And I'd say from the bruising on her head, left shoulder and left side, she was thrown. Hard. And the fall broke her neck.' He cleared his throat. 'Matthew, I know what Harriet will dread to hear – that someone . . . interfered . . . with her. It is my professional opinion that they did not. But oh, the poor child!'

There was another tap on the door. It was Thatcher, ushering in Francis, who collapsed on to the nearest chair.

'Brandy, Dick!' I mouthed.

Thatcher was back in an instant, as silently efficient as ever.

Francis' head was in his hands so he did not notice the decanter and glasses appear on my desk. Page poured, pressing the glass into Francis' unresisting hand. As if as an afterthought, he poured himself a glass and sat down.

At last Francis was able to speak. 'To think that we might have heard something – been able to prevent . . . But instead we were listening to Lady Stanton and indulging her prima donna ways! Dear God!'

Ellis raised a hand. 'And yet – I have no evidence for this surmise, gentlemen, so I urge you not to repeat it – and yet I suspect there is something truly wrong with her. I wonder if she is putting on some sort of an act – no, not like Timpson did, whether to keep a promise or for financial gain – but . . .' He tailed off.

'Do I not recall your suspecting something was amiss when you first examined her?' I refreshed his glass.

'Examined! I took her pulse and asked her to show me her tongue! But a doctor has so many more aids to making a diagnosis these days. Oh, they are not what society at large might approve of, and I certainly would not think of using them on her ladyship, even with a chaperon present. But . . .' This time he sipped from his glass. He fell into a silence as deep as Francis'.

'How are your other patients progressing?' I asked at last.

He shook his head sadly. 'If only I had some magic medicine! To see a young man battling against death with no more than a strong constitution to help him – the herbs I use for villagers' ailments are of no avail against such a severe inflammation of the lungs. Ironically the coachman, though older and less robust in general, is making better progress.'

'What of Olwen, the maid?'

He frowned. 'I understand that her ladyship has ordered – yes, ordered – her to leave her sweetheart's side and take walks, walks alone through the corridors of a strange house, Matthew. I know that ladies in houses like this will stroll in their picture galleries when they cannot exercise outdoors, but the girl is being despatched into a cold rabbit warren.' He shook his head in disbelief.

I made a note to tell Elias.

Francis made an effort. 'What of your other patients? Is his lordship still showing no ill-effects from his unhappy outing?'

'The poor man wants to go out on his toboggan.'

'Is there any reason why he should not?' I asked.

Page snorted. 'I can think of one! Lady Stanton! Imagine if she were to throw herself at him as she does at you. Can you imagine anything with more appalling consequences? All our efforts to keep him from a public asylum might be in vain.'

I nodded. 'So they might! But if we could find a way, Ellis. Young man he might be, but he has a boyish enthusiasm for outdoor activity.' Page clearly did not share this enthusiasm. I turned the subject. 'I understand that Pounceman didn't want visitors at first: might he welcome one now?'

'I doubt it. But when I return to the village, I could send his valet to deal with him. A shave and a fresh set of clothes, then he might actually be tempted to descend from the Family wing and enjoy some company.' He gave a most uncharacteristic growl of laughter. 'Though whether the company would enjoy him is another matter!'

'Harriet worries about how the news of his legacy affected Samuel: he is afraid he is to be thrown out into a distant cottage.'

He nodded. 'I have added my voice to hers in an effort to reassure him. Every great house like this needs someone to act as a repository for all sorts of trivial facts – the sort that never get written down. If anyone was that guardian of folk memory, it is Samuel – and I believe that though he is still frail, his memory is returning.'

'Thank God!'

He got up to go.

'Will you be coming to join us all for dinner? You know you are always welcome.'

He smiled sadly. 'After my work this morning I do not feel fit for company. Matthew, I feel soiled! Illogical I know, but a child! A child needing the sort of investigations I had to carry out!' He stood, but hardly seemed to know where the door might be.

'Ellis, work – any sort of work – done on the dead must surely enhance your knowledge of disease in the living,' Francis roused himself to say. 'As for photographs, one day we may know how to use our skills for many areas of investigation – you will recall that I find them an invaluable record of my excavation work. And remember, Mary had found a family here. She knew she was loved and valued. Harriet has taken her death so hard because she meant her to be one of her protégées. She believed she had a future.'

'Yet,' I added, my mood sinking to reflect his, 'that makes her untimely end all the worse.'

It was his turn to try to console me. 'Think, Matthew, what if she had been left to rot in the workhouse – or worse!'

I nodded. 'There would have been no justice for her then. Gentlemen, we will make sure she gets it, will we not?'

Mr Pounceman's return to the world was going to be more difficult than Page had implied, as we discovered when we visited him in his solitary room in the Family wing. Watched over by his valet, he sported a magnificent dressing gown that put in the shade all the others in the House. Although he was now shaved, apart from his mutton-chop whiskers, a bandage still covered his brow which was outclassed by the bandaging round his right ankle, to fit around which his carpet slipper had had to be cut. There were crutches beside the high-backed chair that someone had found for him, along with a matching footstool. Perhaps to hop round on crutches was not consistent with dignity, though he did not spell that out. Harriet and I nodded our sympathy as we pondered the problem, with Nurse Webb standing by, somewhat offended, I thought, that Pounceman was rejecting her advice on how to manage the usual aids for someone with his injury.

At last Harriet smiled. 'Mr Pounceman, if you cannot come down to mix with your fellow guests, it is not impossible that they should come to you. Not all the rooms in this wing are given over to the sick. Her ladyship's former suite . . . It is the work of half a day, no more, for the staff to remove all the dustsheets from her sitting room – though it might take longer for the fire really to warm it.' She bit her lip. 'To be honest,

I would prefer to take a day, perhaps even two, to clean her ladyship's actual bedchamber. And there are personal effects to . . . consider. If Mr Wilson considers it acceptable, I would like to offer some of them to the maidservants and nurses closest to her.' You could see her calculating what else it would involve, not least, I assumed, replacing the mattress and the pillows. Getting rid of the smell of illness and death would not be easy, even with Harriet's expertise and the number of servants she could deploy. The bed hangings, the curtains, the carpet: where would she start?

I could not think that Pounceman could envisage the work involved, but perhaps he had his own reservations about moving into a dead woman's territory. 'You are too kind, Mrs Rowsley. Not for anything would I put you to so much trouble. If only I might return to my own home – but my valet assures me that the roads are so rutted and pitted that the journey is quite ineligible till my ankle is mended or a true thaw has occurred.'

'In that case we must find another solution, must we not? A different bedchamber for you, and space for your valet, of course. And I have had another idea . . . Would you excuse me for a moment?' With a smile and a bob, she left the room.

Pounceman stared at me gloomily. 'I confess I would be delighted to move from all this . . .' He wafted an elegant hand to encompass the spartan air of his surroundings. 'And my fellow patients . . . as you will have observed, Nurse Webb kindly located me away from *hoi polloi*. But the constant bustle, the knowledge that people are on their deathbeds on the far side of the wall and the wailing of a young woman – none of these is conducive to a decent night's rest.'

'On the other hand, your fellow patients must be cheered by the knowledge that a man of the cloth is close at hand to pray for them. And young Olwen could always come to you for support.'

His gaze lacked enthusiasm. 'I understand that she is a Welsh Baptist, and may be with child. However,' he continued, as if wanting to rush away from his *non sequitur*, 'I do remember them in my private prayers. All three of them. And the villagers that you have invited in.' Perhaps he construed my silence as criticism. 'Of course, when I am on my feet again I will visit each bedside.'

But it was not on his feet that he would be travelling. The slight commotion out in the main ward announced the arrival of Harriet and Luke. He was pushing the chair to which George, the estate carpenter, had attached wheels so that Samuel Bowman might attend the Christmas party. Then Samuel had been able to do no more than smile and tap his foot in time to the music. However, since he was trying so hard to walk again he had rarely used it since.

It was both practical and elegant enough for our rector's needs.

'Here, Mr Pounceman,' Harriet declared, 'your transport of delight.'

Even I blinked at her dubious pun, but any objections to the humour that Pounceman might have wanted to voice were lost in Nurse Webb's exclamation that a lord might travel in such an equipage with no loss of dignity.

'To be sure, one does indeed,' Harriet declared. 'Lord Croft himself has an identical chair.'

As we left, we passed the sick groom, Thomas Davies. Beside him sat, as one might have predicted, Olwen, his sweetheart. I knew that Harriet had done her best to make her comfortable, given her appalling situation, so perhaps I expected her to offer a shy smile. What I saw on her young, fresh face was a glance of the most concentrated venom I have ever seen.

We were dressing for dinner when with some reluctance I told Harriet what I had seen, though in a somewhat diluted form. 'My love, I can't imagine what you might have done to deserve such apparent dislike.'

'The only real contact I have had with her was when I chaperoned Elias while he spoke to her,' Harriet said slowly, biting her lip with the effort of inserting the last of my studs, 'but I took very little part in the conversation. Indeed, I could not have done even if I had wanted to: it was conducted in Welsh.'

I smoothed my shirt and shrugged on my smoking jacket.

'Did you ask him to put any questions to her, perhaps? Ones she might not like?'

A brief smile replaced her frown. 'Why should I need to? He has become such a shrewd young man, has he not? A real credit to the police, and a wonderful asset to our village. I wanted to get up and cheer while he was addressing the guests this morning.'

'Me too. And his interrogation of her ladyship was masterly. Did he tell you what he had extracted from Olwen?'

'Some I could work out for myself. That she was too distressed to answer any questions at all! And I believed her. She is sick with grief. But all he actually told me was that she was born in the village where they were travelling from—'

'Go on! Attempt a pronunciation! My love, respectable women like you do not stick their tongues out at their lawful wedded husbands!'

It seemed that one at least did.

'And that they were indeed making their way to Cheshire,' she continued, almost seamlessly. 'I fancy there is more – but Elias is a good policeman, remember, and not one of the House employees. I felt I must not interrogate him. If there is information he wants us to know he will tell us in his own good time.'

I snorted. 'That is all very well for him. But he is not living under the same roof – albeit a large one – as a killer!' I had fewer scruples than Harriet; I would ask him point-blank when I next saw him. 'Where did you slip off to, by the way, while he was interviewing the guests?'

'To talk to Florrie. Who offered to talk to Olwen. But surely she would say nothing untoward?' Her hands flew to her face. 'Surely a loyal young woman like her – one I taught to read and write . . .'

'What could she say that was untoward? She can have no complaints about you surely? And if she had, none that would impinge on a complete stranger.'

She shook her head almost in disbelief. 'She is an intelligent and loyal young woman; it was her own suggestion that she might approach . . .' She paced round our bedchamber. Why on earth had I mentioned the tiny incident?

'Surely her ladyship is the most likely suspect.'

'She would be if she were on anything like friendly terms with the girl . . . Should I speak to her? Or to Olwen herself? Or should I not?' she demanded, wheeling to face me. 'Matthew, what if it was someone in the Family wing itself? One of Nurse Webb's staff? Even Nurse Webb herself?'

'Why did I ever say anything? I am so sorry, my dear, dear love.' My God, what a fool I was to have mentioned it.

'It's better to know than not. But I would dearly love to know who put the poison in her ear. Oh, Matthew, what shall I do?'

I took her in my arms, not necessarily what she wanted, I feared. She wanted me to dispense wisdom, did she not? And yet all too clearly I had none at my disposal. I needed hers, in fact. But at any moment the gong would ring out and we would be summoned yet again to attend the needs of others, with the added complication of our wheelchair-bound rector. All I could do was hold her, and feel her returning my embrace. This loving silence was the best help I could offer her, just as her presence helped me. As she had observed, this was a most unnatural life, having authority without rank to support it, having no power unless others chose to give it, having no real place in the world of the people we had to organize and entertain. And it was all playing out in the unnatural world of snow that kept us all nominally in one unit – but in a house that enabled people to roam as they wished.

And there was the gong.

SIXTEEN

Harriet

Mr Pounceman was obviously going to be centre stage this evening. His valet had returned him to the fine figure he usually was, and had even managed to undo a seam in his trousers to accommodate the bulk of his bandaged ankle. Having been carried downstairs – no mean feat for the footmen involved – Mr Pounceman and his chair simply dominated the drawing room, a fact that did not displease me. Lady Stanton was an enthusiastic handmaiden, insisting that he had too many or too few cushions, that he needed to be closer to or further from the fire and the table placed at his side for his sherry glass was too low or too high. Since she involved the gentlemen in her endeavours, for a while I could lurk in a less well-lit corner and observe, rather than participate in the proceedings. My all-too-brief moment in Matthew's arms had made me realize how bone-weary I was. In the past I had shared responsibility for the house with Samuel, who had every detail of both our jobs at his fingertips. Good as Dick was, he was not Samuel, and it would take years of experience to grow into his shoes. And he was not hosting a strange group of people considerably above his social station. If only I could kick my boots off and sit and read for an hour. Just an hour. What would I choose?

Dick coughed gently. 'I was wondering about the table arrangements, ma'am. With the wheelchair to accommodate.'

'I'm sorry. Of course. Yes, what had you in mind?'

He looked taken aback. 'I . . . it's usually you or Mr Wilson who works these things out, ma'am. But I'd say we had to put Mr Pounceman at the head or foot of the table, because that's the best place for his chair.' Encouraged by my nod and smile he continued, 'Should I put her ladyship beside him? At the head? And you beside Sir Francis at the foot, and Mr Rowsley

beside Mrs Arden, who asked me to convey her apologies as
she is still engaged in the kitchen?' He dropped his voice. 'And
devil take the rest!'

'What an excellent plan,' I said. 'Every last bit of it!' He was
about to put his suggestions into operation when I called him
back. 'Dick, after servants' supper tonight, can you mention
to everyone the matter of her late ladyship's effects. I meant to
do it today, but it would have been quite wrong in . . . in the
circumstances. Some will have no intrinsic value, but might
mean much to one or another of us. We can distribute them
as soon as we have a moment to call our own. No one must
feel left out, it goes without saying.'

'Ma'am, that would be much appreciated. And may I say, I
believe that Mr Bowman might want an object or two: he
remembers things she said better than he recalls a conversation
an hour ago.'

'Of course! Thank you for reminding me. He would be
proud of you, Dick.'

He blushed to the ears. 'Thank you, ma'am. I hope I would
deserve it. And now, if you will excuse me.' He bowed and
went off to supervise the table.

The seating arrangements were excellent: for the duration
of the meal I could relax in conversation with my friends.

'A play? How on earth can we enact a play?' Lady Stanton
demanded, stranded halfway between her seat and the piano.
Francis could be very unkind if he wished.

And clearly he wished, keeping her there as he replied to
the drawing room at large.

'We read aloud!'

Certainly what he planned would alleviate the gloom which
last night's events had cast over so many of us. Was what he
was doing irreverent? Would an evening with serious poetry
and a tragic piano sonata have been more appropriate? Almost
certainly. But when he had discussed it with me in an undervoice during dinner – 'I see you and Matthew as Beatrice and
Benedick, Harriet. Parts that might have been written for you
in particular' – I found I could not frame any objections. He
would have been able to break the news of our projected

evening with the Bard while everyone was still seated, but
chose not to.

He continued briskly as she hovered in no man's land, 'Mr
Wilson and I have located enough copies of Shakespeare's
works for all of us to have one. We propose *Much Ado About
Nothing*. And to save time we have already drawn up a cast
list.' He flourished a piece of paper. 'Some of us men will
have to double, of course. Pounceman, we know how beautifully you read: you ought to be Friar Francis, but it is too
short a part for you. Would you be Claudio?' He worked
through the other male roles, finally declaring Matthew as his
choice for Benedick. 'As for the ladies – Bea?'

I was interested in her smile. 'Francis, I'm used to looking
after other people and doing two things at once: might I be
Margaret and Ursula?'

To the best of my knowledge she was only familiar with
the very few Shakespeare plays we had already read round the
fire, which had not included this. And she had never addressed
Francis without his title. Something was afoot. He must have
discussed his plans with her already.

'Of course. Thank you for offering.'

'If a servant is to play a servant,' Lady Stanton tittered, 'are
we to ask that clod of a constable to play Dogberry?'

There was a sharp intake of breath; even the professor looked
shocked, but Francis covered her rude unkindness with aplomb.
'My dear Lady Stanton, you must be our Hero – or of course,
our heroine.' Taking her hand, he led her back to her chair.
From behind her back, he winked at me. 'Harriet, since our
Bea is otherwise engaged, will you be Be-atrice.' He leaned
on the joke a little hard, perhaps, but it was nice to be laughed
with, not at.

We had reached the end of the first scene of Act III, where
Beatrice overhears Hero and Ursula praising Benedick and
condemning her for her pride. To my surprise, Lady Stanton
had been quite hesitant at the start of the reading, often missing
cues. However, she claimed the light was too bad for her
to read where she sat, insisted on changing places, moving to
the other side of the fire. To do her justice she improved

considerably, but was never fluent. Bea, on the other hand, managed to be both Margaret and Ursula with no difficulties at all, and schemed with verve. Had she felt so much enthusiasm for matchmaking between Matthew and me? Almost certainly not, but tonight no one would have known.

Matthew got to his feet as the pretty clock chimed half-past ten. 'Sadly I feel we should wait till tomorrow to complete our play. After last night's sad event, Mr Wilson and I have been discussing with Thatcher the best way to ensure we are all safe. You will find that the service doors in all our rooms have been locked. This means that the servants will only use the main corridors, entering your rooms through the main door. Tonight, you will be escorted to your rooms by Thatcher or Luke, his deputy, who will check the room is empty before you go in. This will occasion some delays, of course. We apologize. Perhaps, Lady Stanton, you would prefer not to wait?'

Thatcher bowed, producing a chamber-stick. 'If you will permit me, your ladyship?'

Rather too clearly, she did not wish to permit him, but have Francis to escort her. However, he was deep in discussion with the professor. Wilson was too busy stage-managing the next departure to notice. We agreed to escort Bea, and then, of course, each other.

The valets greeted our arrival in the servants' hall with clean pairs of heels. Our own team, ready to leap to their feet, were settled with a gesture of our hands.

'It's nice and warm down here, isn't it?' Bea observed. 'Now, Mr Thatcher and Luke are seeing guests to their chambers, just in case. And I'd say you should head off in pairs when you're ready.' She responded to a titter or two. 'And don't pretend you don't know what I mean and what I don't, young Harry! You behave yourself!' But her manner was easy. Then her face became more serious. 'You all heard what Mr Thatcher said about the house-staff being allowed to choose a keepsake from her late ladyship's room. I know none of you kitchen girls had much to do with her ladyship face to face, but it was you who cooked her meals, and if any of you want a little something, and the lawyer permits, I'd like you to be able to choose something too.' She looked at me, for a moment as if ready to pick a public fight.

'Of course. Her ladyship would surely have wanted that, as Mrs Arden and I will tell Mr Wilson.' I smiled at her, relieved to see her smile back. 'Sometimes lawyers take a little longer than we would like, but I promise you that each and every one of you will have a personal keepsake. As for now, it is getting late. So goodnight and God bless you all.'

As we left, Matthew said, 'You're still wearing your jet. Do you want to risk leaving it in our room, or shall we go and lock up in the office safe?'

'Oh, surely it'll come to no harm in just a few hours!' I responded, believing what I said.

Nonetheless, as soon as we were out of the hall, he led me briskly, not up the grand stairs but along the miserable corridor to his office. A meagre fire still burned, losing the battle with the cold.

He fell to his knees and unlocked the safe. 'There!' He tucked the jet pieces into their velvet case and stowed it behind some ledgers. In another moment the safe was relocked.

'Why?' I mouthed.

'Just in case. It might be your watchword but it's also become mine. What you don't seem to have noticed is that I put your trinket box in there too.'

'Trinkets! The sapphires are my most precious possessions!'

'In a manner of speaking, trinkets. At least compared with the king's ransom in the House safe. And I put them there – just in case. Dear me, it's cold in here.' He locked the door behind us. 'I hope our chamber is warm!' He seized my hand, and we veritably ran along the deserted corridor, only regaining our decorum as we approached the entrance hall and the grand staircase. The dear Queen herself and her Consort could not have walked up with more dignity.

On the threshold I stopped. Was all well? Had anything been disturbed? An instinct so primitive that perhaps Mr Darwin's apes had shared it told me that we were not the only ones to have been in the room. I could tell myself that it was nonsense – after all, a footman had brought coal and tended the fire – but I could not feel it was nonsense.

Matthew, however, was blithely striding to the fireplace to poke the fire. He turned to look up enquiringly at me, as I stood frozen on the threshold. Then he straightened and came over to me, reaching to close the door, which he then locked. 'My love?'

'I feel . . . anxious. I sense — I sense that someone has been in here. Not to do their job. To do something else.'

He stared, just as I would have stared in his place. But then he smiled, and took my hand. 'Let us just check that there is no one still in the dressing room at least.'

Predictably, it was empty. I shrugged apologetically.

To my amazement, he put his finger to his lips and, striding silently across the room, turned the handle of the service door. As it opened as easily as ever, he flung it open and peered up and down the stairs, which were still, on my instructions, lit.

'No one there. But I am certain the door was locked before.'

'It was. I tried the knob myself before we left.'

He looked as aghast as I felt. 'Dear God, what if you had come back alone and suffered Mary's fate?'

'Come, Matthew, do you not believe I might have put up more of a struggle!' But it was hard to feign cheerfulness, especially knowing that someone under this roof disliked me intensely. 'As would you, I hope!'

'Who on earth could have done it? And how? A maid? A footman? Harriet, they are our colleagues!'

'I prefer to hope it was not one of the staff. Though the choice there is limited.'

He relocked the door, turning to lean against it. 'What were they looking for, I wonder?'

'Apart from my "trinkets"? Thank goodness you were prescient! Matthew?'

He had hit his face in apparent irritation. 'Lady Stanton! Elias suggested that she would be wise to put her jewellery in the House safe. Has she done so yet?'

'Not yet. Even if she had tried to cajole Dick into opening it, he would have to ask me for my key too.'

'I hope she's still got some jewellery to lock up,' he said grimly. He glanced at the clock. 'Should I go now and warn her that—'

'At this time of night? She'd cry scandal at an unaccompanied man turning up. That or eat him alive.' I sat down. 'She is an adult, my love. If she was warned by no less a person than a police constable, and chose to do nothing, I would say she only has herself to blame if anything goes wrong.' Then I snorted. 'Except it would be our job to run any thief to earth, of course. Which we can start doing in the morning, but not at nearly midnight when we are on duty again at seven tomorrow morning. My love, I am so very weary.'

'Are you too tired to deal with my studs?'

I must have been. One dropped from my fingers and rolled away under the bed.

'Leave it!' he said, as I sank to my knees to retrieve it. 'It will still be there in the morning . . .'

SEVENTEEN

Matthew

Having double-checked that the service door was still firmly locked, I retired to the privacy of my office the following morning to deal with an urgent problem with the accounts of one of our tenant farms. I forgot all about the missing stud until mid-morning coffee, which I drank at my desk so as not to break my concentration. Even as I sipped, however, I felt a pang of vicious guilt. In this great building, my own dear wife, still no doubt fretting over my careless words, was the only one who did not have a moment like this to call her own. Even the most menial servant had some free time every day, and with so few guests most had no evening duties. At least, I reflected, as I closed the ledger and left the office, locking the door behind me, I could spare her one task – though as I made my way upstairs, I knew it was a very trivial gesture, and one probably made far too late. Certainly made too late. The maid cleaning our bedchamber should have found the stud during her sweeping, and I would probably find it sitting in state on the washstand or dressing table. I did not. And Queenie, the maid I found polishing the mirror, assured me, blushing and stuttering as she tried to conceal the duster beneath her pinny, that she had swept under the bed and found nothing. No, nor anywhere else neither. But – with a deep bob – she'd keep her eyes peeled, gaffer, Mr Rowsley, she meant sir.

I flipped her a sixpence and left her to it, poor child.

So where on earth was my stud? I did not want to embarrass her or indeed myself by crawling under the bed and checking between the floorboards. But I would assuredly do just that, but in decent privacy. It was not as if I did not have other sets. I had only ever worn this one out of a weird and probably misguided sense of duty, since it was a Christmas present from her ladyship. But abandon it I could not – the same impulse of loyalty to a relative and a principle that my parents had inculcated in me, that one should willingly waste nothing. Even Beethoven could write a piece of music raging over the loss of a penny! One day, when I had time to practise, I really must master it, must I not?

Just as I must conquer those accounts.

I was humming it under my breath as I headed to the stairs. To my delight Harriet was just ahead of me.

'I was just returning to the servants' hall,' she said, slipping her hand briefly into mine. Pale though she was, her smile was quietly triumphant. 'Mr Wilson and I have been going through her late ladyship's effects, deciding what can and cannot be given away. Fortunately he got bored and started nodding things through that he might have thought keeping half an hour earlier, when the fire was still burning brightly.'

'So everyone will get something?'

'Everyone, though I can't guarantee that everyone will find something they really want. Which reminds me, did you find your errant stud?'

'Sadly not. But I have asked Queenie to look for it.' I started down the stairs.

'No. Please. Just a moment together, even if we are talking shop! As soon as we reach your office or the Room, someone will need us. And while we are here we can discuss – how has it slipped my mind? – how we advise Lady Stanton on her jewellery case.'

'Get one of her apparent admirers to persuade her,' I said. 'I really am too busy to worry about her, and she's too rude to you for you to worry about her! Let us instead consider a walk this afternoon. The sun is shining, and we can wrap up against the wind. Even for ten minutes it would be good.' I grabbed both her hands. 'Harriet, did you ever skate on the lake?'

'Once or twice,' she admitted, failing to sound blasé. 'Can you skate?' Her face glowed with anticipation.

'Never successfully. I ended up in the water once; fortunately my cousin was at hand to rescue me. Mark. It would be good to invite him here when spring comes – and when, please God, there are fewer complications and we can be hosts in our own home once more. So, shall we skate?'

'Do you have skates? Oh, there must be some in one of the outhouses!' She paused. Her face changed a mite, as I am sure mine did. Neither of us could face the thought that the other might meet with an accident, even trivial. 'Let us go for a trial walk first. Just where the driveway has been cleared or where it has thawed.' She grimaced. 'But at least it will be out of the House.' It was almost a wail. She took a deep breath, as if to return to normality.

'My love, you are clearly in need of an outdoor adventure to calm you down. I know that I am. But not,' I added with a sigh, 'not until I have finished the Farquharson accounts.' Glancing around us with something like guilt, I bent and kissed her lips. 'This afternoon, then!'

If a woman dressed from top to toe in black could look enchanting, Harriet did. I could see no reason why her bonnet was particularly charming, or why her muff was a playful adjunct, not merely a way of keeping warm. But I had rarely seen her look more beautiful as we descended the main staircase for our afternoon adventure.

'Ah! Mr Rowsley!' a voice trilled. 'I have been looking for you everywhere. But the butler – he is no more than a boy, is he? – insisted that you were busy in your office and were on no account to be disturbed.'

'Good afternoon, Lady Stanton,' I said, as we continued our descent. 'I'm so sorry I wasn't available. And I'm afraid I have an urgent appointment now.'

'Really? But I find I cannot do without you. I need you to open that safe that constable was speaking of. Apparently the butler-boy's key is not enough. Two are needed.'

'That is true, your ladyship. But I do not have one. You need to discuss that with my wife. But she too has an appointment now.'

'Oh! Is that really your wife? She looks unexpectedly . . . affluent. Her late ladyship's furs, no doubt.'

Harriet bobbed a curtsy. It might have been somewhat belated, but after such rudeness, such unkindness, I doubted if my knees would have bent at all. 'Alas, fur always made her late ladyship sneeze and her poor eyes run. You'll have noticed that there are no dogs or cats in the House: that is why. No, these were a Christmas gift from my dear mama-in-law, Mrs Rowsley senior. I should be back within an hour, ma'am, and I will wait on you then – in your bedchamber or in the drawing room, whichever is more convenient.'

'The bedchamber is far from convenient! I discover that fires are only lit when it is time to change—'

A peal on the front-door bell, and a vigorous knocking, stopped her in mid-sentence. She became ashen-pale. 'I am . . . not At Home!' she gasped.

Harriet took her hand. 'Come this way, ma'am.' Whisking her through the nearest service door, she shot over her shoulder, 'I'll take her to the Room!'

Bemused, I waited in the wings, as it were, until Luke had opened the door, to admit no ogre to threaten Lady Stanton but the familiar figure of Sergeant Burrows, Elias Pritchard three steps behind him, as if the sergeant were royalty.

They saluted as Luke bowed them in. When he had taken their hats and oilskin capes, reinforced with non-uniform mufflers, I noticed, I strolled over, offering first the sergeant then the constable my hand in greeting.

'It's good to see you, gentlemen,' I said, quite truthfully. 'And good to know that the roads – or perhaps the railway lines? – are clear at last. Would you prefer a cup of tea in my office or do you wish to speak to the guests immediately, sergeant?'

'It's been a cold journey – yes, I came on the train – so tea would be welcome.' As Luke melted away, Sergeant Burrows looked about him, focusing at last on the grand fireplace. 'I am used to seeing a great blazing fire over there, not that tired-looking heap of ashes.'

I touched my nose. 'Policy, sergeant. I will explain in a moment. This way, please.'

Burrows cast a disparaging look at my office fire too, quickly poking it and adding coal. 'Have you all taken some sort of vow?' He added another piece of coal, then another.

'In a sense, yes. Elias will have explained to you the

difficulty of keeping our guests in one place. Our theory is that the cold will do it for us. There are no fires in their rooms till it is time to change for dinner. The library and document room have an unfortunate infestation of fictitious mice, and are locked until the pests disappear.'

'Human pests,' Elias said.

Burrows studiously ignored the interjection. 'And does this policy work?' he demanded, letting the tongs clatter on to the hearth.

'Not entirely. Someone unlocked the service door in our bedchamber last night. But we could find no evidence that anyone had been in. All the servants have been told to use the public corridors and stairs and to move around in pairs, by the way, and last night each guest was escorted to his or her own room. Elias . . . Mary's keys—'

Before he could reply, a polite knock announced Luke's presence. I waited while he poured and passed round not just biscuits but a cake still warm from the oven. 'Thank you, Luke. Now, will you knock and slip this under the door of the Room,' I continued, writing a brief note to tell Harriet the identity of our guests. 'And,' I added, 'see to it there's a fire lit in our bedchamber, will you?'

His bow might have been conspiratorial as he left.

Sergeant Burrows rubbed his hands. 'Some things haven't changed, I'm glad to see. Bakes a good cake does Mrs Arden.'

I cut him a large slice, with a slightly smaller one for Elias, as if to maintain the sergeant's sense of hierarchy. While they ate, I continued, 'Elias has spoken to all our guests and all our servants, as I'm sure he's told you. I was only present for one interview, that with Lady Stanton. Heavens, Elias, it was like fencing with a tiger! You did very well.' I turned back to the sergeant. 'When you and he have had a chance to discuss and evaluate the material he obviously could not share with us without your permission, my wife and I would be grateful for an update. I presume there will be an inquest very soon?' Keen on detecting the good sergeant might be, he was occasionally slow in his duties – and on a not too distant occasion had sadly delayed the official investigation.

He snorted. 'A lot of deaths this snow has caused. The

coroner'll be a very busy man, I fear. But at least this village doctor of yours has done his job with this waiting maid. Elias tells me that he'll have the report on what he found waiting for us when we go down to the village. Nice idea, having your private railway station here on the estate, isn't it?'

'It's a great privilege. But I hope things will change when we have built the new village, and that the people of Stammerton will be able to use it.'

Another snort. 'Wages'll have to go up a bit before they do! Though third class is cheap enough, I suppose. Right, I feel the better for that.' He put down his cup and saucer. 'Drink up, Pritchard. I need to see the place the poor wench died.' He glanced at me. 'And I dare say I'll need my muffler to go there, if you please.'

'Won't take that long, gaffer,' Elias ventured. 'You'll find I've jotted down all the details: number of stairs; dimensions of stairs; location on the stairs; lighting—'

'On the stairs. Very well. But what about your bedchamber, Mr Rowsley? I shall need to look at that too, mind.'

'You may have heard me tell Luke that the no-fires rule can be briefly relaxed – I suspected you would need to investigate there,' I said, not meeting anyone's eye.

To do the sergeant justice, he was as thorough as if Elias hadn't prepared his notes, checking in particular the two handprints.

'One right hand, in your room. The other her left hand,' he declared. He was so close to it he was almost drawing the fire, a job normally done with a newspaper or even a board held in front of it. I hoped it was not singeing I smelt. 'So the little mite was actually bouncing downstairs on her back. Funny if she was pushed.'

'Perhaps she somersaulted,' Elias mused.

I frowned. 'There were no bruises on her face – none that I recall. Dr Page will have noted any, of course. But her neck was certainly broken, and he says there were bruises on her shoulders where someone applied force to push her. I saw those on her arms for myself.'

'The question is, when were those bruises inflicted?' Without moving, he gazed at the mark on the door jamb. 'Very small to be heaving coal around, I'd have thought,' he added accusingly.

'Unnaturally poor growth is a product of the workhouse system, sergeant – a result of malnutrition. So although she looked nine at the most, she was actually twelve. Her brain was mercifully unharmed by her awful diet – she was as sharp as could be. Harriet was teaching her to read and write – if ever a child should have been educated, it was her.' I told them the tale of my slippers and the cushion. 'As for the coal, she was in the room simply to make up the fire; a footman would have refilled the scuttle earlier. And you know that footmen are usually chosen for their height, with broad shoulders to match.'

'Make good fast bowlers they do, eh, Matth– Mr Rowsley?'

'Indeed.' But cricket was not uppermost in my thoughts now.

'Very well, we'll be on our way now, Mr Rowsley,' Sergeant Burrows declared. 'And maybe the good doctor will be able to cast some light on that bruising.'

'Did Dr Page pass you a bunch of keys, Elias?' I asked.

'Indeed he did sir. But Sergeant Burrows hasn't seen them yet.'

'Evidence must be examined,' Burrows said, even before I could open my mouth to ask for their return.

EIGHTEEN

Harriet

My impulsive act, my lèse-majesté, indeed, was so foreign to my nature I believe I was more shocked than Lady Stanton.

We did not get as far as the Room before she pulled away from me. 'I believe I would prefer to return to my bedchamber, despite the cold.'

'That surely depends on whom you did not wish to see,' I replied gently. 'If such persons are likely to rampage through the House looking for you, I should imagine a bedchamber is an obvious target, locked or not. But if that is what you wish, I can escort you up the backstairs and rekindle your fire. I can even station a footman in the adjoining room to come to your rescue if necessary. I think he might need a fire, too,' I added with a smile, to no immediately obvious avail.

She clasped and unclasped her hands.

'Or you might prefer to think about it in the warmth of my office.' It was the first time I had used the term, even to myself. Yes, that was what it had become; just as Matthew's was the administrative heart of his lordship's estates, so the Room had changed from being a sitting room to a place for all the meetings and decisions to be made about the House and its occupants. 'Whatever else, it will be completely private, secret, even, and there I can offer you a cup of tea.'

Her nod was not entirely gracious, but it did seem to signify agreement. I led the way; we were in my territory after all, and in our staff corridors there was no room to walk two abreast.

Accepting my invitation to sit down, she looked around her, blank-faced. No, despite all the refurbishments – and my pride was grateful the place looked less shabby – it could never be taken for a room on the far side of the green baize door. Perhaps refreshments might thaw her.

'I believe Mrs Arden has been teaching her staff how to make cakes today; would you care to try one of their efforts? I assure you that no one could tell that Bea herself had not made them. And tea? Perhaps some of the very fine blend her late ladyship preferred? Very much a lady's choice, she used to say, wasted on gentlemen. Ah!'

A slip of paper appeared under the door, which I had locked. 'A note from Matthew: the impatient visitors were Constable Pritchard and his sergeant, who came by train from Shrewsbury.'

Her rigid shoulders dropped a little, and I thought a little colour returned to her cheeks. Perhaps it was not the police she was afraid of.

'Thank you,' she said, ambiguously.

'One moment, then.' I let myself out, slipping as unobtrusively as I could into the kitchen.

Bea was astounded. 'Her ladyship in the Room, Harriet! Well I never.'

'She's terrified of something. Someone. So might I ask an enormous favour – that you bring the tea tray yourself. And sit down with us to see if together we might work out what's afoot? I know this is your busiest time . . .'

She returned my conspiratorial grin. 'I don't see her as a candidate for a good gossip myself, but I'll see what I can do. Only ten minutes, mind.' She turned away to start giving orders.

Lady Stanton greeted my return with such indifference that I could not doubt the accuracy of Bea's judgement – not that I often did.

'You are missing your appointment, Mrs Rowsley,' she observed at last.

'Indeed. And my husband is missing his, too. But the arrival of the police must mean the postponement of other engagements. Today, of course, it also means that the railway line between here and Shrewsbury is clear, which suggests that the roads are also improving.'

'Alas, my groom's health is not. I understand that my coachman, however, is almost out of danger, so we may have to proceed without Davies. I'm sure one of your men will act as his replacement.' It was not a question, not even a request.

Perhaps one might, and perhaps again one might not, I thought but managed not to say. At this point a tap on the door announced the arrival of Bea, with a laden tray and a table cloth over her arm. Normally a maid would have laid the table: today's apparent need for secrecy meant the task fell to me.

Her ladyship accepted the cup of tea I offered, but did not taste it. She accepted a slice of feather-light sponge, but did not taste that either. She looked from one to the other of us, concentrating, with some disbelief, on Bea's working dress. Bea was never less than neat and tidy, but clearly this gown was not of the same order as her evening wear.

Bea responded to the scrutiny, of which she must have been conscious, with a reminiscent smile. 'Seeing you down here, your ladyship, reminds me of the times the late Lady Croft came down. Before she was ill, of course. You should have seen the House in those days – always full of guests! Heavens, the house parties we've had here. Her ladyship would always sit over there in the window, with her list of things she wanted seen to. Most meticulous, she was. But then she would laugh, and roll the list into a ball and throw the paper on to the fire. "You two have thought of everything," she would say. As for his late lordship, the times I had to chase him out of my kitchen! He'd wander in after a day's shooting, mud to his eyebrows, and pretend to be a schoolboy stealing my little cakes – of course, we both knew I'd only made them because he liked them. What a lovely gentleman he was. You knew him even better than I did, didn't you, Harriet?'

I nodded. 'I still find it hard to speak of him without emotion, your ladyship. The kindest of men, a real scholar. But as at home on the cricket pitch as in the House of Lords, he'd always say – adding he knew which he preferred.' I paused. 'Did you ever meet him, ma'am? Until he became frail, he and her ladyship would always spend the Season in London. They entertained all the great families.'

'I did not have that pleasure.' She might have been discussing a visit to the dentist.

'What a pity. They hosted the most wonderful receptions,' sighed Bea. 'I was in charge of all the refreshments – not that

I was expected to do all the cooking, of course. But it was my job to deal with the caterers we had to bring in – my goodness, I miss those times.'

For the first time, Lady Stanton made an effort to join in. 'Is this how two – servants, for a better word – have come to run the establishment here?'

'Forgive me, but you are mistaken, your ladyship,' I said firmly. 'The House and all of us in it are actually answerable to a board of trustees, since, as we told you, the present Lord Croft is suffering a chronic illness. We were faithful employees, as I am sure you understand, and that is why we keep the place as it is. We continue our routines as if the Family were about to step through the front door as you did.'

'But you are involved in what one might call the upstairs life.'

'There'd be precious little of that if we didn't!' Bea said. 'And, forgive me if I'm blunt, ma'am, but you'd be in a very awkward position – you'd be closeted with a band of strange gentlemen from breakfast to dinner and beyond. Unchaperoned. That wouldn't be pleasant, now, would it? It'd be that or keep to your room, presumably.'

'I am glad you have been able to meet our rector, Mr Pounceman,' I said. 'And I understand that Sir Francis has been enjoying your company, too.'

The look she shot me suggested I had overstepped a mark I had not even seen.

'It was a pleasure to hear you and Mr Pounceman read so beautifully together,' Bea said, jumping in valiantly. 'I have never seen a Shakespeare play on the stage, but I am sure it could not be more enjoyable. As for my reading, you made me sound a complete bumpkin.' Which was untrue: she read as well as if Francis had coached her. Which I am sure he had.

'Do you often read aloud with your family, ma'am?' I asked. 'I should imagine you are much in demand for musical evenings,' I rushed on, over her look of astonishment. 'It is one of the great regrets of my life that I can neither sing nor play, but I cannot even imagine matching your accomplishments.'

A silence grew and deepened. A spurt of anger flared in my head: she alone of the three of us was trained to make light conversation, to put others at their ease.

Sighing, Bea got to her feet. 'Forgive me,' she said, 'but I must return to the kitchen if we are to have dinner tonight. Let me say this, ma'am, though I suspect I shall offend you. Bluntly, if we do not know what is frightening you, we can't protect you.' She curtsied, gathered the china and cake on to the tray, and headed for the door, which I got up to open. We both froze as her ladyship spoke.

'There is . . . someone . . . I do not wish to meet. And . . . I would be grateful . . . Perhaps you would instruct the butler not to admit anyone directly into a room in which I might be seated, and to warn me who the visitor might be.'

It was hard to warm to her, but at least we could see the effort her words had cost her. Still holding the tray, Bea stayed where she was.

'Indeed I will, your ladyship,' I said. 'Now, do you care to remain here while I speak to Thatcher? And I will find out if we have had any visitors beside the police officers.'

'Let me be even blunter, ma'am,' Bea said. 'I know you think young Elias Pritchard is no better than a hayseed, but I for one would trust him with my life. If you can't tell us your troubles, you might think of talking to him. Or,' she added, at least sounding sincere, 'perhaps you might turn to Mr Pounceman, as a man of the cloth.'

Slowly, Lady Stanton rose to her feet. 'Thank you for your hospitality. I would like to return to my bedchamber now – ah! No, the salon has a fire, does it not?'

'In that case, ma'am, I will ring for Thatcher to escort you and we can speak to him together.'

NINETEEN

Matthew

Sure though I was that our mischievous friend Wilson would have loved me to invite the two policemen to join us all for supper, I resisted the temptation. They had their work to do, as I did, though I would be the first to admit that going through fraudulent accounts might not be as morally valuable as running down a murderer. It was hard to settle. I felt like a schoolboy, kept back to do work when he should have been running around with his classmates. The only consolation for losing my walk with Harriet was that she would have been as disappointed as I was. On the other hand, she was presumably having an indoor adventure, as it were, spending time with Lady Stanton in the Room. Or perhaps, given her ladyship's propensity for stonewalling, a very frustrating adventure. Why should I not postpone the rest of my investigation and go and see how she had got on? Moreover – I glanced at the illicit clock – I must lock away my paperwork and go and change for dinner. And yet, I could spare a moment, must spare a moment, to look at the painting that I had appropriated at the same time as the clock.

So far, moving it had achieved nothing, beyond filling a gap on the wall. Moving my desk lamp this way and that, I peered harder, hoping the brushstrokes would vouchsafe me an answer. Why did it worry me? Why had Harriet and I, standing before it, not discussed the matter? At least she would have given an opinion on whether I should mention my unease to Francis; at most she would have observed something that had escaped my notice. The frame? I removed the portrait from the wall, turning it this way and that. Nothing about the back looked anything but old. Nothing about the gilt looked anything but new. But I could imagine no possible reason to paint a frame which would then make it look out of place. I tried telling myself that one oddity in a house crammed with treasures should be treated as no more than an oddity and forgotten about. I tried, but did not succeed. I must indeed raise the issue as we dressed; perhaps she could even inspect it before we had to forgather in the drawing room.

My thoughts were interrupted by a strange noise in the corridor and a tap on my door.

'Mr Pounceman,' Luke declared, easing the wheeled chair into my office. He glanced at the fire, and made it up again without being asked. Then, with a bow to us both, he withdrew.

'It's good to see you among us,' I said, shaking his hand formally before taking a chair opposite his. Had he observed my preoccupation with the picture? Somehow I doubted it: he was a man whose own actions would always be of more interest than others'.

'Thank you. It is in no small part a result of the expert care of the young women in the Family wing. At least Dr Page seems to have chosen better for his head nurse this time,' he said. 'I hope to see her in the congregation next time I am able to lead divine service.' I suspected his hopes might be in vain. 'Meanwhile, my dear Rowsley, I came to discuss the tricky situation poor Lady Stanton is in!'

'What a tricky situation we are all in,' I agreed, deliberately misunderstanding. 'Rattling round the House as we are with a murderer on the loose. Are the guests as vulnerable as the maids? Are the valets – I am glad yours had managed to get here, by the way – at risk too? Part of me wishes that Sergeant Burrows and our good Elias could stay to guard us, but they are busy, of course, with their investigations.'

'Where better to investigate than here?' he demanded, reasonably. 'But to return to her ladyship, would it not be better if she kept to her room? Under the protection of some sort of guard?'

I took a risk. 'Entirely between ourselves, Pounceman, we thought it better if all the guests were kept herded together, as it were. It's harder to kill someone in a room with other people in it, is it not? Which is why we are trying to discourage our guests from wandering around. Hence, I'm afraid, the cold corridors and unheated bedchambers.'

'But her ladyship in particular – remember that she is unchaperoned! How uncomfortable for her.'

'Which is an additional reason why I am so pleased to see you up and about. The company of a respectable churchman must be irreproachable. And your social credentials are better than any of ours, Francis excepted, of course. Wilson is a lawyer, Fulke-Grosse, a professor, Mrs Arden and my wife – exemplary characters, all of us, but middle-class professionals, not even gentry. We all work.' I was aware that I was simply saying what he was thinking, even if he might have omitted the words about our characters.

He bowed in acknowledgement.

'I believe her ladyship has another problem too. Something frightened her today. Terrified her. I know she has this hard carapace, this absolute reluctance to treat her underlings, particularly my wife, as she should – as anyone should—'

'For such a beautiful woman she has an unwelcome harsh side. I could not admire her mockery of your wife and Mrs Arden, and the unkind reference to Constable Pritchard. Wit is a fine thing, is it not, but not if it becomes hurtful – indeed, unladylike.'

'I have suspected that this is because she is genuinely reluctant to admit to any weakness, but after an incident this afternoon I believe that something, I know not what, actually terrifies her.'

His glance was surprisingly shrewd. 'Something or someone?'

'I suspect the latter. I know that Harriet spirited her away from the entrance hall when she was afraid of who might be coming in – but since then I have not had a chance to ask her what transpired.' I gestured at the paperwork. 'There is something I wanted to ask you. Mary's death. May I ask you to take the funeral – at the estate's expense, of course – and offer the kindest and most loving words at your disposal? All the servants will be there, some only a few years older. She was their sister, in all but blood.'

'The sister of all but one of them, don't forget,' he observed. 'I will of course take the service, though I will tell you now I do not think that ladies or women should attend funerals, since they are prone to hysteria, and I fear I must veto the presence of young women especially. I would only be adhering to the norm, would I not? Now, on reflection, Rowsley, I believe you are right to consider her ladyship safer with us. Now, if you would be kind enough to ring for Luke, I will be on my way.'

'I can do better than that,' I said, putting the fireguard in place. I did not want a stray spark destroying my efforts. 'I will push your vehicle myself.'

'I believe your wife coined a better term for it: my transport of delight.' He seemed genuinely amused. 'Thank you, Rowsley, let us sally forth!'

So we did. But not before I locked my door behind me.

Having conveyed him to the foot of the stairs, I left carrying him to his new bedchamber to the strong footmen who had managed him before. On impulse I headed to the Family wing; it was a few days since I had sat with poor Samuel.

He greeted me with the gentle smile he always used these days; he seemed simultaneously to welcome me and to apologize for not getting up. In the past I had read passages from the Bible, slowly and clearly so that he could recite them under his breath. But now he was able to talk, Page had told us to engage him in proper conversation. We talked a little about the bequests, with me adding my reassurances to Harriet's that he would never be forced to leave the House.

'You recollect that we have redecorated the Room, do you not? What did you think of it?'

He frowned. 'There was one change of which I did not approve – but, bless me, Matthew, I cannot recall what it is. I will look in on it tomorrow when I come down for servants' dinner. Something struck me. Yes, indeed . . .' Then he caught sight of my watch. 'My dear boy, is that the time? You should be dressing for dinner!'

Delighted to be reminded, I had to run to our room: there

was little time to change and I did not want Harriet to have to deal with our gallimaufry of guests on her own.

I called out cheerily as I opened the door – the fire burned brightly but no candle was lit. And on the bed, flat as a corpse, lay my dear wife.

TWENTY

Harriet

'Heavens, you scared me!' I said, struggling to sit up.

'Heavens, *you* scared *me*!' Matthew countered, clasping my hands and kissing them. 'The room in darkness, you motionless on the bed – my darling, I did not see you now, I saw as you lay near to death after that vile poisoner's efforts. But you live. Thank God, you live!' He was near to tears.

'And thank God,' I said, desperate not to weep too, 'that I neither dribbled nor snored.' I swung my legs to the floor.

At last he smiled. 'I did not say that. Why, your snores might have echoed down the corridors for all you knew!'

'In which case you would have had no cause to worry, would you? Heavens, we will be late – and the jet necklace is still locked in your office!' I dragged off my day-dress, stepping into the dress I had laid out for the evening and turning my back to Matthew so that he might hook it up. The moment he'd flung on his shirt, I attached the studs – a set his mother had given him. I was determined that none of these would go adrift. My hair! It had slipped its moorings and become hopelessly tangled: once again Matthew turned lady's maid. Except that he let it all down first, burying his face in it and running it through his fingers. In that moment there was nothing either of us wanted less than to have to proceed calmly downstairs to become social martyrs once again. At least, as I whispered to Matthew as we ran to the stairs, we had our roles as Beatrice and Benedick to look forward to.

'And we are more than halfway through the play. Let us not linger afterwards,' he added in an urgent undervoice. 'Ah! That damned jet!' Still hand in hand, the moment we were in the office corridor we sped along.

To find the door unlocked.

Swearing under his breath, Matthew flung open the door, braced, I could see, for battle. I seized an oil lamp from its sconce: what I would have done with it heaven knows, since hitting anyone with it would have sent burning oil flying all over Matthew's tidy paperwork. But such folly – it was unlikely a fire would have confined itself to his desk or even his office – was unnecessary. The room, as my gently-raised lamp showed, was empty. Using its light, Matthew checked his desk, while I lit candles and made up the fire. 'Nothing seems to be amiss, though I can't see my paperweight,' he said slowly.

'That ugly onyx thing?'

'It's not very lovely, is it? But her ladyship gave it to me, one of her strange off-hand gifts, and I keep it – out of respect, I suppose.'

'Like those shirt studs. It must be here somewhere – I can't think why you should, but did you stow it in your desk for some reason?' I rifled through the only unlocked drawer – the one over the kneehole. I got nothing for my pains but several pencil stubs. 'What worries me more is how someone got in. My keys are still on my chatelaine. I must check who was on cleaning and fire duty and have a word with them.'

When I looked up, I found him already on his knees by the safe. 'Your jet necklace, my love, is safe. Here: let me fasten it for you. And the bracelet? There. Now, please watch as I lock this: I want to be sure. And please watch me lock the door behind us. I don't want lingering doubts that I somehow forgot my essential routine. After the missing stud, I begin to doubt my memory. Even my sanity.'

I put my hand on his. 'I don't doubt either of those. And I don't doubt my own. I've been meaning to ask you: that clock – I've seen it before, but not in here. And the picture, of course. It was in one of the guest bedchambers. What on earth made you want that old thing on your wall? You can't even see what it's supposed to be!'

'It's got a remarkably nice frame, though.'

I held the lamp closer. 'It has, hasn't it? I wonder why. Have you asked the professor?' I asked casually.

'Dick Thatcher counselled caution.'

'Dick? Why on earth should he do that?'

'He might have used your phrase, "just in case".'

'Might he indeed?'

'The impression was that both the professor and Lady Stanton were prowling too much – inspecting too closely, remember. I know that our cold corridor regime has limited that, but I still don't feel inclined to ask for his advice – in case, to be frank, he himself knows anything about this mismatch.'

I bit my lip. 'I have a terrible thought. No. I won't share it even with you yet.' He stared and I was ready to explain after all when the clock struck. 'We're late for sherry, and – heavens! That late!'

We ran. But Matthew definitely locked up first.

'But everyone can sing!' Lady Stanton stated in the middle of dessert, her declaration shared with the entire table, not just her dinner partner, Francis. 'Even birds sing!'

'Especially the Swedish Nightingale,' Francis said, evidently trying to divert her. 'Did you ever hear her sing? An altogether magical experience.'

'No. Never. They say her lower register was sadly wanting,' her ladyship added, 'and frequently out of tune.'

Mr Wilson frowned. 'That was not the voice I was privileged to hear. But to the point. I believe that entertainment in which everyone may join in is more appropriate. And it is such a long time since I read *Much Ado* I should be disappointed not to complete it.'

'Indeed,' Mr Pounceman said soberly. 'Though in fact I wonder if our choice of play might not have been a little indelicate. Perhaps a tragedy . . .'

'But then—' Bea stopped abruptly.

'But then the parts for women would have been very limited,' I finished for her. 'And, to be honest, I wonder whether we need more murder and destruction at the moment. If I might add my voice to Mr Wilson's, I would love to finish the reading. We could enjoy your music tomorrow evening, perhaps.' Even as I used the possessive adjective I knew I was giving her ammunition. How foolish of me. But this was perhaps the moment to return to more conventional dinner table etiquette. I turned pointedly to Ellis Page, who had accepted an invitation to dine at least. 'I am sure one of the gentlemen would gladly surrender one of the many doubling parts. I believe at one point last night at least two of them were talking to themselves and would be grateful if you took a part or two.'

He smiled equivocally.

'Tell me,' I continued more seriously, 'are the roads any clearer? If you have any doubts about making the journey back to the village your usual room will be ready within the half-hour.'

He raised his voice to the usual social level: 'I believe a thaw may be setting in—'

'A thaw? Thank God! I may lead my flock in Sabbath worship!' Mr Pounceman said, in what I suppose was a forgivable breach of the conversational rules – after all, serving the Lord was more than a whim, it was his calling.

Lady Stanton declared, less appropriately, 'And I, thank God, may at last be on my way!'

A slight frown appeared between Pounceman's elegant eyebrows.

Ellis shook his head. 'Alas, I hate to disappoint either of you, but my gardener sucks his few remaining teeth and assures me it will be but temporary. So while I hope you can lead Divine Service, Pounceman, I fear her ladyship would be ill-advised to assume she could travel yet. As for her servants, the life of her groom still hangs in the balance.'

We all shook our heads sadly, Mr Pounceman promising further prayer.

When conversations restarted, I dropped my voice so that only Ellis might hear. 'May I ask – something I do too rarely, I am the first to admit – how his lordship does?'

'As I have said, some time in the open air would do him a great deal of good. But not while you have a visitor whose presence and behaviour might upset the even tenor of his life.'

I nodded. 'Once he used to wander round the place – do you remember the anxiety we suffered when the portrait of Queen Bess disappeared? And then where it reappeared? Is it possible he might have left – I don't like to use the term, *escaped* – again?'

'Why would you think that? Ah, it's not something you can talk about over the dinner table. It would be best to talk about it next time I come to the House. But the answer to the original question is no. He is well . . . cared for. Supervised. The guards may be dull of speech but they know what they must do.'

'Indeed. Thank you.'

'But your brow has not cleared. Indeed, your frown is deeper.'

'If he is not responsible for some – let us call them minor irritations – then someone else must be. And the question would be, who? But you are right: this is a conversation for the Room. Ah, I believe that Lady Stanton is signalling that Bea and I should withdraw.'

Like the other gentlemen he rose as we did. 'Stick to your guns over the acting,' he mouthed as I turned to thank him for easing back my chair. I managed to suppress a snuffle of laughter. All our lives Bea and I had managed to get up unaided; now we were temporary ladies, we needed assistance.

Lady Stanton ensured she had the same seat as the previous evening before engaging in conversation with us. 'I hope we can regard what was said this afternoon as confidential?'

Still on her feet, Bea bridled. 'Your ladyship, do you not think we are used to holding our tongues? It is what a life in service teaches you: think of all the conversations the footmen are privy to, waiting hour upon hour to do your bidding. Think of the confidences ladies' maids share. I should imagine Harriet knows to a penny how much is spent, how much is owed in the House. So no, we will say nothing. But our advice would be the same: if you feel unsafe, talk to Constable Pritchard. Failing that, to Harriet and Matthew, together with Thatcher, so that a plan for your protection can be devised.' She sat, with some emphasis.

'Who said I needed protection?' her ladyship demanded. 'I did not.'

It was time for me to intervene, though I sat first. 'I recall, ma'am, that this afternoon you needed us to lock away your jewellery. Other matters intervened, did they not? Would one man be able to carry what you need to have locked away? Because Thatcher is still on duty, and although technically I am not, I would happily take five minutes to share the unlocking and relocking duties with him.'

'Is there any point, if I am to leave soon?'

'Ma'am, did you not hear Dr Page's warnings?'

'Oh, he's such an old woman, isn't he? Ah! Here come the gentlemen already!' Her face and her posture changed perceptibly. Then, extraordinarily, in view of the conversation that had taken place but half an hour before, she left her seat to take possession of the piano stool. Her fingers were running up and down the keyboard even as Matthew pushed Mr Pounceman through the double doors. His knuckles whitened and his face closed in a way I knew meant he was battling with what I knew could be a terrifying temper.

I stood. 'Ah, gentlemen, Lady Stanton was just entertaining us until you actors arrived. But before we open our books, I need some kind volunteers to convey her ladyship's strongbox to our safe. Thatcher and I will await you there.' I swept out, a bemused Thatcher following in my wake. At last, I paused and looked back. Yes, Francis, her ladyship on his arm, was leading Mr Wilson and Matthew up the stairs.

Dick Thatcher shot a sideways look at me. 'Safety in numbers, ma'am? And may I say, ma'am, you deserve a round of applause for that. Saved a nasty scene, didn't you?'

'For now. But later I may well regret provoking her temper.' I had not meant to say that aloud. And I knew I could not bear to ask Dick if he knew who in the household hated me enough to drip poison in Olwen's ear.

Dick touched his nose, grinning like a schoolboy. As one, before the safe, we stood like twin guards, our keys raised like swords. The gentlemen might appreciate the parody, but I doubted if Lady Stanton would.

And so it was back to the play. Once again there was a little awkwardness when perhaps by chance Bea sat in the chair by the fire her ladyship wanted, but with tactful aplomb she declared the place was too hot for her and vacated it. If she was disappointed that Ellis Page had declared that he could not join us, his place being where villagers could easily reach him, she did not show it, concentrating instead on our evening's entertainment. So, thank goodness, did we all, helped, perhaps, by the champagne Matthew requested. At last, our motley group was united, if only for a couple of hours.

TWENTY-ONE

Matthew

I happened to be alone in the breakfast room when Francis appeared. He joined me at the window, admiring a large icicle which had formed overnight. Although we were now friends, I knew that he and I would never share the ties between him and Harriet. But I felt I might trust him enough to talk about Professor Fulke-Grosse, even if I did not start the conversation about him directly.

'Harriet has found me out in a theft,' I began.

'Confession is good for the soul – you should speak to Pounceman before he leaves. What a wonderfully self-righteous Claudio he made last night!' But his face became serious. 'I cannot believe that Harriet would not forgive you.'

'She takes her responsibility to the House and its treasures very seriously,' I said. 'Rightly. I think I could have helped myself to the Holbein if I had asked her first. As it was, I absconded with a pretty clock and a painting I now think is ugly.'

'So why did you take it?' he asked reasonably.

'Have you a moment to come and see? Before the others join us?'

'You are serious, are you not? Very well. *Andiamo!*'

The office fire had been banked up with what the locals called slack, a mixture of coal dust and little pieces of coal, but soon responded to the poker and blossomed into flame. The clock chimed the half hour as if in relief.

'My spoils,' I said pointing. 'And this is the painting.'

He lifted it down and took it to the window, turning it this way and that. 'What,' he asked quietly, 'was your real reason for choosing this?'

'My puzzlement,' I said. 'And from your expression you see the mismatch as clearly as I do. You know that we keep all our rooms locked these days, after his lordship was found to have tried to throw our portrait of Queen Bess out of the window.'

'Allegedly. He has a most devoted valet-cum-attendant, does he not?'

'Yes. Hargreaves. A young man who has made enormous sacrifices for a master most young men would have walked away from.'

'Is he well paid?'

'By my standards no. But he is paid as much as Thatcher, some sixty pounds a year, with no deductions for board and lodging which some employers still make,' I added with a shake of my head.

'Either derisory or generous, depending on your viewpoint. When the portrait was found, do I not recall it was tucked away in a wardrobe somewhere?'

'Yes. In Hargreaves' room. But there was so much else going on, and afterwards so many bruises to lick, I fear he was never questioned properly. To be honest, I suspect if he had simply asked for a picture, then it would have been given him with hardly a second thought. There are a lot of pictures in the attic,' I added dryly.

'Might it be possible for Fulke-Grosse to inspect this?' He sighed, more with disappointment than asperity. 'Matthew, why did you ask me to look at this strange amalgam, not him? He is an expert, is he not? His expertise is the reason why he is here.'

I felt my temper flare as it often did when he spoke so reasonably. But I confined myself to a shrug. 'Can I be absolutely frank with you? In this strange half-world, with Mary's murderer still at large, I do not know who to trust.' I raised my fingers to count on them. 'Except Harriet. Bea. You. Me.'

'Page and Timpson can surely be added to that list – except I suddenly recall why you might have reservations about Timpson. And all you know about Fulke-Grosse is his reputation, and the fact it was I who introduced him. How well do I know him?' He spread his hands. 'He is a charming acquaintance, at times irritating in the extreme, of course. Not a friend as you and Harriet are my friends. And,' he said, extending his hand, which I happily shook, 'I apologize for my earlier rebuke. Let me see how your thinking went – a painting is tampered with. Who might have the skills to tamper? An art expert. And God knows he has had plenty of opportunity. In fact, of course, when the House was in turmoil after her lady-ship's death, he made himself scarce out of tact, he told me.'

'I think it was his tactful withdrawal and the way he prowled around the House that alarmed one or two of the servants,' I said. 'But Francis, if you felt able to be here when I ask him to look at my acquisition, my mind could easily be put at rest. And Harriet's. Given what I gather was the Family's conserva-tive taste in visitors, I don't think she's ever met anyone quite like him before.' I added, 'To be honest, my own acquaint-anceship with aesthetes is limited. My professors were much more conventional in dress and behaviour. They might have been models – stereotypes, indeed – of one's notions of what academics should look like. Hudson Fulke-Grosse would not.'

I earned a bark of laughter. 'And you, dear Matthew, conform so very closely to the notion that an estate manager should be a wizened, be-gaitered, retired farmer with an accent impen-etrable to anyone but his neighbours. Harriet should be a roly-poly old dame entirely preoccupied with nagging the servants.'

'If there were a stereotype for you explorers of the past – dear me, I don't know what it would be. Thank God for individuality. I shall try to appreciate Fulke-Grosse more. And now it is certainly time we presented ourselves for breakfast.'

He smiled. 'If you issue the invitation to Hudson, I shall busily ask permission to join you both. But I fear we may be joined by another party – and it would be sad to deny her ladyship the chance to be in a room with two eligible gentlemen, would it not?'

'Were there space, we could make Pounceman a third! I never thought I would say this, Francis,' I admitted, as I ushered him out of the room, locking it behind me, 'but his presence here has been invaluable.'

'Dealing with her ladyship? It's given me time to take a breath, at least. Having to be charming all the time, always

under Wilson's eagle eye, exhausts one so! Just thank your
lucky stars you are safely married!'
'I do,' I said. 'Every single day.'

Whatever the professor's reaction to the picture might be, we
would in fact have to wait until Pounceman had left us. He was
not sufficiently high on the social scale to merit a full-scale
turn out of the domestic staff, but Thatcher and Luke were in
attendance. Harriet and I were joined by Francis and Lady
Stanton on the broad sweep of steps down to the best sleigh.
Our estate carpenter, George, had fashioned a long ramp from
top to bottom of the flight so that his wheelchair was less of
a burden on our footmen, who nonetheless were needed – to
act as brakes – and Thatcher and Luke walked alongside as
escorts. It was, as Francis remarked as the sleigh disappeared
from sight, all very elegantly done.

Harriet snorted. 'I suspect our progress to and from church
tomorrow will be considerably less stylish. But go we must.
Or we may find ourselves with unwanted renovation work on
our hands: he wants us to re-open the Family chapel so the
servants can attend every day for morning and evening prayers.'

'Us too, no doubt, to set an example,' I added gloomily.
'Heavens, there may be the slightest of thaws but it's still too
cold for this!'

Harriet led the way inside, she to supervise, with Bea and
Thatcher, the distribution of her late ladyship's keepsakes and
I . . . Francis and I exchanged a glance. Clearly he and the
professor were now required to entertain Lady Stanton. In that
case I might as well join Harriet and the others as an impartial
witness. I made my way to the Family wing and her ladyship's
drawing room.

Harriet's team had worked wonders, though she quietly
observed that there was still much to do in the bedchamber.
Here the elegant chairs and sofa had been pushed back to
accommodate two long narrow tables, on which lay a collection of handkerchiefs, hat pins, gloves and trinkets far too
inexpensive to have been stowed in the jewellery casket but
still of some sentimental value to her servants. There was
also a small pile of books, none of them improving, but most

hardly opened. The black-clad men and women stood in silence, but you could see flashes of desire as eyes fell on this or that. Florrie rushed in late, bobbing to us and gasping that Lady Stanton had wanted her to redo her hair after her trip outside.

'I'm glad you're here, Florrie, since you actually knew Lady Croft better than most,' I said ambiguously. 'Accordingly I would like you to make your selection first, and then Mr Thatcher will select a memento on Mr Bowman's behalf. Then Mrs Arden's chief assistant. After that, we will have a simple queue.'

Florrie's reaction was not one I had expected. Her eyes filled with tears, and she almost gibbered her thanks. Harriet's arm encircled her shoulders. 'Would you prefer Mr Thatcher to make his choice first? Very well.'

With all Samuel's dignity weighing upon him, Thatcher stepped forward and looked at her ladyship's two prayer books, one old and battered, the other almost pristine. With a bow, he picked up the older. 'This is the one Mr Bowman will recognize, Mrs Rowsley.'

'Of course. Thank you. Florrie – are you well enough now?' As her tears dripped, Harriet reached for one of her ladyship's handkerchiefs and pressed it into the girl's hand. 'Dry your eyes, my dear: her ladyship wouldn't have wanted this distress. I wondered if you might like her nightdress case? You were probably one of the team who embroidered it for her last birthday.'

'Isn't that too much?' But she held it to her as I have seen women hold babies.

The other maids' responses were less dramatic whether they were Harriet's staff or Bea's. I suspected that many of the items might be sold the next time the pedlar called: even handkerchiefs would fetch much needed coins, especially those as finely embroidered as these. But I could not argue with that. Her ladyship had always been a remote figure, and as her health declined, her tongue had grown sharper.

Thatcher still had nothing, but I had seen his eyes on the newer prayer book. I whispered to Harriet, who scooped it up and pressed it into his hands.

'It's not for me, ma'am – I wanted it for Hargreaves. He'd have been here but it seems his lordship's not at his best today.'

'Of course. But you served her ladyship too, and must not be left out. Do you know what I think she would have liked you to have? That little notebook and pencil.'

The cover was tortoiseshell. He glowed with disbelieving delight.

'And the rest of you men must take something,' she added. 'Even if you keep the items to give to your sweethearts.'

Soon everyone had something to keep and – perhaps more important – something with which to barter with the pedlar. The room emptied but for Harriet, Bea and me.

'Thank God that's over,' Harriet said quietly.

Bea looked at her. 'In just one morning the vicious old bat becomes a saint.' She turned to Harriet. 'She's probably spinning in her grave. Give stuff away? She'd sooner have burnt it.'

'I know. But I could hardly have said that, could I? And what else would we have done with it? Given it to the poor? Our people have a little more claim on it!' At last she smiled. 'I feel we all deserve a cup of coffee.'

Hardly had we sat down in the Room when a maid tapped on the door to announce the arrival of Constable Pritchard. A fourth cup and a plate of biscuits arrived before he had even sat down.

'I thought you would like me to report on what we have found so far – but it must stay between these four walls.' His voice was solemn.

'Of course,' Bea replied, rather spoiling her calm response by snarling, 'Have you found the murdering bastard yet?'

'No. There is nothing in any of the statements I took from the household and the guests to suggest that any of them were not where they said they were. Sergeant Burrows and I have been over them with a fine-tooth comb. Nothing. We are left with your theory that someone wanted to remove her ladyship's jewellery from your room, Matthew, and that poor little Mary interrupted him or her. But we have no more idea than the Man in the Moon who. However,' he said, raising his finger with some authority, 'we have looked into Lady Stanton's story, as much as we can, given the state of the roads. One of my Chester colleagues has been to interview her friends and they confirm that she was indeed their acquaintance.'

'And?' Harriet prompted.

'And PC Clarke – that's my colleague there – saw no reason to ask any other pertinent questions,' Elias said with quiet fury. '"They were ladies and gentlemen" apparently – so couldn't be challenged! If only I'd been there!' he added savagely, conveniently forgetting his own qualms about interrogating the gentry.

I frowned. 'So he got nothing out of them at all? I wonder why . . .'

'Exactly what I'm doing, Matthew, and that's the truth. Apparently they asked where she was, that's all. And if Clarke did ask whether they knew where she'd been staying before, then they didn't say. What a waste of time! The sergeant isn't best pleased, I can tell you.'

'But perhaps we need to look under the words, Elias,' Harriet said slowly. 'Do we know what sort of people they are? Their names, their address? Strictly between us, of course.'

'Lord and Lady Silverland. Doughton Hall. Big place. Not as big as this, of course.'

'But aristocracy? Old money or new?'

The poor man pulled a face: how would he know? Harriet did not press him; I suspect she would be looking them up in the *Peerage*, or questioning Francis about them. Or possibly both.

'So we don't know whether they're the sort of people who'd take umbrage at being questioned by an officer of the law or if they don't want to give away secrets because they've been asked not to. Very frustrating. I wonder if you might ask Lady Stanton herself. She might confide in you,' I added, doubtfully.

He jutted out his lower lip. 'And maybe I see a pig flying past that window. But I'll try. Maybe I'll take the line that her posh friends are worried about her, and that I can get a message conveyed to them via the telegraph.'

Harriet looked up, her face very serious. 'Bea and I promised, did we not, Bea, that we would reveal nothing that she said to us.'

'I'll make it clear that this was a police enquiry, as indeed it was, ma'am. There's no need at all for either of your names to be mentioned. And if it is – but not by me – then I can tell her that you didn't know what was happening. Which is more or less the truth.'

Harriet nodded slowly. 'Thank you.' She looked at Bea. 'She needs to know she can trust someone, does she not?'

'Trust them if not like them. Heavens, she goes out of her way to upset people! Now, if you good people want luncheon, you must excuse me.'

We all stood.

'If Thatcher will announce me, I must go and talk to her ladyship,' Elias sighed.

'And I will look up her ladyship's friends in the *Peerage*,' I declared.

She took it, managing to ignore his part in its appearance. Through the open doors I could see Matthew and Francis ready to do anything necessary; equally a number of servants were watching the most interesting sideshow for years. With a cool head, Luke put the tray on the nearest table and, picking up the broken chair, went off to shoo away the audience. All but Matthew and Francis inched away.

By the look of them, Thatcher and Elias could have done with a nip of brandy too, but they would have to wait. Thatcher slipped into the salon; Elias subsided back on to his chair at the far side of the table, as Thatcher materialized with another, presumably medicinal. Once again he withdrew, but I suspected only to lurk with Matthew at the far side of the doorway. If only I could signal to Francis to come casually to our rescue.

'My dear Lady Stanton,' I began, wishing that I did not have to say such words to a woman who did not inspire me with any affection, 'what has caused you such distress? No, quietly now.' I pressed the brandy into her hand, hoping I could inch it towards her mouth. I did not want it thrown over her ladyship's favourite silk hangings. There. The first sip. 'Constable Pritchard? Have you delivered bad news?'

He took his cue adeptly. 'No, Mrs Rowsley. I brought good news. I came to tell Lady Stanton that the police have located her friends in Chester and told them not to worry, because she was safe here. And it seems I was wrong to do so.'

'To tell her? Or to talk to her friends?'

'*I* did not do that, ma'am. That was what the Cheshire constabulary chose to do. After all, lives have been lost in the blizzards – they must have been sorely anxious.'

'You – *they!* – had no right! None at all. And now I am in dreadful danger! What can I do?' To my surprise, she clutched my hands, which were still holding the brandy balloon.

I managed to remove it and my hands from her grasp. Placing the glass safely on the table, I asked, 'Could you perhaps explain why you did not want them to know? Are they in fact not your friends? So why did you say they were? You insisted, still do insist, that you want to continue on your journey – to Chester. And yet you don't want to go there at all?' Ashamed that I was overstepping the mark, that more than a note of

TWENTY-TWO

Harriet

I ran. Every rule in the House forbids running, but hearing a scream I ran. Please God, not another death in the House! I reached the great entrance hall, where sounds bounce weirdly from all angles, amplified, muffled by marble and tapestries. Where, where were the screams coming from? No. Here on the ground floor? No. Up the grand staircase? A man would have taken it two at a time, but my skirts kept me to a more decorous pace. There! The drawing room? Dimly I registered men on their feet. Perhaps they followed me. The blue salon? Or the little anteroom just off it, where Elias had interviewed the guests before? Yes! Pausing only to gather my skirts more tightly – it would never do to sweep the Dresden or Limoges from the fragile occasional tables – I sped as fast as I dared.

I found Elias looking totally appalled and, still screaming, her ladyship literally lying on the carpet, thumping it with her fists. The pretty gilt Regency chair lay beside her, one leg broken.

By now the gentlemen and the servants must be coming too – yes, Thatcher was there a yard or so behind me.

'Get another chair. Yes, that will do. Now, you and Elias are going to take her by one arm each and help her on to it. Luke! Cold water. And brandy.' I went to her head, stooping to look her in the eye as, now seated, she kicked and tried to scratch the men. 'Lady Stanton. Be quiet. Or I shall have to slap you. Hush, now, hush.' Now she was crying in good earnest. Luke approached with two glasses on a tray. I knelt, putting an arm round her shoulders, either to comfort her or to support her head as I released the vinaigrette from my chatelaine and wafted it under her nose.

At last, with the indignity of streaming eyes and nose, she subsided. With aplomb, Thatcher produced a handkerchief.

exasperation was creeping into my voice, I got to my feet, turning away and gesturing to Elias to continue.

'I am sure my colleagues really thought they were being helpful,' he began. 'And I apologize on their behalf if they have brought trouble to your door. But now,' he said, his voice becoming stern, 'as a police officer I would like to know why you felt it necessary to lie to me.'

'I do not need to explain anything to you! You fool! You cannot know what you have done!' Getting to her feet, she turned to me. 'A fire in my room, if you please. And I require Olwen's presence. Now.' Gathering her skirts, she sailed out just as I would imagine a great actress would quit her stage.

'Not so fast, ma'am, if you please!' Elias spoke quietly, but with an authority that stopped her in her tracks. Moving the chair she had just left and placing it on the opposite side of the table to his, he gestured. She was to sit.

And sit she did.

I caught his eye: was I to stay or slip away?

Lady Stanton settled the point. 'If I am to talk to you, it will not be in front of these people.'

Accordingly I curtsied and left the anteroom, closing the doors behind me. The three men, faces both aghast and intrigued, were clearly about to question me, but I touched my lips and cupped my ear: could we shamelessly eavesdrop? But the House was built too solidly to accommodate listeners-in, so we made our way from the room and across the painting-hung landing.

'Downstairs, Harriet?' Matthew asked, clearly puzzled.

'To your office. To look up the mysterious non-friends. The Silverlands of Doughton Hall. Know thine enemy—'

'Or in this case,' Francis put in, 'Lady Stanton's enemies. What on earth do we make of all that?'

'Whatever it is, perhaps we should discuss it in my office. The acoustics . . .' Matthew gestured at the great dome. 'Even the quietest words can carry unexpectedly.'

'Let me ask Luke to bring us coffee,' Matthew said, as I sank less than gracefully on to the nearest chair. 'All that drama was exhausting to watch, let alone take part in.'

'Indeed.' Francis paused in his examination of the reference books' spines. 'But we were primed, absolutely primed, to jump in and rescue you if necessary. I was even rehearsing a convincing proposal of marriage to distract her, so you can imagine how wonderful it was to hear you calm her down.' He paused while Matthew spoke to Luke. 'Ah. Here it is. *Burke's Peerage.*'

SILVERLAND OF DOUGHTON HALL. Line established 1666. Edmund Silverland, born March 1, 1813, married June 11, 1825, Bronwen, daughter of Lord Machynlleth, of Plas Newydd in the county of Montgomery; by which lady he has issue Thomas, born August 8, 1827.

'Blah, blah, blah . . . So nothing of any use there.'

'There's the Welsh connection,' Matthew corrected him. 'Elias needs to know that – assuming her ladyship does not tell him. Dear me, I hope he'll be able to reveal some at least of what she's saying.'

There was a tap on the door. Mr Wilson appeared, his face serious. 'Might I?' he stepped in almost furtively, waving a dismissive hand when Matthew raised the coffee pot. 'I thought I should tell you – I've mislaid the professor. We were both sitting reading in the drawing room when he excused himself. But he never came back. Could it be that he has become unwell? I took it upon myself to ask one of the footmen to check if he was in his bedchamber but the answer he came back with was in the negative. Imagine if he is indisposed in one of these icy corridors!' As if he himself had not endorsed the scheme to keep people together. 'So I despatched the same young man to search the corridors for him, again with negative results. Where can he be?'

'Perhaps he went for a walk,' Francis suggested, with barely concealed irritation. 'It looks very beautiful out there, does it not? I fancy a stroll myself. Would you care to join me?'

'What an excellent suggestion. But perhaps we should defer the pleasure till after luncheon – or more importantly until Fulke-Grosse has reappeared. I apologize. I have interrupted your meeting.' But he did not budge.

Francis said, with what I suspected was deceptive calm, 'Perhaps in this weather, in this cold house, in seeking warmth we have been too much on top of one another. Perhaps we need more time to enjoy solitude without the lingering suspicion that we are being watched by our fellow guests. I quite understand the need to economize on fuel. And I understand the problems with rodents in the library. But—'

'My dear Sir Francis,' Wilson began. I could veritably see the high horse he was ready to mount.

'Mr Wilson,' I intervened, putting my hand on his sleeve, 'I will tell Thatcher to ask all the servants if they have seen the professor. Since we need a moment to talk over a personal matter, he will report to you in the drawing room. Meanwhile, I think Sir Francis' suggestion that we go out for some exercise this afternoon is an excellent one, which he could raise at luncheon. We can stroll off on our own or dawdle in groups according to our whim. As long as we all avoid the area near the lake. I would hate any of us to take an inadvertent bath.' I gave him my most dimpled smile.

He bowed low over my hand and took the hint. And his leave.

As one we sighed.

'Perhaps I should discover we have had another delivery of logs,' I said dryly.

'I think the concept is right. We should be spying on each other. But not as overtly as Wilson, perhaps. Let us return to our *moutons*. Forgive me, Harriet – I always forget that you did not have a chance to learn French. Let us return to the subject of Lady Stanton. The performance was wasted on so few of us, was it not? She should have been on the stage.'

'Except that she does not read aloud well enough,' Matthew said. 'One would expect her acting to outclass Harriet and Bea's – but there is a disconcerting lack of fluidity. Yes, I know you coached Bea – but an educated lady with nothing but time on her hands to acquire accomplishments should have been better.'

I shook my head slowly. 'She read her speeches well. Elegantly, indeed. The problem surely lay in her ability to react to her fellow actors quickly enough. Perhaps she was not concentrating. She made it clear she was only joining in reluctantly, and heaven knows she seems to have enough on her mind to stop anyone giving their full attention to the work in hand. Poor woman. You may think she was play-acting, but I think she was genuinely outraged.'

Matthew looked doubtful. 'Is outrage the same as terror?'

'In her case, I think the two were there in equal measure, merging into hysteria. Oh, dear – how would she have reacted if I had slapped her face?' I could not suppress a grim laugh before I added, 'Though I do not think it would have made matters much worse – she made it quite clear, did she not, that she trusted none of us.'

'But the corollary is that Elias will now find it hard to trust her. And she has made a potential enemy of one of the few people, one of the two women, who were ready to protect her,' Matthew pointed out. He glanced at the clock. 'It will soon be time for luncheon. Is she able to eat in her bedchamber?'

'I've not yet had the chance to have her fire lit. And as for her demand to have Olwen return to her service – I would prefer to ask Ellis Page's opinion before requiring the poor young woman to leave her lover's side.' My face went stiff. 'Matthew saw, as I did not, Olwen's expression when she looked at me, up in the Family wing. Pure loathing, he said. And neither of us can work out why.'

Francis looked appalled. 'It seems to me you should ask Page that too! Or get Elias to speak to the girl – Parker reports that he is brilliant at dealing with servants, getting them to talk despite themselves, as it were.' Then he smiled. 'I will pursue her ladyship with a plea that she join us for lunch. I will cajole her with a promise to beg you for wood or coal, and offer to start it myself with books I can no longer value if she is not happy. I will be a veritable Shakespearian lover!'

'And when she sues you for breach of promise?' Matthew snorted.

'I shall rely on your forensically eloquent cousin to dig me out of my hole. But I cannot think that anyone wants to leave such an unstable woman alone in her room unsupervised – especially with a servant who wants manners if not sense! No, much as Wilson and his constant hovering irritate me, I fear we must keep her ladyship under surveillance. And, of course, find Hudson Fulke-Grosse.'

'And openly consult him about that picture,' I said. 'If he panics, we know where we are. If he can give us the benefit of his knowledge, we will be able to make better decisions. Meanwhile, I want to go and talk to Florrie: I was worried that she was so upset when we were distributing those little mementos. And I really do not like the thought of her being compelled to spend so much time in Lady Stanton's cheerless dressing room. In fact,' I added, 'I have the beginnings of an idea I would like to discuss with her.'

TWENTY-THREE

Matthew

'Elias – what the hell is going on, man? No, I'm not going to ask you to betray secrets, but this woman is living under the roof of the Family that employed me. They may not be my masters now, but I am as answerable to the trustees as I was to her late ladyship. We did the right thing to rescue Lady Stanton in that storm, but now – now she is repaying our limited but freely offered hospitality with behaviour that seems nothing short of bizarre.'

Poor Elias, cornered as he walked apologetically through the entrance hall, spread his hands. 'I can't speak of this here, Matthew.'

'You can speak of it in the Room or in my office,' I retorted. 'Please.' I ushered him firmly towards the latter. 'Just tell us,' I said, nodding him into my visitor's chair before taking my place behind my desk, 'what we should do with her?'

'Do with her?' he repeated, almost stupidly. 'What can you do, but let her stay here?'

'She doesn't want to stay here! She's made that embarrassingly plain. Heavens, the performance that we've just witnessed! She was fit to be confined!'

'Isn't that just the gentry for you? Always want and get their own way. And a lady too – can't be surprised if she gets an attack of the vapours, can we? They say even our dear Queen has what I would call tantrums if a child of mine behaved that way.'

'We can be surprised if she is an uninvited guest. We can expect decent behaviour. She expects it of us. More, she expects us all to dance to her tune, Harriet and Bea in particular. If her coachman and her groom were well, we could have sent her on her way with a flea in her ear – an upper-class flea, if you prefer.'

He looked dumbfounded. 'Never expected to hear you speak like this, Matthew. You've always been such a peaceable man.'

Peaceable? That word was very far from accurate, especially in my youth. 'I do my best to keep my temper under control, but the events of this morning have made me very angry, especially for Harriet, to whom Lady Stanton had been extremely rude in the past. Elias, tell me where we can send her or take her and I will verily drive the coach myself!'

'Ah, but where would that be?'

'Surely she has told you!'

'Not exactly.' He shifted uneasily.

'She's told you nothing, has she – not a single hard fact. Nothing you can verify. The woman is as slippery as an eel.'

He clearly resented my tone. 'I know where she can't go, and that's Chester. And another place she can't go, because it's still cut off, and that's Cwmbach Llechrhyd. So where would you suggest, eh, Matthew? Out into the cold? Yes? Because I smell more snow in the air.'

I stood. 'Very well – let me put an idea to you. She arrived from nowhere. She cares not a snap of her fingers for her servants, not one of them. One of our servants dies. Might you see a connection there?'

'There is no evidence, Matthew. None at all. Or any evidence against any one,' he said ruefully. 'I've not given up. But I simply don't know who could have done it. And I'd wager a week's wages that you don't either.'

'It's true. I don't. But I do know that everyone is on edge. We have a murderer on the loose. Someone who killed an innocent child who believed, probably for the first time in her life, that she was safe and cared for. Someone who must be found!'

'Well . . .'

'We are doing everything we can to control people's movements. It is as if we were under siege – from within. And then there is that picture.' I pointed. 'We believe someone has tampered with it.'

'Nice bright frame for such a dingy old picture, isn't it?' he said, getting up to look more closely.

'Even you and I, no art experts, can see there's a problem. It's only a few weeks ago before there was all the kerfuffle about the missing Queen Elizabeth portrait. Thank goodness there was an explanation for that—'

'Were you ever convinced by it?' he asked with a shrewd look in his kindly eyes. Shrewd and anxious. 'Or would you like me to question the most likely suspect again? And I don't mean his lordship, Matthew.'

'You mean Hargreaves, I gather.' I could not suppress a sigh. 'His dedication to his lordship is almost saintly. His lordship relies on him utterly and completely. What would happen if he did confess?'

'It would probably be up to the trustees whether or not they pressed charges.' He grimaced. 'And I'd wager they'd let him get away with it. They'd have to. At least it might stop him doing it again. And we might discover if he had an accomplice.' His face went white. 'Matthew, what if young Mary found out and he killed her to shut her up?'

'What indeed? But I would be grateful if you would question him about the picture. Start with that.' My laughter was grim. 'I ask you to help me solve one problem and all you do is give me another. But I tell you sincerely, Elias, we need to deal with Lady Stanton sooner rather than later. She tells us she is afraid of something, but not what. She havers about having her jewellery stowed and waits till the most inconvenient moment to ask for the safe to be locked. I have to say, I admired Harriet's aplomb in getting it transferred there after supper last night. She is terrified when you and your sergeant knock at our door, but won't say who she fears so we can't protect her properly. She wants the privacy of her room – but would need protection from our already stretched staff. I wish you could take her away to the privacy of your lock-up!'

Instead, we had to watch her quaff far too much wine with her lunch and flirt with arrant determination with Hudson, who had returned with no explanation after his absence, with Francis, with Montgomery and even with John Timpson. She saved the most blatant attempts for me, smiling at Harriet at each point she felt she scored. I would cheerfully have tipped the bottle over her.

As we all dispersed to dress for our expedition, I could not resist taking her on one side. 'Your ladyship, I can understand that you are in a serious situation—'

'That bumpkin of a constable has broken his word!'

'Constable Pritchard has said nothing. He is a good, wise officer whom we all respect.' Perhaps I had not thought all that an hour ago. 'Please do not interrupt me again. Your behaviour is not worthy of a guest under this roof. It is causing me and my wife embarrassment, and—'

She tapped my cheek. 'Oh, you have no sense of fun. It is time you grew accustomed to the ways of the world now you have taken over this house.'

'Madam, allow me to correct you. We have taken over nothing. This great House is not our home. We stay here when we have guests, to ensure their comfort and—'

'And spy on them. And treat them as prisoners. And deny them the essentials of decent living. Tush, Mr Rowsley. Do not take it on yourself, a mere employee, as you yourself point out, to criticize how others choose to behave.'

'I asked you not to interrupt me. I urge you to listen for your own sake.'

'And now you threaten me? What will you do if I don't conform to your notions? Throw me out? A gentlemanly act indeed. Except, of course, you are not a gentleman but a jumped-up farmhand.'

'You will find a fire in your new bedchamber, Lady Stanton,' came Harriet's icy voice. 'Constable Pritchard fears you are at risk now your whereabouts are known. I have transferred you to the late Lady Croft's suite, where you cannot be anything other than warm and comfortable. Your luggage has been moved and Florrie awaits your instructions. Mr Thatcher will escort you up there now.'

In silence, we bowed as one as her ladyship swept out. When I was sure she had indeed left us, I turned to Harriet. 'What will she say when she finds she is guarded?'

'A great deal. But it is not as though she won't be joining us for meals and, of course, if she wants, on our walk. But to reduce the chances of that, I suggest we use the outdoor clothes we keep in the servants' entrance and veritably scarper!'

We set off at a spanking pace across crisp unsullied lying snow. Still almost blind with fury I had no idea of where Harriet was leading me. At last, our pace slowed. I found we were in the garden Lady Croft had loved so much; as if she might still want to stroll there, the gardeners had cleared the paths as best they could – the surprisingly warm sun had done the rest. Harriet released my arm and bent to the ground – and the next thing I knew was that she was bombarding me with snowballs. And I her! We hit and missed and laughed aloud like children. At last, our outer clothes soaked and her bonnet awry, we stopped and hugged like children. Then we were kissing in an entirely grown up way. Taking my hand, she ran not back to the House but to our own home. A fire burned in the entrance hall; another warmed our chamber. And for the first time in many days, we were completely alone with each other.

It was already snowing when we made our way sedately back to the House; big wet flakes settled on the fur trimming of her bonnet and on her eyelashes. One landed on her lips. I removed it in the obvious way.

As I set us in motion again, she stopped and stared. 'My love, we have left it to its own devices for two whole hours and yet it still stands. Look, there are no cracks in the portico, no chimneys toppling down, no flames leaping from the windows.'

'More important,' I said, irreverently but truthfully, 'we are whole again. As individuals and as the couple we are. We must abscond again. Soon.'

TWENTY-FOUR

Harriet

We were back on duty, of course, the moment we stepped through the servants' back door. A note from John Timpson lay in the centre of the Room table. Might we favour him with a word as soon as it was convenient. He would remain in the muniment room until he heard from us.

'This is most unlike him,' I observed. 'Since the disaster before Christmas, he has been so self-effacing as to be almost invisible. Shall we invite him to join us for a cup of tea here or in your office?'

'It'll be warmer in here. I'll go and fetch him while you order tea, shall I?'

There was no sign of Bea in the kitchen; Saturday afternoons were her precious time off. But the duty team was working like clockwork, and there was no doubt that she would be there to ensure that dinner was its usual impressive standard. Meanwhile, there were freshly-baked fairy cakes and a sponge that I knew from experience would be so light it was amazing that it did not float.

The delights waiting him when he came into the Room did not appear to cheer the young man at all, however, and Matthew's face was grim once more.

'I only left the muniment room for three minutes, four, no more, and – oh, ma'am – someone's been in and done I don't know how much harm.' He was almost in tears.

I looked at Matthew, who nodded. 'To be sure, all John's careful annotations and filing are . . .' He threw his hands in the air. 'It is as if a giant snowstorm had descended on the room.'

'Has the intruder stolen anything or simply created chaos?' I asked, as Matthew eased him on to a chair.

'Until we have redone the work of weeks it's hard to say,' Matthew said. 'We have half an hour, maybe longer, before we need to be fettled up for duty – shall we go and help?'

'Let John drink this tea first. He can eat some cake as we walk – you look ready to faint, young man, and that would never do.'

The idiocy of the person who had undone all of John Timpson's work was beyond belief. Parchment, either in sheets or in scrolls, was everywhere. The envelopes that had protected them were torn in pieces. Clearly John had had to pull some documents from the fire itself, which was mercifully banked up rather than showing flames. But any extra damage to parchments as fragile as this was distressing even to us – and worse to a man who loved them as he so clearly did. Matthew and I gathered everything from the floor, leaving John to sort everything into piles, some of which promptly rolled back on to the floor.

'I can do better than this,' Matthew declared, leaving the room. Soon he was back with an armful of empty filing boxes. 'John, as you put your piles into these, tell us what to write on them.' He took a pencil and passed me another.

We worked very quickly, encouraged by the relief that seemed to be appearing on John's face.

'I believe these are the real treasures,' he breathed, as he unrolled three or four documents. 'And these – look at the illumination!'

'It wouldn't do to write "Treasures" on the box, however,' Matthew said dryly.

John bit his lip. 'Write "Northumberland". I believe these pages resemble the Lindisfarne Gospels. Is there room in a safe somewhere?'

'I'll make room.'

John passed me another sheaf. 'Land deeds. How the Crofts made their money.'

I wrote his first two words, not the rest.

It was only as everything was tidy that I asked, 'Do you have any idea if anything is missing?'

He shook his head. 'Do you know what I think? I don't

think it was an attempt to steal, because in the world's terms, there is nothing of value here. I think it was . . . I don't know. Perhaps a warning, or perhaps even wanton vandalism. But who? Why? I know I am not liked but . . .' Head on hands, he collapsed on to his chair.

Matthew looked at his watch. 'We have to change for dinner, all of us.'

'I really can't . . . Not facing—'

I shook his arm gently. 'If you don't dine with us, whoever did this will think they won. We'll get as much of this as we can into Matthew's safe. Come on, if we all carry a few boxes . . .'

'Good God – look at this!' I cried as he let us into his office. 'It's as bad as the muniment room!'

Matthew looked shamefaced. 'I just wanted John to have the boxes as soon as I could. Every pile is as I left it. I've run out of boxes so we'll just have to tie everything.' He put his head round the door. 'Luke! Bring some string, some scissors and two lads, will you? There, soon have it all put to rights!' He patted John's arm. 'We'll just stow the precious stuff in the safe, shall we? There. Ah, the jet that Harriet will need.' He passed it to me. 'Now go and change for dinner, both of you, and look extra spruce. Go on! But John – perhaps we say nothing of all this until we have some idea who did it.'

John obeyed, but I dawdled behind. 'I'd rather wait for you to escort me,' I admitted, slightly shamefaced. We finished my sentence together: 'Just in case . . .'

I decided to ignore the tension emanating from Lady Stanton's end of the table, where chance had placed the professor and John on either side of her. There was little pretence of conversation. John had every reason not to talk too much, of course, and Hudson was keeping his counsel. Her ladyship embarked on a tittering monologue about being summarily decanted to far better accommodation. Perhaps – yes, indeed I should have been more tactful, discussing the change beforehand. I had let myself down again. I might even have explained much better when I broke the news – but I was in a rage threatening to overwhelm me as she cordially insulted Matthew.

Now her ladyship, getting little response from her companions, resorted to complaining about each dish she was offered, thus offending Bea. I caught my old friend's eye. She who responded with an elaborate shrug and beneath the table-top a tiny gesture with her hands, suggestive of wringing a chicken's neck. We exchanged most unladylike grins.

At our end of the table, despite my apprehension that I might sooner or later be on the receiving end of a vitriolic diatribe, we were far more relaxed, and laughter broke out from time to time. But that made us perhaps more aware of the deficiencies of our colleagues. At last, when all of us had dwindled into an uneasy silence, I said, 'Ladies and gentlemen, before we adjourn for coffee, I believe that I should explain to those of you who might be unaware of it, the House tradition of Sabbath morning church. All are invited, from the highest to the lowest. Mr Pounceman will, of course, lead the service. Some of us may choose to walk down to the church. But two sleighs will be available for those who would prefer them.' I paused. There was no obvious enthusiasm. An imp inside me made me add, 'If, of course, the threatened snow arrives, then you are cordially invited to the very short service that we always hold in such circumstances. Ten o'clock in the red dining room. All the servants will attend, and it is lovely if our guests set a good example. Matthew will lead the worship using the *Book of Common Prayer*.'

In truth, the tradition of guests attending was more honoured in the breach than the observance, but they were not to know that. Nor were they to know that Matthew had never led the service before: it had always been Samuel Bowman's proud duty if the Family was unable to attend. Should I have asked Dick Thatcher? Perhaps. But though his gravitas grew daily, I could not imagine his feeling secure. Nonetheless, I would ask him before we adjourned to the drawing room.

In fact he approached me. 'Thank you for saving my bacon there, ma'am. I know how Mr Bowman loved to do it, but I wouldn't, I promise you. All those chances to stumble over long words!'

Did he protest too much? 'Nonetheless, if the situation arises in the future, even next Sunday, I believe you should attempt it. Because if you don't, you may well come to resent the fact that someone else has taken over, willy-nilly, part of your role. Now Dick, walk with me a little way down here – out of earshot – if you please. Has rumour reached you about anything untoward?'

'Mr Timpson's office? Indeed it has, ma'am.'

'Are you able to tell me the gist of the rumours?'

His flush reminded me how young he was. 'There are several. You have to remember, ma'am, that the gentleman is not universally popular. If gentleman he may be called.' His sniff was worthy of Samuel.

'People resent how he came here?'

'Aye! And more to the point why he stays.'

I drifted us further away from the drawing room. 'It is a conundrum, isn't it? On the basis of his behaviour, he should have been sent packing the moment he confessed. But it would have been hard for me to despatch into the snow someone who had helped save my life, especially so close to Christmas. And my husband was really desperate for an experienced clerk – which we know Mr Timpson is.'

'With due respect, that's what he says he was. And with his history—'

'Dick, do you really think we would have appointed him even on a temporary basis without personally checking his references?' I asked quizzically. 'Both those when he worked for the late Mr Brunel's team and those from the shipping line? He has lightened my husband's load considerably. He would be the first to admit that he knew absolutely nothing about what seems to have become his passion – the old papers and parchments he found in the attic. But in his spare time he is writing to experts in the field and gaining knowledge all the time.'

'But is he putting that knowledge to good use or bad? Who's to say he didn't make all that mess himself just so that he could steal the most valuable pages and imply one of us had done it?'

'That's a very good question, Dick, to which I have no answer. But there's something else troubling you, is there not? Something rankling still?'

He grimaced. 'This sounds really petty, ma'am. But – well, he dines with you and the gentry! Him, a common clerk, and like to have been a common criminal!'

I nodded. 'You're quite right. "Neither flesh nor fowl" might be the best description.'

'He's not even a good red herring!'

Again I nodded. 'As Mr Rowsley's clerk, he would have dined with any tutor or governess, would he not? Other people in social limbo. But we have neither. Or with the chief nurse, perhaps – but in fact she is far above me in the social scale as I am sure you know, and though she is more than welcome to mix with us, she says she prefers to eat with her staff. There is no right or wrong to any of this, Dick – perhaps it will solve itself when the snow thaws and Mr Timpson can seek employment in a town or city, where indeed he would be more at home.'

'Ah, he's no countryman, that's for sure. But there's no guaranteeing he'll want to leave such a cushy billet, is there?' He looked over my shoulder. 'Ma'am, they have all gathered in the drawing room – shouldn't you be with them?'

'I'm sure they can manage without me for a few more minutes. Dick, can you convey all I have told you to everyone in the servants' hall? Or should I come down myself? However it is done, I want to make sure no one is tempted to . . . copy . . . to repeat . . . the business in the muniment room. Fun it might be, but some of those old papers have a value beyond what we can imagine, perhaps as high as some of our pictures, and they must not be damaged. Do you understand me? And if it was none of our colleagues, then I need their help to discover who it was. None of us, none, wants to harm anything in this House.'

'Except whoever put Mr Rowsley's dirty old picture into the shiny frame. I don't suppose you've found who did that, have you?'

'You'd be the first to know – as Mr Rowsley's partner in crime when he brought it down to his office!' I laughed. 'That clock too! I have spoken very firmly to him, Dick! There is something else I would like your help with. It seems to me that some of us are getting careless over locking rooms, or returning keys promptly to the proper hook. I am there so little now I wonder if you could keep an eye out for miscreants and tell them off.'

'I've not noticed – but I'll certainly warn people. Sternly.'

It was a horrible thing for a young man to have to do. But I was sure he would take his duty seriously. 'Thank you. And now,' I sighed, 'I suppose we must both go into battle . . .'

TWENTY-FIVE

Matthew

T impson and Fulke-Grosse might almost have been cele-
brating their release from Lady Stanton's company, as
they sat talking quietly but with great animation.
Fulke-Grosse had apparently let slide his previous chivalric
adoration of his dinner companion, which interested me. What
had caused his change of heart? Better acquaintance, perhaps.
He had made a point of speaking to Bea, I noticed, as they
had left the dining room together, reassuring her, I hoped, that
the dishes that had reached the dinner table were as excellent
as usual. Indeed, I had caught the words, 'You surpassed
yourself.' He even kissed her hand.

She reacted to his flourish with a smile I was relieved to
see was no more than amused. Of all the men of my acquaintance, the professor was the least likely to make an offer of
marriage, but I fancy she had realized that herself. It was
good to see her growing in confidence at our strange social
evenings, as was my lovely Harriet, who had drifted away
from us as we had all left the dining room together, eschewing
port and cigars. It was almost as if we men had made a tacit
pact not to let her ladyship bully those she no doubt thought
of as mere servant women. Mere! Bea was graciously inviting
Lady Stanton to sing while we waited for Harriet to arrive
– which, come to think of it, was less of a compliment than
I thought.

Francis, with a slight air of resignation, took his place as a
page-turner. Lady Stanton sang, but one could not say she
sang well. Had she again drunk too much wine? Was her mind
elsewhere, perhaps on some petty act of revenge on Harriet
and me for our hostility and then defection this afternoon?
Dimly I recalled Ellis Page saying that he had discovered
some ailment that perhaps he should mention to her ladyship's

physician. What might that be? I could scarcely ask him – and if I did, he would never betray a professional secret, any more than I would in my role on the estate.

If only her coachman and groom – and Olwen, her maid, of course – might recover enough to travel. For a terrible second, the words 'or just hurry up and die' flitted into my brain. Horrified, I pushed them aside furiously. Why was I so desperate for her to leave? Apart from being an unpleasant person, she was doing no active harm. Was she? She had been here less than a week. Even if she had had evil intent in descending on a strange house – this strange house – she could not have wandered round stealing items. If she had, how would she have eventually got them away?

In her huge jewellery casket? In the luggage that Florrie was not allowed to unpack? There was room in her trunks for a very great deal. And there was, after all, a very great deal within easy reach. On Monday – I would not ask him to work on the Sabbath – I would ask George, the estate carpenter with the extraordinary visual memory, to walk along all the corridors. Every last one.

Harriet slipped into the room, as silently as her silk skirts would allow, but the great billows of fabric made enough noise to cause Lady Stanton to break off in discord. I am sure I was not the only one braced for a tantrum.

But Harriet managed to speak first. 'My apologies. I was unavoidably detained on a matter of household importance. Before I ring for tea, would you be kind enough to repeat that song, my lady? I would hate to think that I spoiled everyone's enjoyment.'

Lady Stanton complied. And then she applied herself to a Chopin nocturne, which was beyond her abilities. 'You see, I cannot concentrate! Perhaps you would prefer me to adjourn to my new prison cell so that you might fidget as much as you wish!'

Harriet made no response – I could not think of anything that she could say that might not inflame the situation – except to ring the bell. There was a collective intake of breath: was she about to have Thatcher escort her away? Thatcher certainly responded, but received a quiet request for the tea tray to be brought in. Francis asked Lady Stanton to join him in a duet. Fulke-Grosse abandoned Timpson and offered to turn their pages. Wilson, who had sat in furious silence throughout, ostentatiously moved to Bea's side, engaging her in quiet but perceptible conversation. I took Harriet's hand and kissed it before strolling over to talk to Timpson, which did not feel quite right, since it meant abandoning Harriet, the last thing in the world I wanted to do. But so it came about that the only person not making any noise, sitting statue-still, was the person her ladyship would want to accuse.

The Chopin stuttered to a halt. The musician swung round and faced the room. 'I suppose that we will have no music tomorrow. Nothing but silence or readings from improving sermons.'

'Is that, my lady, what you are used to in Wales?' Wilson asked, startling us all.

'Worse. Church three times a day. Chapel, I suppose I should say. Every meal a cold collation – a hair shirt of a meal. God knows why religion was ever invented!'

Francis and Wilson assumed she was making a witticism and laughed, while Fulke-Grosse applauded. I braced myself.

It was almost as if she did not hear them. She returned to the keyboard, optimistically embarking on a piece by Liszt. Conversation rose to cover her slips. Eventually it dawned on her that she was not carrying her audience with her. She smashed a chord. 'No one answered my question! How do you Puritans spend your Sundays?'

'As Christians all over the country spend theirs,' I said. 'As my wife explained over supper, we try to attend at least one service in our parish church. Thereafter we may find our meals are simpler because all of us are entitled to a day of rest.' I nodded towards Bea, who responded with a smile. 'How you guests choose to spend your time is up to you – but of course, the House is still in deep mourning and this is the first Sunday after her ladyship's funeral. Often people favour a quiet reflective walk: the paths in the formal gardens have been cleared and, so long as you stick to the paths – we don't want you wandering anywhere near the lake! – anywhere in the estate should afford views of interest. You could even get as far as the Roman remains which are Francis' particular interest,' I added with a smile in his direction.

He shook his head firmly. 'I would not attempt it, not when it is under such deep snow. It would be all too easy to fall in and break a limb in one of the trenches. Perhaps, Matthew, since we eschew all but sacred music on the Sabbath, I might give a short talk instead, and show you some of the finds?'

We joined in a general murmur of thanks, with the exception, to my surprise, of Lady Stanton. Personally I thought he was making a big mistake: there were enough beautiful objects in the House without drawing the attention of the light-fingered to even more. But I recollected that he had already dispatched what he regarded as the most important finds to his home and to the Ashmolean Museum. Surely he would risk nothing of value in the present situation. Perhaps Harriet had the same fear: she shot an alarmed glance at him.

He wilfully misunderstood her. 'Worry not, my dear Harriet: I will show nothing *indecent* on the Lord's day. Indeed, perhaps, if the weather is not too inclement, it would be possible to invite both Dr Page and Mr Pounceman to join us – or would that cause you too much trouble, Bea?'

'Not if you promise to peel the potatoes and whip the egg whites for a meringue.'

'And I could have rooms prepared for them should they prefer not to make the journey home,' Harriet said.

'"Aired for them"? Would not that involve using some of the fuel you claim is so short?' Lady Stanton demanded.

'There is a difference between heating long corridors, ma'am, and heating two guest rooms for one night. You will observe that tonight we are using logs, not coal. There are plenty of logs on the estate, but I do not care to use them in unoccupied rooms, for obvious reasons.'

As if on cue, the fire threw out a shower of sparks, most of which were caught by the mesh fire curtain. Wilson stamped on one threatening the carpet. 'You will understand now, your ladyship,' he said in his dry way, 'why the trustees do not encourage log fires.'

I braced myself for a lecture. Instead, he turned towards Francis, with an enquiry about his photographic equipment.

Perhaps the evening might pass without a serious incident. Perhaps it might simply and mercifully pass.

Fortunately for me, although the clouds were heavy with snow, we were able to go to church next morning – all our guests, including her ladyship, ravishing in exotic furs, were happy to travel by sleigh, with hot bricks for comfort. With Harriet, whose beauty in my mama's gifts eclipsed her ladyship's in my prejudiced eyes at least, I joined the servants on their slower trudge, falling into step with first one group then another.

Pounceman used a walking stick as a bishop might have used his staff, actually ensconcing himself in the bishop's chair, a fact that did not go unnoticed by some of his flock. In the circumstances, however, I hoped that God would understand and forgive him for not trying to scramble up the pulpit stairs, never a dignified movement. He did not rush the service, especially his sermon, however, and even I, wrapped up to my ears, was thinking of warm fires. I resolved to trek to Stammerton as soon as lunch was over, with a sleigh full of any food and blankets the House could spare. Logs, too, and anything else Bea and Harriet could think of. Possibly—

But Lady Stanton had fainted!

Harriet, who had once notably staged a swoon at the start of one of Pounceman's sermons, was already on her feet, joined in an instant by Ellis Page. They seemed to be taking the illness seriously, Harriet once again producing a vinaigrette and wafting it under the aristocratic nose. There was no shortage of advice when that remedy failed. One of the footmen slipped out of the church, admitting a blast of even icier air as he did so. He soon returned, with the news that the sleigh would be brought round as soon as the horses were back from the inn stables, where apparently they had been sheltering from the cold. Ellis smiled his approbation. 'She will be better off in the Family wing,' he said.

And she was. Her recovery was apparently complete, according to Harriet, returning from her ladyship's new quarters. She had despatched all the servants to the servants' hall to get warm; we were gathered round the drawing room fire, wishing we could wrap our hands round the cups of tea with which Bea had provided us before she descended to her realm. I believe we were all tempted to join the servants with their steaming mugs. Ellis soon joined us, his face expressionless until he smiled at Thatcher, handing him his cup.

Then Thatcher approached me. 'I understand, sir, that Mrs Arden will be making soup for luncheon, instead of the usual cold collation.'

'What an excellent suggestion. Could you ask her if she can make extra – I could take some to Stammerton when I go this afternoon, and anything else she could spare. Thank you.' I turned to Ellis. 'Would you care to join me? I can't promise you a warm ride but I am sure we will be well provided with hot bricks. Unless Lady Stanton needs your constant care, of course.'

'I am more than confident that the nursing staff will be able to do all that is needful,' he replied, his voice as blank as his face.

After a very informal lunch, we set off swathed in sheepskin rugs, John Coachman's nephew taking the reins and, I suspect, a fine opportunity to demonstrate his skills to what he hoped was a potential employer. We spent a chastening hour there, Page trying to reassure the sick and encourage the weakest to consent to be nursed in the Family wing. Only two accepted the offer, the others preferring to die, as they said, in their own homes. He made little attempt to change their minds, observing to me quietly as we turned for home, now empty-handed but with the rear sleigh carrying the new patients, that he could have done all too little to help them. We had a sober but thankfully uneventful journey back to the House.

As the orderlies took the patients indoors and the horses led to what was in all truth better accommodation than the villagers', I put my hand on Page's arm to detain him. 'I have done my best not to ask any questions I should not – about any of your patients, not just Lady Stanton. But there is one question I must ask.'

He frowned with embarrassment.

'Or rather, one I would like you to ask. It concerns young Olwen—'

'The groom's sweetheart? What about her?'

'It is nothing to do with her health or otherwise. It's . . . how can I put this? Let me tell you simply this. On one occasion when Harriet and I were in the Family wing, I saw an expression of dislike, even hatred, in Olwen's eyes as she looked at Harriet, who fortunately – or otherwise – did not notice. Hatred. Yes, hatred, pure and simple. Do you know any reason for this? Can you even guess at one?'

Clearly nonplussed he shook his head. 'I could imagine a servant here with a grudge, real or imaginary, against the housekeeper or butler, in the way of things. But why someone else's maid should take a stranger in dislike defeats me. I will keep my eyes and ears open, I promise. Now, however, my patients need me – and we both need to go in out of this wind.'

'Indeed! Now, Page, do you care to join us for our plain supper tonight?' I tapped my head in irritation. 'Botheration. I meant to invite Pounceman but it quite slipped my mind this morning.'

'It is my professional opinion,' he said, as I closed the servants' door behind us, 'that a jolting ride would not be good for his ankle. In other words, we can manage without him.'

'We can indeed – though I am sorry that he will miss Francis' little talk tonight. He is going to show us some of his Roman finds and talk about them.'

'Excellent! I shall look forward to it – and your plain supper.'

TWENTY-SIX

Harriet

Predictably, Bea's plain supper was a feast. A good old-fashioned salmagundi opened the proceedings to be followed by a chicken pie and then cheese and biscuits. In the spirit of picnickers, we abandoned the etiquette surrounding which dinner partners one should address. Rarely have I enjoyed a meal so much: for the first time I felt truly at home.

But that pleasant state was not to remain long. As the gentlemen sipped their port – Bea and I preferring madeira – Thatcher brought us word that Lady Stanton was awaiting our presence in the drawing room, where she expected to hear Sir Francis' lecture.

Mine were not the only eyes turning in Ellis's direction. It was Bea who spoke for us all when she observed, 'That is a remarkably swift recovery, is it not? You have magic powers, Ellis.'

'I have no powers at all, it seems. My strong recommendation was she keep to her bed for forty-eight hours – it was good of you to install her in such a charming room, Harriet, with a sitting room too! I believe Bea prepared a light supper for her – just what would tempt an invalid.'

'But something must have tempted her a good deal more,' Bea pointed out. 'Were you aware she had a deep interest in Roman remains, Francis?'

'Heavens, no. I was simply clutching at a straw to avoid tantrums over the vexed issues of music or a Sabbath reading. May I be embarrassingly frank? If Mr Thatcher could conjure a piece of baize to cover this table, I would prefer to speak in here. If all the items are in one place, not passed from hand to hand, I can keep an eye on them.'

Thatcher bowed. 'I will endeavour to find something

appropriate, sir. Perhaps I might suggest that you and your fellow guests adjourn to the drawing room while we make the changes. And then, if you do not mind, sir, I will ask you if everything is acceptable. Then I can make arrangements to have the items brought from your study.'

The staff worked very quickly. Scarcely had we sipped our tea than Francis left us to supervise his display. Lady Stanton, who had been perhaps unnaturally bright – and indeed, disconcertingly polite to everyone including me – suddenly lost her energy, something which brought Ellis to his feet to check her pulse. Pettish, perhaps justifiably, at this public reminder of her fragility, she shook her wrist free.

As if by magic, Thatcher appeared, bidding us to return to the breakfast room. The incident was over. Clutching her reticule, she led the way. Perhaps to my surprise, she chose to sit opposite Francis, not beside him. I did not exactly find myself sitting next to him: I made sure I did so to enable me to act as his supplementary eyes. John Timpson sat on his right. I smothered a little smile as Bea and Ellis, deep in conversation as they entered the room, chose to sit together. Their conversation continued uninterrupted until everyone was seated. We stared expectantly at each other, and at the table itself, covered not only by a baize but also by numbered squares of card. On each was a small item. The footmen worked their way round the table, offering and serving wine.

Francis entered the room as I imagined a great actor would take command of the stage. Silence was immediate. The footmen gravitated as one to the edges of the room, but could still hear what he said and see what he showed. Many of their items had, of course, been dug up – excavated! – by members of their family, but they were in any case intelligent young men. There were intelligent young women too – several maids had joined the group, but not Florrie.

'On the Sabbath,' he began with a serious smile at everyone, whatever their rank, 'where better to start than with the Chi Rho? Let me emphasize that we did not find this item in this area, but I am in hopes that we may well discover something similar here. I know most of you have seen it before, when I showed it to the trustees. But some of you were not present then, and I believe it merits examination. Mr Pounceman in particular was entranced by it, as it is a Christian symbol used by Romans: you can see an X crossed by a P. Let me explain as you pass it round . . .'

The evening passed very quickly. Even those seeing the small collection for the first time were entranced. But, as we prepared to disperse, there was one tiny problem. One of the squares of card was empty. The one for the Chi Rho stone.

The conclusion was inescapable.

Francis was no longer a genial lecturer. His face hardened, his blue eyes icy. 'Gentlemen,' he said to the footmen, 'would you ensure that no one leaves until I have located the missing relic. And perhaps,' he continued, addressing us, 'you would remain in your seats. It may well be that it has slipped on to someone's lap, or on to the floor beside them.'

There was a great deal of movement – a patting down of clothes and a gathering up of skirts. John Timpson seemed as anxious as if it was one of his treasured manuscripts. He even dropped to his knees, crawling under the table with markedly less dignity than the footmen, who had confined themselves to squatting and peering. His face as he surfaced empty-handed was distraught.

Or was he overreacting – or even, over-acting? Matthew was the first to turn out his pockets – not that there was much room for anything in a tightly-fitted smoking jacket. The other men followed suit – including the liveried footmen. The maids turned out their apron pockets. I tipped out the far more extensive contents of my reticule, as did Bea. Lady Stanton stared, but then, getting to her feet, threw down her reticule – to the imminent danger of the other artefacts.

'There! Search it! I know you won't believe it if I do it myself! Go on!' She stamped her foot. 'Don't think I know you don't trust me! Why else would you place me in a wing full of lunatics and guards with keys?'

Now Ellis was on his feet. 'Dear lady, calm yourself. This will not do. It really will not. You will make yourself seriously unwell!' He signalled to a footman for more wine, in my view a mistake. But she was persuaded to sit as she drank it, and the commotion subsided.

And somehow, as we returned our attention to the table feeling rather embarrassed, we found that the missing Chi Rho was back in its place.

There was a general exodus, the maids and footmen leading the way to ensure that we could all find fires lit and hot water when we reached our bedchambers. Soon the gentlemen escorted each other, as it were, to their rooms, and Ellis Page returned Lady Stanton to her new quarters. At last, the room empty until Matthew returned for me, I could turn to Francis. 'How did all that happen? Do I need to look further than you to find the perpetrator? Why, Francis, why?'

He hung his head, but with the residual smirk of a naughty boy who had got away with something. 'How did you guess?'

'You didn't look shamefaced when you did something very similar at your aunt's. You don't now. And you played such a cruel trick! Why did you do it?' I almost shook my finger at him. It was time to sit down and lower my voice.

He sat down too. 'Shall I tell you the truth? I do not believe anything she says, not one word. And I hoped that she would reveal . . . something. And in my opinion she did. She introduced the notion of trust. No one else did. And to my mind she is betraying the fact that she is concealing something – yes, we knew that already. She is concealing a great deal of truth. But is she concealing objects as well? I venture to suggest that our good police constable should insist on inspecting the contents of her cases.'

'I fail to follow your logic,' I said.

'There may be something in it,' Ellis Page said, making us both jump. 'You may recall, both of you, when a certain lady, anxious that her friend was about to be condemned from the pulpit, staged a swoon. I am convinced that – and I realize I should not be saying this – you were not the only one to pretend to faint. I can understand why you should, Harriet, and honour you for it.'

'As do I,' Francis said, reaching for my hand to kiss it. 'She did it to stop Pounceman inveighing against me as a heathen.

But that is all in the past, it seems. This morning, however, surely all that Pounceman was doing this morning was his job: taking a service when he, like the rest of us, would probably have been far happier by his fireside. He was as mild as I've known him. I was preparing to be lulled to sleep by him — except it was far too cold in that iceberg of a church to close one's eyes. The lids might have frozen together!'

I regarded Ellis closely. 'I promised myself not to ask . . . I know Matthew refused to ask this afternoon. But is there anything seriously amiss with her?'

'You know I cannot answer that. But I can tell you I can think of no physical reason why she might have sunk so dramatically to the floor.'

My eyes narrowed. 'I observe that you did not use the verbs "to faint" or to "swoon".'

'Did he not?' Francis, a satirical smile on his face. 'He must have forgotten. I understand that you stay here in the House tonight, Page. I cannot imagine you will be permitted much sleep. You will be summoned on the hour every hour.'

'I think you may trust the nursing staff not to let that happen,' he said. 'Ah, Matthew! I was hoping you would return, so I may talk to the two of you together.'

Francis' bow was ironic. 'In that case, I will wend my way back to my chamber. Do I need an escort, or shall I take my chance?'

'Thatcher and Luke will ensure you are safe.'

As Francis left us, kissing my hand once more, Matthew made up the fire. We sat at the end of the table nearest to it. Perhaps Matthew expected what I did — a dramatic revelation about her ladyship's condition. Or — would it not be lovely? — the news that he and Bea were to be betrothed. As it was, it was neither. But it was good news.

'Thomas Davies recovering? Thank God! That's wonderful news! And wonderful for that sweetheart of his.' My disinterested joy changed to something more selfish. 'So we can legitimately send her ladyship on her way!'

'It's not quite as simple as that, I'm afraid. Davies may have got through the worst, but that emphatically does not mean he can resume his activities for many days yet — maybe many weeks. And he may always have a weakness of the lungs and never work as a groom again.'

Matthew grimaced. 'Do you see her ladyship pensioning him off or making sure there was a job on her estate that he can manage? Quite. So I certainly cannot imagine her letting him share the coach with her and Olwen when eventually they do set off.'

'But that is surely a problem that can be dealt with nearer the time,' I said.

He rolled his eyes. 'Page, are you in need of a pair of new servants and their baby? No? I suspect that my kind-hearted wife will try to find them positions here. Ah. Olwen,' he added grimly.

'Olwen indeed. Olwen and her seeming anger at Harriet. I have been trying to talk to her. To get to the bottom of that matter.' He smiled kindly at me. 'She says no more than that she has heard things, things that clearly cast you in a bad light. I tried to find who had been filling her ear with poison, but she refused point-blank to tell me. Can it be Lady Stanton? I hardly get the impression that her ladyship has spent time talking to her, but can't imagine it could be anyone else. Can you?'

I shook my head. 'So she probably wouldn't consider a position here anyway. Which gets one possible problem out of the way. But it raises a very uncomfortable question, does it not? If it is not her ladyship – and truly she seems the most likely source of the trouble – it must be someone here in the House.'

Matthew took my hand. 'Surely it must be her ladyship. She has never treated you with any respect; in fact you have borne the brunt of her tantrums. As for Olwen, the only person who has really supported her pleas to remain at Davies' bedside is you. Is the baby safe, by the way?' he asked Page.

'Apparently. I hope so. But it makes their situation even worse, does it not?' He paused as the clock struck. 'But as a physician I would say that this discussion can wait till tomorrow. It is time we escorted each other to bed.'

Neither of us argued. I am sure that the four footmen still

ould not either. They would bank up
out, according to the room. They
or lamps were still alight. Then
dors all over the House to see that
oom – naturally we were accom-
men set off more than briskly ahead
ure they would be thorough, however: dear
had been a martinet in such matters, and Thatcher
was certainly not the man to let standards slip.

Still in gentle conversation, we were halfway up the main
staircase when one of the young men came hurtling down
towards us.

'Sirs! Ma'am! There's a terrible screaming in the servants'
corridor. Fit to raise the rafters, ma'am!'

He raced back up to the area that housed all but the most
senior servants. Samuel and I had persuaded the late Lady Croft
to abandon the dormitories that she had favoured, replacing
them with bedrooms for two, three or four. We followed.
Hampered by my skirts, I waved them on. Irk me how it
might, I must follow more decorously.

The noise was over when the men reached the door the
young man was pointing at. But there were women's voices
and perhaps the sound of sobbing. Both the footman and
Matthew were looking at Page; unhappy women were surely
more his area of expertise than theirs. And then they all looked
at me, still, to my chagrin, panting after forcing my skirts up
the stairs.

'Florrie, Dorcas and Beth's room,' I said, still trying to
catch my breath. Ellis and I exchanged a look – but it seemed
that I had lost the silent argument and had to see what was
afoot. I called out, knocked the door quite gently, and let
myself in, leaving the door slightly ajar – I might have urgent
need of Ellis's skills.

I was braced for . . . something. I knew not what.

What I found was a tearful, tousled girl, grasping her friends'
hands as if they were pulling her from a deep pit and must
not drop her. 'Florrie!' Gently I pushed back her hair. 'My
dear child. Are you all right?' When she could not speak for
her tears, I turned to Beth. 'What has happened?'

'Please, ma'am, we think she had a dream. A[...]
Fast asleep we were, and then came these terrible scr[...]
couldn't wake her, not no-how, until Dorcas dashed so[...]
water on her face. But she says that whatever she does, [...]
ever we do, the horror stays with her.'

'Poor child.' Still getting no response, I turned to Beth agai[...]
'Has she been having these terrible dreams long?'

Beth and Dorcas looked at each other. 'Not really, ma'am.
Since the snow came, really. Since we've all been stuck inside.'

'Perhaps some fresh air tomorrow will help. See if you can
persuade her to go for a walk with you, even if the weather
isn't ideal. Her health – everyone's health – is more important
than dusting empty rooms. Now, can you help her into a dry
nightgown and settle her down? And I might ask Dr Page if
he can give her something to help her sleep. Good night and
God bless you all.'

When I emerged, the footmen were shifting their feet. They
still had more corridors to patrol, of course, but had no authority
to slip away. I smiled at them. 'Bert and Christopher, thank
you for waiting. There's nothing to worry about – one of the
girls had a nightmare, dreadful enough, of course, but nothing
more. But you did well. Thank you.'

The two lads made themselves scarce as soon as they had
bowed themselves off.

I turned to the men. 'Yes, a terrible nightmare. Florrie –
apparently the others had to shake her awake so that they could
stop her screaming. You can imagine what a state they were
all in.'

Page, trying not to dither with the cold, asked, 'Do they
need anything to help them sleep again? Not that I recommend
anything like that for the young. I dare wager that they will
be sleeping like babies before we reach the warmth of our
bedchambers!'

'I'm sure you are right. But I would be grateful if you could
just check on her.'

Matthew took my hands and chafed them while we waited.
'What now?'

'A day or two off, I should think – but I'll act on Ellis's
advice. I need to talk to her in any case about returning to

her usual duties if Olwen is able and willing to return to Lady Stanton.'

Ellis emerged, overhearing my last words and giving a snort of laughter. 'I had better talk to Olwen first, then.'

And I had a terrible feeling I must talk to Florrie – or perhaps to Elias Pritchard first.

TWENTY-SEVEN

Matthew

Despite the overnight snow, it looked as if a thaw might be setting in. I dearly hoped so, not least because at last the earth would be soft enough for the gravediggers to get to work; it was more than time for poor Mary to be laid to rest. And for the inquest into her death to be held. My first task was to send a note down to Elias to prompt some action. I also mentioned, because I felt we all needed some good news, the improvement in the health of her ladyship's groom, Davies. Another note brought George, the estate carpenter, to my office.

We talked for a few minutes about the daily trivia of the estate, and then I turned to the reason I had summoned him.

'Check the House, gaffer?' he repeated. 'But I don't know about fancy stuff.'

'I bet that you can tell me what is different about this room, however, George.'

'That's different. I've been in here many a time without seeing that clock. Nicer than that ugly old bugger you had last time.' He walked over to take a closer look. 'Nice piece, that. Anyway, I'd best be starting on this job.' His hand was already on the doorknob.

'Nothing else different?' I prompted him, disconcerted.

'Oh, ah – that picture. Used to be in one of the bedrooms. One of the smaller rooms.'

'Could you take a look at it and tell me what you see?'

He grimaced. 'Well, 'tis old, by the looks of it.'

'And the frame too?'

He took it down, jabbing a strong finger at the back. 'Old too, though you wouldn't think so to look at it.'

'Any idea why there's a mismatch?'

Why on earth did he flush brick red? 'I'd say one wasn't made for t'other. About an eighth of an inch out.'

'Really? Yes, you're right. You see, George, you notice things I never do. In the last few years you've walked pretty well every corridor in the House. All I'm asking you to do is walk down them again and tell me if you think anything is different. My wife will know about most of the official changes, so I suggest you team up with her for your stroll.'

He nodded. 'A good woman, your wife, sir, if I might make so bold. But if it's all the same to you, sir, I'd rather go on my own – I know I shall start chatting to Mrs Rowsley about my family and such and that'll mean I don't listen.'

'Listen?'

'To something up here' – he touched his head – 'that tells me something's amiss.'

'Very well. I'll let her know you're here so that she can tell the staff not to disturb you. But you might need her to unlock the rooms.'

He pulled a face. 'That'd be nigh on a day's work, gaffer!'

'My grandfather had a saying, "If a job's worth doing it's worth doing well".' I smiled. 'I think that's your motto, isn't it?'

He nodded. 'Maybe it is. It's a good one, anyway. Now, best be on my way. Will you be here if I need you?'

'If I have to go out I'll leave word with the footmen and with my wife.'

He nodded. 'Need to watch your step out there, gaffer. Very treacherous it is under foot.'

For some reason, that casual mention of treachery reminded me that I had not yet invited Hudson Fulke-Grosse to tell me about the painting. I could hardly despatch Luke to summon him and Francis. I would have to go myself. Naturally I locked the door, even leaving a note pinned to it – I could hardly imagine that George would need me so soon after his departure, but one never knew. I also told Bert – today's footman at large – where I was going, and to tell anyone asking after me that I would be back within minutes.

The gentlemen in question were still breakfasting, the professor consuming a plate covered by so much ham that I could not imagine his dandyish clothes fitting him much longer, especially when he followed it up with three of Bea's wonderful breakfast scones, liberally spread with her incomparable strawberry jam, the quality of which she always attributed to the addition of champagne. To have one myself would be greedy – I had already breakfasted well enough an hour or so before – but I could not resist.

In fact, the treat gave me an excuse to start what I feared would be a difficult conversation.

'Smelling the jam, Matthew? Are you afraid we're being poisoned?'

'On the contrary! I'm savouring the aroma, and also trying to detect the presence of his lordship's champagne,' I explained.

The notion caused some hilarity, as we all decided we needed to taste another. The bonhomie gave me the chance to raise the issue of the picture.

'I'm sure it's a trivial problem but I can't work out why I have a picture, the frame of which doesn't match. Or even quite fit. Would you two gentlemen care to look at it and give me your opinion?'

Did either look uncomfortable? Did either tense? Certainly neither blustered or protested. Soon we were in a jovial enough procession.

Perhaps they exchanged a glance when I told Bert I did not wish to be disturbed. Perhaps not. I ushered them in, but did not invite them to be seated. Instead I gestured at the picture.

'How strange,' Francis commented, as if he had never set eyes on it before. 'There seems a small but perceptible mismatch there. But,' he continued, taking it down and tilting it to the light, 'surely the wood and the nails are contemporaneous. What is your opinion, Hudson?'

The professor took it. 'Has someone been trying to clean it? Or restore it? And why the sparkling and quite vulgar frame? It's old, to be sure – you see this, Francis? – but surely the gilding . . . No, it would take a proper framer to achieve a result like that. My theory, for what it's worth, is that someone . . . no, look, this wasn't the original frame. You see? Here at the edges – you can see where it came to. The new one is a fraction of an inch smaller.'

'Why would anyone reframe this anyway?' I asked.

'It depends on what was written on the original that might suggest the artist. I couldn't see a signature, but perhaps there is one under all this varnish and the centuries' worth of dirt. What I really need is my loupe, so I could look more closely.'

I handed him my magnifying glass; Francis moved the curtain a little further aside.

'No. Nothing to suggest anything except that it has been reframed. Whoever did it was skilled enough to re-use old pins.' He touched it and raised his index finger. 'I would love to solve this little puzzle, however. I know a very good picture restorer in Oxford. I am sure he could remove some of this veritable disguise and tell us what lies underneath. When I can leave, I'll take it with me, shall I, and ask him to work on it?'

I shook my head. 'Sadly, much as I would like to accept your offer, I am not able to authorize anything to do with the House. Or with the estate, apart from day-to-day matters. Much as I wanted to tell Francis to start work on his Roman remains, I could not: he had to convince the trustees first. All I can do is put your offer on the agenda for the next meeting. But,' I added, a malicious sprite dancing in my ear, 'you might like to discuss the idea with our chairman, Montgomery Wilson. I'm sure he could give you invaluable advice on how to prepare your submission. Or Francis could?'

'If you have a week to prepare it!' Francis laughed – the champagne in the jam, perhaps.

Hudson did not laugh. 'I am trying to help you, not submit myself to trial by yokels!'

'Of course. My apologies. I expressed myself very badly. The idea of getting permission from the trustees is to stop people like Harriet and me removing beautiful furniture, say, to furnish our house. Or Francis absconding with a cartload of Roman gold – do you expect to find treasure like that, by the way?' I asked, trying to lighten the moment.

'If I did, I suspect that neither I nor the Croft estate would benefit. I would have to report it to the coroner, who would determine – eventually – if it was treasure trove. Have you found any obviously interesting pictures here, Hudson? I know you spent time exploring before we had the cold regime thrust upon us.'

He accepted the olive branches we had thrust at him. 'There is that fine collection of Lely portraits, of course – and a couple of portraits by Mary Beale. Now, your Harriet should be interested in those, Matthew. She was the first English artist to make her living painting portraits. Italy had Gentileschi, of course, and Switzerland produced Angelica Kauffman, who also worked here, of course. But Mrs Beale was thought to be as good as her illustrious contemporary. Many men would have hated the idea of their wives working, but Mr Beale seems to have become her assistant – her manager or administrator, as it were.'

'Many men still do object to the notion of women working,' I agreed. 'But my dear wife is capable of far more than I am, and much as I would love her to rest and enjoy life, I truly believe I would take away what she loves best if I tried to cabin, crib and confine her.'

Francis nodded, 'And, as her ladyship never ceases to remind her, her social position is . . . shall I say, vague? She falls between the great ladies who have no need to do anything, and the wives of working men in trade unions who are quite reasonably arguing that they need a fair wage to support a whole family – what is the clarion call? "A fair day's wage for a fair day's pay?" As long as you have two such strong pressures against women working—'

'With the exception of Miss Nightingale's saintly nurses,' Hudson interjected, with a modicum of irony. 'And governesses. So long as women have a tendency to do jobs we think are less than manly, then it will be hard for them to fight to work alongside or even above men. I wonder what Page would think of women as doctors. Or artists, not just using them as models but studying under their tutelage?'

'I can think of several women writers who could teach some men how to improve their craft . . .'

The discussion continued long enough, I hoped, to take away any grievance Hudson might have had. At last I ventured, 'Did you notice anything else of note? There is one portrait I should particularly like to show you, but it is in his lordship's suite and I do not know if he would care to have it removed.'

Catching my eye, Francis raised an eyebrow, mouthing, 'Hargreaves?'

'Yes: the Elizabeth portrait,' I said. 'Apart from that, we have more old works as filthy as this one. We really must talk to the trustees, must we not?'

'And soon,' Hudson, who had not ceased to turn the picture this way and that, declared. 'I smell one of your rodent visitors, Matthew. Of the metaphorical variety. I really do. Meanwhile, I've always been an admirer of the Virgin Queen, so I would more than welcome a glimpse of her portrait.'

TWENTY-EIGHT

Harriet

'I was telling Matthew,' Samuel said, as he finished the last of his morning coffee, 'that you had done something to the Room that I did not approve of – but I cannot for the life of me remember what it was.'

I smiled, not exactly with pleasure. It was the first time I had had anything approaching free rein to decorate a room – those in our home were still as the previous agent had left them – and I did not want criticism, especially from an old friend whose loyalty to the Family and the House eclipsed even my considerable devotion. But since I had been praying long enough for his memory to return, I could not legitimately object when it did, even if it might inconvenience me.

'Why not step inside now,' I said, passing him his walking stick, 'and see what has offended you.'

It took him all of thirty seconds. Turning to me, he shook his head as if I were a new tweenie who had disappointed him. 'Mrs Rowsley, you should not have touched the House paintings. You have far exceeded your powers. Return them immediately to where you stole them from and I will say no more of the matter.'

'Mr Bowman, they are not stolen. They are attached to a wall of the House. The ones they replaced are still in the House.' I could feel my face redden with anger, but I tried to keep my voice calm. And myself calm. In an instant I would be in tears.

'And what was wrong with the Room that you had to change it?' His voice was more querulous now.

'It was a disgrace, that's what,' Bea's voice rang out. We both jumped. 'So was mine. And so is yours. Drab. Dirty paint. Faded curtains and worn-out carpets that were cast-offs from someone's bedroom. If you ask me, the reason you like the Family wing so much is that it's clean and bright. Come on,

Samuel, sit down and have a good look round. And then come and look at your room, which we have not presumed to touch, and see the difference.'

He turned on her. 'Neither of you had any authority to make changes. Any at all.'

'That is not quite the case,' I said carefully. 'We had the trustees' agreement – at one of the meetings which you were too ill to attend. Neither of us would have done anything that we felt to be wrong: you know that. And you must admit that the whole place looks brighter, the servants' hall particularly.' He nodded, albeit reluctantly. 'Why do you not do as Bea suggests and look at your room. Then you could consider how you might want it.'

He took my arm and, with Bea following behind carrying his walking stick, peered into his sitting room and then his bedchamber. The unforgiving light of the snow picked out every last scuff of paint, every last stain on the carpet. We had kept it aired, but the cold was palpable.

'You're sure we have permission? Not that I'd want any pictures!'

Not quite idly, I asked, 'Do you remember which room they were in?'

'I fancy they were in his late lordship's dressing room.'

Which was why I had brought them here, of course. I said nothing.

'I wonder if that will ever be opened up again.' He sighed, and turned away. 'Always fond of you, his lordship. And now you're his librarian! My goodness, what a responsibility. I wouldn't want that for all the tea in China.' This from a man who had assumed personal responsibility for all the House plate. I turned him gently back to the warmth of the servants' hall. He cast a doubtful look in the direction of the Room, but said nothing. Two of the footmen bounced in, making a beeline for the fire – but as soon as they saw Samuel they stopped short, bowing and behaving with not just decorum but kindness, seating him and finding a footstool.

As Thatcher came in too, I caught his eye and smiled: yes, he was maintaining House standards.

* * *

It is no exaggeration to say that I was amazed to see Queen Elizabeth making a slow and careful Progress down the main staircase. I was just as surprised to see her being carried to Matthew's office. At a respectful distance, naturally, I followed her.

Christopher put her down gently on one of the visitors' chairs. Matthew, Francis and Hudson bent as if in homage. Christopher took a step backwards, to stand beside me.

Straightening, Hudson whispered, 'This is so like the portrait of her by Marcus Gheeraerts the Younger. See, she is standing on the globe – because the artist's patron wanted to flatter her. She ruled the whole world!' He exhaled deeply. 'Thank goodness this did not go out of the window, Francis. It could be, probably is, almost beyond price! It is almost certainly of national, if not international importance. And it has been kept in a madman's wardrobe!'

I was glad that Samuel was not present to hear his lordship thus described. I coughed gently. 'In his lordship's valet's room. Yes, in a wardrobe. But the Family wing is so closely guarded – am I right, Christopher? – that is probably in the safest part of the House.' I nodded at the young footman – he might leave us now. And the lift of my eyebrow suggested that it might be better if he did not share the professor's ill-advised observation. He bowed himself silently out.

'But no one can ever see it there!' the professor exclaimed.

'His lordship can,' I said gently. 'Before he took a fancy to it, it was simply stored in the attic. Propped up in a pile of others.'

'Even so!' He spread his hands in apparent despair. Then he brightened. 'There are others up there? As good as this? Good God! So why in Hades are all the walls hung with what can only be called – in far too many cases – dross?'

I could not stop myself saying, 'Because tastes change? Also in the attic is a huge amount of furniture that previous generations admired enough to buy – but which later ones consigned to oblivion. I daresay his lordship's heirs will disdain what is in the House now.'

Francis laughed. 'The sooner everyone disdains this vile regal passion for vivid tartan the better!' His face straight again, he asked, 'Do you and Matthew – even the full board of trustees

– have any control over what hangs on the walls? Over what new furniture needs to be purchased?'

'I think that we would all agree that that exceeded our brief,' Matthew replied, 'unless there were a catastrophic flood or fire, which Heaven forbid. We already have agreed to install proper plumbing as soon as we can. Apart from that, we can agree to your excavations, for instance, and we can probably agree to have a picture restored or otherwise investigated.'

'And – assuming he can one day attend meetings again – Mr Bowman would fight radical changes tooth and nail. Only this morning I offended him deeply with a trivial change.' I explained. 'Goodness knows how he will react if he ever sees that hanging here, not in its rightful place!' I pointed to the picture with the bright frame.

The professor narrowed his eyes. 'If he knows so much about where items should be, does he know anything about the items themselves? Might he recall when and why that was reframed?'

He spoke to Matthew but I replied, 'He almost certainly would. But one thing is certain – we cannot let him find it hanging here. The clock must go back to its original place – for a while, at least. And we must choose our moment to ask – there must be a reasonable excuse.'

'But he is a mere employee,' the professor responded, anger making him less than tactful, perhaps.

'Indeed. Just as I am. But just now Mr Bowman is far more than that.' I paraphrased what Ellis had once said, 'As long as his lordship is unwell, Mr Bowman is, apart from myself, the only person able to recall the Family's immediate past. Mr Timpson is digging into the further past, but no one except Samuel can give us information that may one day be vital – and would be very useful now,' I added with a rueful smile at Matthew and Francis. I had overstepped the mark once again.

'When do you suggest we talk to him?' Matthew asked, as if I had not.

'Tomorrow? And there must be a reason he will accept. And,' I added, 'I should not be the one to ask him.'

Until the trustees had discussed and agreed some changes in my role, there was no one else to check on the state of all the rooms, occupied and unused. So, donning a thicker shawl, I set off as usual. In one of the corridors I ran into George, pencil behind his ear and notebook tucked into his belt. He was staring at one of the big cabinets holding some of her ladyship's favourite china – a Meissen dinner service richly decorated with exotic birds.

'Did they ever use this, ma'am?' George asked.

'Just once, as far as I know. One of the dessert plates was cracked as it was being washed up and that was that. You see the hairline there?' I froze as he peered intently at each item in turn. 'Is something missing?'

'Not as far as I can see. They are just so lovely. Like real birds – but not the ones round here.'

We stood in silence absorbing the colours. Eventually I had to ask, 'Is everything else where it should be?'

'In the corridors at least, ma'am. I've not made a start on the rooms yet.'

I looked at my watch. 'It's almost dinner time down in the servants' hall. There'll be plenty if you care to eat there. But I'm afraid you'll need to think up some excuse for being in the House. Ah, the chair Lady Stanton broke the other day! I believe it's still in the anteroom off the Blue Room. Shall we go and see?'

As he shook his head over the damage, I looked round both the anteroom and the room myself. A tantrum like Lady Stanton's would have diverted everyone's attention and been the perfect chance for someone to seize one of the miniatures. But they were all there, including the Nicholas Hilliard that had been his late lordship's favourite. I owed him so much, with his gentle and subtle ways of teaching: now I understood the import of Jane Austen's comment about the little piece of ivory in the context of miniature painting. Sadly he had been by his own admission tone deaf, so he had been unable to guide me through the intricacies of music – not least because music needed performance, and evening concerts were always held in the drawing room after servants like me had withdrawn. If ever we had time and opportunity, I would look to Matthew to help me understand, or at least love it.

'Can you repair it? I'm sorry, if anyone can repair it, you can, and probably invisibly.'

He grinned. 'Ah, I do enjoy a bit of gilding. Next time you see it, ma'am, you won't be able to tell it from the others in the set. I'll see you after servants' dinner for the keys, then, ma'am.' Picking up the chair, he set off down the corridor.

'One moment, George!'

He turned back. 'Ma'am?'

'Gilding, George. Have you done work on other items in the House at any time?'

'Me, ma'am?' I had known George for ten years at least and never known him look shifty before.

'Yes. Have you done repairs, for instance, on any other items in the House which you had to regild? Repairs or restoration, perhaps?'

'Oh, plenty of that. Those pretty chair legs get kicked often enough.' He looked more confident. 'That big mirror in the ballroom. I don't know why but folk seem to put things down beside it and lift them up all careless like. You must have seen, ma'am.'

'Indeed. And sometimes picture frames get bruised, you might say, by the handle of a feather duster – come to think of it, you've touched up things I've asked you to look at, haven't you?'

'I have indeed, ma'am.'

'And – I want the truth, George, let me make that clear – you might have worked on the very bright frame round the picture Mr Rowsley moved into his office. Don't look like that, please. You know about the picture. All about it, don't you? Yes?'

'I do and I don't, ma'am and that's the truth of it. Please don't ask me any more, ma'am. A promise is a promise, see.'

'I see that someone has put you in a very difficult position. George, you have worked for the Family for far more years than anyone I know here except Mr Bowman' – did I imagine it, or did his eyes change? – 'so you know more about loyalty than most. That's one reason why my husband asked you to do this strange walk through the corridors. Because he knows you're a man of honour, of truth. I won't press you now – but

I beg you to reflect so that if a wrong has been done we can right it.'

As I walked back towards the Room, I fell into step with Hodge, the professor's valet, looking quizzically up at him. 'Florrie?'

He responded with a dry smile. 'I'm biding my time, ma'am. Thought I might suggest a bit of fresh air would do us both good – though it wouldn't be tactful to say I thought she was looking peaky, which she is. The trouble is when we might go – afternoons off don't seem to occur to Lady Stanton.'

I had to be careful in what I said. I hoped I was jumping to an unwarranted conclusion, but cared share it with no one – not even Matthew as yet. 'Who does not approve of followers anyway. But bear in mind, Mr Hodge, her ladyship does not employ Florrie; she is employed by the House. And is entitled to some free time each day.'

'And so I shall remind her, ma'am. Thank you.'

'And I will remind you of something, Mr Hodge: you are older and more experienced than she. Don't break her heart.'

He looked me straight in the eye. 'She is more likely to break mine, Mrs Rowsley.'

TWENTY-NINE

Matthew

Sergeant Burrows presented himself at the House late on Tuesday morning, with the welcome news that at last there could be an inquest into Mary's death. But his next piece of information was far less welcome.

'The coroner wants to hold the inquest here!' I repeated in disbelief. 'In the House? The very place the poor child met her death? And whom would you have in the jury? The staff here? Surely you joke.'

'It has been known. I've heard of a case where the chairman of the jurors was the lord himself,' he concluded ambiguously.

'Divine justice, perhaps.' He did not laugh. 'They're more usually held in inns,' I added.

'But the Royal Oak doesn't have a big enough room.'

It didn't. 'Mr Newcombe has a fine house – I am sure he would be able to host it.' He would probably be delighted – it would clearly establish him as the leading man in the village. I would assume that topic had been exhausted. 'While you're here, Sergeant, George has presented me with this list of items which appear to have gone missing over the past weeks – you know his skill at recollecting anything he has seen, do you not?'

Burrows nodded. 'If he was a bit younger I'd welcome him into the police.'

'Thank goodness he's too old, then – we couldn't spare him! Here: you can see that small things seem to have gone astray.'

'Broken by a housemaid and tipped into the rubbish.'

'Possibly. But there's always been a policy in the House of not punishing people who have genuine accidents and own up. I understand his late lordship was an unusually benign employer,' I added. 'But my wife tells me that the missing things were associated with her late ladyship. A hideous agate paperweight, for instance, that sat on my desk, vanished without trace. Quite big compared with the rest, I'll admit. And a tiny thing: a dress shirt stud.'

'A tiny stud? Wide cracks between floorboards?'

I knew where he suspected it had gone. But I still had doubts.

'Where have you searched for all these bits and pieces?'

'Assuming I wanted to, would I be within my rights to do so? Legally?' Perhaps I was being unusually truculent today. I was certainly irritating the sergeant.

'Ask your wife to. She's in charge of the House, after all.'

'I think she might respond that searching people's property is the job of the police – though she might baulk at the notion of strange men rifling through women's things. You must discuss it with her. Shall I ask someone to fetch her? Or would you prefer to go to the servants' hall, which is very much warmer? I will accompany you myself.' I stood, gesturing. I locked up behind us.

In the Room, Harriet's response was unenthusiastic. 'Is there any evidence that the servants might have taken these missing objects?'

'Who else would? Come, Mrs Rowsley, if things go missing, they must be somewhere, and being stowed in some-one's cupboard or drawer is the obvious answer.'

Even I could not argue with that.

'In that case, we should implement his late lordship's policy, and ask people to come and see me privately to confess. And the stick will be that if no one owns up, then we will involve you and Constable Pritchard, and they will feel the full force of the Law if they are found to have stolen anything.'

While I was horrified by the thought of what punishment might result, I sensed that Burrows was rather relieved by the offer. 'Do you think it'll work?' he asked hopefully.

'We shall soon see. But there are other people whose prop-erty should be searched. You would, in all fairness, have to start with Matthew and me, and include our guests and our patients. In two minutes' time the bell will ring for servants' dinner: perhaps you would speak to the gathering yourself and tell them what we should all expect.' She gave her wonderful smile. 'In fact, if you cared to eat with them, you might learn more than we've been able to. But – might I ask you something? – could you return poor Mary's keys?'

'They are evidence, ma'am.'

'Indeed. And as soon as I have seen them I should be able to return them to you. Thank you, sergeant – ah, it smells as if steak and kidney pie is on the menu today . . .'

We, of course, had to adjourn to the breakfast room for lunch with our guests. John Timpson had excused himself – he said he was still trying to deal with the chaos inflicted on his treasures, but I was coming to realize he was not insensitive and was as aware of his anomalous position as the servants were. I looked around. It was time for me to say Grace. But even as I opened my mouth, there was a din so loud we could hear it even in this distant room: the furious pealing of the front-door bell. The door itself was being subjected to a series of thunderous knocks.

'Francis – could you see Lady Stanton to her room, please?' Harriet suggested quietly. 'Just in case,' she added, with a strangely comradely smile at the lady in question. 'Thank you.'

Wilson and Fulke-Grosse were on their feet too, but more out of courtesy, I suspected, than in response to a possible call to arms. I, however, felt obliged to go to support Thatcher and Luke. I caught Harriet's eye.

'How fortunate we have Sergeant Burrows here,' she said quietly.

The professor eyed us with obvious misgiving. 'Are we invaded by some rural militia?' he asked.

'If only Lady Stanton had been happy to explain to us all . . . We believe she is in some danger. But she admits nothing and denies nothing. That was the reason for transferring her to her late ladyship's suite in the Family wing, which as you probably know is guarded on his lordship's account. Ah, Luke!'

'Sir, ma'am, there's trouble afoot. A gentleman is demanding to see her ladyship, and says he'll search the place if necessary. He's got a couple of likely-looking footmen with him too – looking ready for a mill, if you ask me.'

'Where is he now?' I asked.

'Still in the entrance hall with Mr Thatcher and Christopher and a couple of others. But for how long—'

'I'm on my way. Summon Sergeant Burrows if you haven't already. My apologies, gentlemen.'

'Perhaps I might offer words to calm the visitor,' Wilson said dryly. 'Professor, will you stay here to protect Harriet?'

She curtsied. 'Thank you. But technically I am in charge of the House and my place is with my colleagues.' Her back as straight as I'd ever seen it, she swept through the door Luke still held open.

The professor might have raised an elegant eyebrow, but he said only, 'In that case I might adjourn to the muniment room where I suspect Mr Timpson will be working. There is much of value there. I will support him if necessary. After you, Rowsley.'

Was he mocking me as I set off in my wife's wake? I could feel my anger rising as I strode down the corridor, wishing the carpet did not muffle my strides. But as I reached the stairs, I made myself pause. Who was I angry with? The interloper? The professor? My own dear wife? Yes. With all three. And with myself. Mostly now with myself. However much I wanted to play the great hero, she was right, of course. This was her domain, just as the rest of the estate was mine. And it might well be that a controlled, calm, elegant woman might just prevent the fisticuffs that Luke was anticipating.

There she was. Perhaps she had been flanked by Luke and Thatcher, but now she was on her own, facing the leader of the would-be invaders. Was that an exaggeration? They certainly did not look like men making a belated morning call. She addressed the tallest, holding what looked like a visiting card at arm's length – with a pang I realized she might soon need spectacles – and then dropping a curtsy.

The strange acoustics of the hall meant her voice carried up to me as clearly as if I stood beside her. 'Welcome to Thorncroft House, Lord Hednesford. I am Mrs Rowsley, the housekeeper. How may I help you?'

'You can tell these oiks to get out of my way so I can speak to my wife.'

'Your wife, Lord Hednesford?'

'You did not hear? I am here for my property. And for my wife. Now get out of my way.'

'Indeed, my lord, I cannot give anyone the run of this House. We have much sickness here. Lord Croft is indisposed. Lady Croft died only two weeks ago. We are preparing for another funeral even now.'

Wilson now stood beside me, trying, I suspect, not to gasp at the panache with which she lied by telling the absolute truth.

Hednesford took a step backward. 'My wife can come to me then. Now!' Now he stepped forward, looming over her.

She coughed, turning from him and covering her mouth. 'I beg your pardon. Indeed, my lord, to the best of my knowledge we do not have a guest by name of Lady Hednesford.'

'You lying bitch!'

'I beg your pardon, sir, but I would prefer you not to use such language in the House. It is not at all appropriate, especially in the circumstances.' She gestured at the footmen's mourning clothes, and at her own dress. She probably observed as she did so that Sergeant Burrows was now in attendance. Yes, she did. She made the tiniest of gestures to suggest he bided his time.

Wilson touched my arm. Was it time for him to descend? Was it? If anyone was going to get hurt, I would infinitely prefer it to be him, not Harriet. Most of all I should like it to be Hednesford, by my hands. Swallowing hard, choking my pride in my craw, I nodded.

I had to admit, he played his role to the hilt, the busy-busy lawyer, with at his disposal all the skills of a lawyer – his quiddities, his quillities, his tricks – as he bustled down the stairs. Even his gait was prissy.

Before Harriet could perform introductions, Hednesford squared up to the little man, ready, I feared, to grab him by the shirt. Now, surely, Burrows and I must intervene. Glancing at each other, we moved closer.

'Lord Hednesford, may I present Mr Wilson, the Family's lawyer, here to deal with probate? And Sergeant Burrows, of the Shropshire Constabulary, and Mr Rowsley, the estate

manager. Lord Hednesford believes Lady Hednesford is a guest
here, gentlemen. I fear I am not able to help him. Perhaps you
might escort him to your office, Mr Rowsley? And Thatcher
might take these gentlemen to the servants' hall for a slice of
cake. On consideration, to the Room.'

Thatcher nodded his obedience and his understanding: any
meetings in the Room might excite all the interest in the world,
but no one would dare interrupt.

Hednesford's henchmen – I could think of no better word
– sloped off.

'Ah! Mr Thatcher! Could you bring tea to Mr Rowsley's
office, please? Thank you.'

She looked at me. Yes, it was my turn now. I led the way.

THIRTY

Harriet

'Sergeant Burrows – this Lady Hednesford must be our Lady Stanton, must she not?' I said, laying a hand on his arm. 'She must be warned!'

He did not quite shake his arm free, but he frowned at me. I removed the hand at once.

'I'm not sure about "warned", Mrs Rowsley, so much as spoken to. If Lord Hednesford is her husband, then who are we to come between them?'

'If he is a loving husband, we have little right – but did that seem to you like affection, or simply a desire to retrieve property? And by that I do not refer to the extensive luggage she has brought with her, which must indeed be discussed, but to the lady herself.'

He blinked. 'If he is her husband, he has rights, Mrs Rowsley – just as Mr Rowsley has over you. You, having been a maiden lady so long, have most likely forgotten that. Goods and chattels,' he added, as if making some sort of threat.

Perhaps it would be better if I spoke to her on my own. We had reached Matthew's office, so I gestured. He was to go first. First and on his own, as it turned out.

'Get your coachman. I order you to. I must leave immediately. Oh, and fetch my jewels from the safe.'

I looked about me. Her tight-set face pale, Florrie was frantically trying to compress all her ladyship's belongings into too small a trunk. Surely the rush basket into which her boots were going was Florrie's own.

Uninvited I sat down. 'Your ladyship, I cannot obey you. Even if you did leave the House, the police would catch you before you had gone five miles – yes, a sergeant is even now with Lord Hednesford, who alleges that he is seeking property that you have stolen. If you did flee, it would add credence to his tale. Why do you not sit down too, and tell me precisely what is going on? Or tell Sergeant Burrows, if you prefer? I know Constable Pritchard believed what you told him, and he is not a stupid man. In fact, we could send for him, if you wished him to intercede.'

She turned on me, pointing a quivering hand at me, as I had imagined Lady Macbeth might do. 'I would rather die than go back to my husband. And it is all your busybodying that has brought him here! Yours!'

I got to my feet. What I wanted to say was far from what I did say: 'Very well, ma'am. If you will excuse me, then.' I could control my mouth, and I would not lower myself by slamming the door behind me, but I could not, would not, force my knees into a curtsy.

And yet I had to compel myself back into the room. 'Your ladyship, would you prefer to speak to Sergeant Burrows up here, in private, or in front of Lord Hednesford?'

I had persuaded her to let Florrie return the room to order, so when I brought Sergeant Burrows up she could sit like a lady to talk to him. It was he who insisted I remain to chaperone her, a solution clearly neither she nor I liked. At least as I made myself as invisible as I could on a chair by the door, I would have the satisfaction of hearing her version of the story I had missed when Lord Hednesford had told his to the men.

Perhaps his was shorter.

Time and again Burrows had to bring her back to the point. But in essence it was a strange mixture of privilege and tragedy. After an idyllic childhood, with all the advantages anyone might dream of – travel, education, almost unlimited leisure, dancing, music and parties – for some reason she did not 'take' on the marriage market. She ended up, to her family's and her own chagrin, on the shelf. It wasn't until all her friends were married with children that she caught the eye of a man everyone considered dashing and handsome. He was rich. He could offer a continuation of the life she had hitherto enjoyed. I heard the echo of *Jane Eyre*: 'Reader, I married him'. But the hero ignored all his wedding vows, so she decided to match his adventures with those of her own. But society was unfair: his affairs were peccadillos; hers sins. He was enraged. He hit her.

'So all the time I have this terrible ringing in my ears. It never stops. Ever. And I can hardly hear half the time. And my teeth hurt. And now my beauty and my fortune have all gone!'

At last he threatened to divorce her. With a final burst of spirit, she stowed as many valuables as she could into trunks and valises and fled the marital home to friends in Wales. They, however, disappointed her.

'They have turned Baptist! Puritan, in fact. No music. No drink. No fun. And then they turned round and told me that my place was with Hednesford. It was my duty to return and be a loyal and devoted wife. In short, they said, they did not want a scarlet woman in their home. My servants — my own servants — had already returned to what they still considered their home. So my *dearest* friends dispatched me with their servants.' She turned on me. 'And all the time you wanted me to be kind to them, to sit with them! With Olwen, who had spied on me — and who is no better than she ought to be. Carrying a bastard baby!'

I found I could say nothing.

Fortunately Burrows could. 'But why did they bring you here?'

'Ask them! The snow was coming down and I presume they just saw the gates open — you see how lax standards are! — and drove in. *She* knows the rest, she and her pious friends. Country ways! Dear God, they're worse than the damned Welsh Baptists!'

'There's no need for language!' Burrows snapped, genuinely offended — but perhaps more by the religious slur than by the accusations about me and my friends and colleagues. 'Now, your ladyship, what interests me now is what you have in those trunks of yours.'

She rose, crossing the room to put her hand on the top one. 'My property. It is all my property! Ask Hednesford. Under oath,' she added with a hiss.

'Lord Hednesford and I have already spoken,' he said. 'I

suppose the obvious thing would be to have the two of you together while we examine the contents.' For the first time he looked at me.

For the first time I spoke. 'The judgement of Solomon?'

He nodded. The situation was too fraught for a smile, but one was implied in that little gesture.

Lord Hednesford seemed to fill the room, but something had calmed him down – perhaps the presence of Montgomery Wilson beside him might have been a factor. His height now seemed less intimidating than imposing – but I had to remember what his wife had accused him of, and we had had evidence, of course, of her hearing difficulties. Why had I never asked her in a kindly way? Because, of course, she would have responded unkindly. Across the room, Matthew looked at me with concern – perhaps some of my emotions still showed in my face. Returning his smile, I fought for my usual composure. We were merely onlookers now, after all. The time for my resentful account of Burrows' interview might come later – or, if we could laugh together, might not come at all.

The two protagonists in the domestic drama squared up as Florrie, catching the keys flung at her, opened the first trunk. It was like watching two children diving into a toy box, both claiming the plaything in the other one's hand was theirs and that they wanted it, now.

At last Mr Wilson stepped forward. 'I have to end this unedifying spectacle now. It is clear that some of the contents are indeed items personal to Lady Stan . . . Lady *Hednesford* and I doubt if any judge would award them to her husband. But I venture to say, your ladyship, if this marital . . . discussion . . . does end in divorce by an Act of Parliament, a hugely expensive and scandalous affair, then the outcome will not be at all equitable. Unless you had a marriage settlement, your property is indeed your husband's. Might I suggest that you sit down and have a rational discussion, perhaps in the presence of a third party?'

'A lawyer such as you, no doubt!' she flung at him. 'Ready to make money at our expense.'

'I will not favour that imputation with the honour of a reply,' he said calmly.

Hednesford turned to me, his demeanour quite different, I was glad to see. 'Mrs Rowsley, I misunderstood the situation when I spoke in such haste earlier. I beg your pardon. Could you direct me to a local hostelry where I might bespeak accommodation?'

Before I could speak, Lady Hednesford said, 'No need for a hostelry, Hednesford. There's room here aplenty. It might be as cold as a tomb, but the cook is sound. Though you may find yourself escorting her into the dining room for the dinner she cooked.'

He looked blank.

'My lord, as your wife points out, there are rooms here which can be aired,' Harriet said coolly. 'And the cook is indeed excellent. But I must warn you that we do mix in ways that do not appeal to your wife and may not to you, so you might prefer to dine in your bedchamber.'

'Oh, he can share this. And we can eat a deux, can we not, George?'

I managed not to gasp aloud.

Mr Wilson raised an expressive eyebrow. 'My fellow trustees have excellent notions of hospitality, however.' He smiled at Matthew and me. 'Might I suggest, dear Mrs Rowsley, that while you have a room prepared for his lordship in case it is needed, he and her ladyship and I adjourn to a neutral room so that they can discuss their next moves. The breakfast room, perhaps? Unless it would incommode anyone? Sergeant Burrows, does that meet with your approval?'

The poor officer simply nodded.

Hednesford gave Montgomery a long, slow look, from head to toe and back again. 'As Lady Hednesford has just observed, there is no need for anyone to try to profit from our dispute.'

'My lord,' Matthew said, not even trying to disguise his asperity, 'you would not negotiate the fate of even a tenant farmer without legal advice. One would have thought the resolution of this current situation absolutely demanded the presence of a third party – someone neutral, sensible and discreet. I know Mr Wilson – who is the Croft family lawyer – to be all these things. In fact, knowing her ladyship's propensity for – shall we call it *extravagant* conduct? – I would hardly countenance any sort of discussion without someone there to keep watch. I will ask the butler to serve tea there in ten minutes.'

'We gather in the drawing room for sherry at six thirty,' I added. 'I am sure that Mr Wilson will be happy to clarify the details of life here. Thatcher will await you at the door to the Family wing.'

THIRTY-ONE

Matthew

Accompanied by a silent Burrows, we were heading downstairs to the sanctuary of my office. Much as I wanted to hear all about what my pale and shaking wife had endured, I had to say, 'My dear, Mr Hodge is trying to catch your eye.'

Indeed, the valet looked anxious and unhappy as he hovered in the corridor that housed our guests, only approaching in response to her smile of acknowledgement. Burrows and I moved away, but I certainly would not go down without her. I did not want more tasks inflicted upon her until she had had time at least to draw breath.

'Poor Hodge,' she murmured as she rejoined us. 'Unrequited love, I fear. But . . .' She led the way downstairs and along the back corridor towards my office. 'He is sweet on Florrie. Wants to walk out with her – quite literally, a romantic walk in the snow. But she has rebuffed him. And he is concerned about the manner of her refusal.'

'The manner? Not the refusal itself?' I repeated. 'She has hurt his pride, to be sure.'

'I thought so too, but something he said to me earlier implied that she had truly won his heart. A young woman does not usually burst into tears and take to her heels when an eligible male expresses his admiration. Truly her ladyship's death has hit her harder than I would have expected. That nightmare, Matthew! Poor child – I really believe we should ask Ellis Page to speak to her and offer her help.' Even as I made the suggestion, a tiny germ of niggling doubt sprang up. If only I might physically dash it aside.

Burrows coughed, as if to remind us of his presence. 'Were you serious, ma'am, when you offered her ladyship a haven here if she did not wish to travel with her husband? If so, I think you need to limit her stay to a week, at most. She is a wilful, destructive woman, and even if her bad behaviour springs from unhappiness, she cannot be allowed to regard this as her home. I would not like her to speak to my wife as she spoke to you.'

'I am sure she does not want to stay. She was certainly eager to leave earlier – and the bonus is that as far as I could see she had purloined nothing from the House. But now, you know, I actually think she wants to be reunited with him, absurd as that seems in the face of the violence she says he has inflicted on her. But we should adjourn to Matthew's office for a conversation like this.' She stopped. 'I must speak to Florrie. I will order tea and join you as soon as I may.'

But it seemed she could not do so immediately. George, looking anxious to the point of hang-dog, was lurking outside it. Had he been outdoors, his cap would have been in his hands.

'Ma'am, might I have a moment of your time? And yours, gaffer?'

Matthew grinned at Burrows. 'You're a dab hand with a fire, sergeant. Can you deal with it?' As the sergeant closed the door – almost – George coughed.

'It's about the picture and its frame, I gather,' he said, Matthew prompting him.

'Ah. Well, the mistress said the truth ought to be told, lest someone else be blamed. So while I was up in the Family wing, I took my chance, see. Had a word.' He must have registered the anxiety in Matthew's face. 'No, don't worry yourself, gaffer. I talked to Mr Bowman. He'll want to tell you himself, but his memory being what it is, I thought I'd reassure you – so long as you act surprised when he speaks to you.'

We nodded as one. 'What did he tell you?' I asked gently.

He jerked his head up the stairs. 'The young master – he had his wilder moments, didn't he? I mean, not as wild as now, but . . . well, you know what young men are. And it seemed he had a bet – ended with a big debt of honour, Mr Bowman says. So he took a picture from the attic. A filthy old thing. Took it out of its frame, and was ready to pawn it. Mr Bowman spotted him lowering it from a window – well, his lordship could scarcely have carried it down the main stairs, could he? Mr Bowman got the idea it would be noticed, so they got another one out of the attic and got me to put it into the original frame – only that was damaged, see, so I had to regild it. And then, blow me if the young master didn't put the pawn-shop money on a nag, instead of paying back the loan. And it came home fifty to one. So the picture's back in the attic – I can show you exactly where it is – and the debt got paid. Maybe . . .' he added with a rueful grin. 'That's what I was told, anyway.'

'Why on earth didn't you tell us? You weren't to blame!'

'It wasn't my story to tell. But all's well now that ends well, isn't it?'

'Of course. It's late now, and you ought to be getting on your way. But next time you're in the House we'd like to see the other picture.'

'So you shall.' He touched his forelock and went on his way.

Harriet was clearly torn – who mattered more, Florrie or Burrows?

'I will send the tea up immediately. But I must speak to the poor girl.' She was off like the wind – without ever once breaking into a run.

'Do you believe that cock and bull story?' Burrows demanded as I entered the office.

'For now, we have to. And Professor Fulke-Grosse will be able to give his opinion. However, we have other things to worry about: that fire, for instance. This has been a sad load of coal – all smoke and no heat. Ah! Here's Luke with the tea. Thank you.' He poured out and passed us our cups. There was cake, too, which distracted him for a few minutes. But if Harriet's talk to Florrie took much longer we would have to proceed without her. 'About this afternoon, Burrows . . . Ah, Harriet! There is still plenty of tea.'

She took a cup, but her face was still troubled. Whatever the problem, we would have to discuss it later.

'Mr Burrows was just about to tell me what happened this afternoon, but he hasn't quite finished his cake yet.'

She took the hint. Her succinct account, with occasional

contributions from Burrows, made me shiver. I was all too capable of acting with violence – she had been appalled once by my cold anger, and repelled by my violence to myself. What if I had ever touched her?

'How can a woman love a man who is so cruel?' she concluded.

I had no answer.

Burrows had. 'She can love his money,' he said. 'Now, if I might change the conversation, you will recall that I joined the servants for dinner – and very good it was too. I had occasion to mention that certain items had been reported missing, and it would be better for all concerned if they were returned forthwith. I happened to mention the penalties for theft. But there was no queue of servants waiting to confess, shall we say – though I suppose there might have been had I not been interrupted by this new lord's arrival.'

'Sergeant Burrows,' Harriet began slowly, as she did when her idea was not yet fully-formed, 'can we return to the Hednesfords for a moment? What if there is a tender reconciliation between them? Do you think they would linger here if there were? Or would they drive off as soon as they could?'

'Why do you ask, ma'am?'

'Because I would not trust her an inch.'

'We have a wonderful way of stopping her going anywhere, my love,' I ventured. 'We forget to open the safe. It takes two keys, after all.'

'And I can think of another way,' she said, her smile deepening. 'Sergeant Burrows, do you need to return to Shrewsbury tonight? Or would you care to enjoy our hospitality?'

'You mean catch them in the act?' He rubbed his hands. But his face fell. 'I don't know how to arrest a lord, ma'am. And I know they don't go to court like ordinary folk.'

'Not even if one of them has killed a servant?' I asked.

He looked so appalled I almost laughed. 'But she's a lady! Not a nice one, I'll admit. But lady all the same.' He frowned, then turned to Harriet. 'Ma'am, if it takes two keys to open your safe, and you are one of the keyholders, who is the other one? Mr Thatcher? If he was at the far end of the House, how long would it take you to summon him?'

'Not as long as it would take to summon Elias Pritchard, sadly. Who is surely far less equipped to arrest a lord.'

The sergeant was visibly torn. At last his face cleared. 'You have a very decent inn here, do you not? I might just bespeak a room there. Then I can come here if necessary.'

'Thank you. And when you do come, sergeant, you will remember your promise to show me Mary's keys, won't you?' Her smile was more dazzling than anything Lady Hednesford could have given.

'Hm.' You could almost see his brain working. 'Didn't her ladyship say your gatekeeper had left the gates open during the blizzard? Do you think you might order them to be kept locked?'

'Just in case,' she agreed blandly, not daring, I suspect, to look at me.

At last in the privacy of our bedchamber, Harriet could ease off her boots and enjoy the tea Luke had brought up.

'Not an easy day,' I observed, as she collapsed on to the chair by the fire.

'Not at all. And my little talk with Florrie has left me puzzled. No, I didn't talk about her reluctance to walk out with Hodge. I talked about what she might want to do after the Hednesfords have gone. In particular, I said that I needed to train someone up as my deputy—'

'Ah! You admit you can't do everything!'

'I do, freely. Anyway, I said that I needed someone like her. It would mean her working closely with me, of course – but would be excellent for her future career.'

'And?'

'She said all that was polite – but there was no sign of enthusiasm in her voice, quite the reverse, and I would swear I saw panic – no, fear – in her eyes. I said everything I could to reassure her and to show her how much I trusted her – but in the end I had to suggest she could give me her reply tomorrow or even the day after. To insist on an immediate response would have been unkind. Matthew, I am really very worried about her.'

'Do you want to tell me? Or is it women's troubles?'

Before she could reply, there was a tap at the door. Hot water and a plate of cakes. I turned with an ironic shrug – only to find her already dozing.

After a very stilted gathering beforehand – even champagne failed to add any sparkle – dinner was again taken in the breakfast room, his lordship having the grace to offer his arm to Harriet. He installed her beside him as he took the head of the table, his wife sweeping to the foot, demanding Francis' attendance beside her.

It was all so civilized that we might all have spent the day in peaceful amity. Civilized on the surface, at least. I could see that much of Hednesford's conversation was not at all pleasing to Harriet, but, since I was seated towards the other end of the table, I was powerless to draw his fire. At last she quite deliberately turned away from him to speak to Timpson. Thus the professor was now forced into conversation with Bea, who claimed her only motive for attending was to watch this Blue Beard of a lord in the flesh. I now had Wilson as a partner. For the first time in our acquaintance, he looked terribly weary.

'With all due respect to all your usual valiant efforts at post-dinner conviviality, Matthew, I could wish that this wonderfully regulated household might run out of candles and that we should all be despatched to our chambers for an early night. Though tomorrow promises to be interesting. *The jewellery casket*,' he mouthed. 'And, of course, there will be speculation about where his lordship spends the night.'

'Of course. I think you should know that Burrows has made some precautionary moves.'

'Ah! The gates? Excellent. My opinion, for what it is worth, is that they will leave together and continue this unseemly marital battle for years to come. Which,' he added with an impish smile, 'could make some of my colleagues very happy. No, not me, I assure you. I do not understand the premise on which they base their lives. Their philosophy. Do not accuse me of class prejudice. Look at Francis: as decent a human being as you would wish to meet. His late lordship – a gentleman in every sense of the word. But they . . . they defeat me.'

We withdrew. We had music. We had readings. We had a great deal of ennui.

And finally Lady Hednesford declared she was dropping with fatigue. 'Ah! Mrs Rowsley! Perhaps I might trouble you for my jewellery, now I have Hednesford to protect it.'

'Alas,' Harriet said quietly, 'as you know, Mr Thatcher holds the other key, and he has already retired for the night.'

There was the tiniest of noises from outside the door. No doubt Thatcher was taking the hint.

THIRTY-TWO

Harriet

I was going to the Room, still chatting with the staff who were breakfasting, when one of the outdoor lads came bustling up with a package. 'Please, ma'am, these are for you, ma'am. From Sergeant Burrows. Mary's keys, ma'am.'

I knew from the weight that there was something wrong, but tried to keep my voice normal. 'Thank you, Robin. Now, it's very early – have you had breakfast? Yes? Well, would you like some more? Sit yourself down.'

Once in the room, one glance told me that only two of Mary's many keys remained. Someone had removed the others, and was almost certainly using them. I must talk to Burrows urgently. I wrote a note and sealed it.

As soon as he had finished that enormous bowl of porridge, Robin must be on his way again.

'There's no need for all this palaver,' his lordship declared, gesturing at the breakfast table. 'My wife and I will leave now. Be so good as to have my carriage brought round and despatch my servants up here to carry our luggage down. Oh, and I see your butler is awake,' he added with a sneer. 'He may put her ladyship's jewellery straight into my barouche.'

'One moment,' I said. I caught Matthew's eye, imploring his silence. 'This has to be said: if her ladyship is disinclined to return to your marital home, then she may stay here – with Constable Pritchard's protection if necessary. And of course,' I added, aware I was about to create more than gentle ripples with my next statement, 'she will in any case need his permission to leave. A murder has been committed in this House. Until the culprit has been arrested, we are all suspects. All of us. And without the express permission of the police, none of us,' I concluded as I took my place at the table, 'may leave. None.'

'Do not mock me!' Hednesford did not sit.

'I do not mock anyone, sir.'

Thatcher coughed. 'Sergeant Burrows, ma'am.'

Thank God he was here. And at least he now knew my concerns about the keys. Perhaps he had dealt with them already?

The sergeant entered, bowing low, yet dignified as he straightened and stood tall. 'Anyone wishing to leave here,' he said, sounding as if he had conned his speech by heart, 'may do so.'

Had he been a child, Hednesford would have stuck his tongue out at me.

'Provided that,' Burrows said, 'he or she – or they, of course – furnish me with evidence of their permanent abode. Credible evidence, your ladyship,' he said, bravely nodding at her. 'Not a tissue of lies and half-truths. And furthermore, given other unlawful activity in the House, any person desirous of leaving must submit their luggage for a search by me or my constable, who will be here within the half hour. Trunks, valises and any other receptacle, including reticules and jewel boxes,' he added meaningfully.

Hednesford took two steps towards him. 'Do you not know who I am?'

'I believe you are Lord Hednesford of Darlaston Park. But I believed your wife was Lady Stanton of somewhere in Yorkshire. The constabulary have to deal in evidence, your lordship, and I need evidence. I also need evidence that nothing is leaving this House that should stay.' By now he was brick red and sweating profusely but he held firm. 'So, at your convenience, please provide me with said evidence.' He bowed and, helping himself to ham, sat down next to Matthew.

It cannot be said that his intervention improved the morning conversation. As the original bearer of bad news I was particularly unpopular, with comments directed at, rather than to, me. But I had dealt with rudeness before, and in my own time would finish my meal. Then – I leapt to my feet.

'What in Hades is that?' Hednesford demanded, as if the loud tolling were a personal insult.

'It's the House alarm bell!' Soon it would be echoed by

those in the gatehouse, in the home-farm yard, and even in the village. 'Please excuse me! Sergeant, Matthew!'

We got no further than the corridor. Thatcher ran towards us, his face in agony. 'Ma'am. Florrie's missing. And there are footprints leading to the lake! Elias is there!'

'Send someone for Dr Page and someone to alert Nurse Webb.' Though of course they would hear the alarm, of course, wouldn't they? I turned to the others. 'The main entrance is quickest!'

As one, we turned and ran.

Hodge, dripping wet, was struggling to escape the hold of Elias and two estate burly men. He was crying out, reaching towards the lake, where the cracks and hole told their own tragic story. Dared we hope it was a false one? Already men were racing across the grass carrying skiffs and pleasure boats. Someone was hitting the ice as hard as he could with a long pole. Another came with nets, boat hooks and lifebelts, never used before but always at hand for a boating accident. Someone called for ladders and crawling boards. Behind us, a crowd of staff was gathering. One or two broke into hysterical tears, but were quickly silenced. This became a tragedy silent but for the shouts and instructions of the onlookers.

Ellis arrived, to my amazement with Mr Pounceman as his passenger. His prayers floated above the other words.

At last – how long was it? – a shout announced success, of a sort. At risk of falling in themselves, half a dozen men grappled a woman's form on to a punt. Now we were quiet enough to hear the lapping of water on the boat, the occasional knocking of ice on the wood. And we all knew the worst.

Or nearly the worst. What we did not know till Ellis had given her a preliminary examination was that she had stones in her pockets. He broke the news to us all, including Hodge, in the servants' hall. She was weighed down with stones and an agate paperweight, and ornaments of no value except that they had once belonged to her ladyship. She had not wanted to emerge from the lake.

One of the maids handed me a note she had found under

Florrie's pillow. In her best copperplate hand, learnt in the Room, Florrie declared that she had meant to end her life. How could I read it aloud? But I must.

Dear Mrs Rowsley

I am sorry to put everyone to more trouble.

Why did no one care when her ladyship died? Why would you not let us go to the church to bid her farewell? I loved her. No one else seems to have done. Why did you bring that Lady Stanton to swan round in her ladyship's suite? I hated every minute with her, trying to smile and be nice.

I needed to keep something of her ladyship's, because I had nothing, and I am sorry to have inconvenienced you. I am sorry about Mr Rowsley's stud. It is in my ribbon box. I really wanted something that she had worn – so I had to try to open her jewel casket. But then you were kind and gave me more treasures, and I could not bear it. I did not deserve you to promote me, not after all I had told Olwen about your taking her ladyship's things. How could I be your deputy with all this on my conscience? No one knew what I had done. No one even seemed to guess.

Now you have the keys you will know about Mary. I am sorry. I didn't mean to hurt her. But she swore she would tell. So I shook her, to shut her up. Then she wriggled free and she fell. I promise I only wanted to scare her. I wish I had confessed, but I knew they could not let me off, and a hanging would have brought disgrace on the House and on the Family. I had to have the keys so I could save her ladyship's things.

I hope I have not damaged Mr Rowsley's paperweight. Maybe the lake will give it a good clean.

Goodbye from your unfortunate employee.

I remain yours sincerely,

Florence Murdock

Then there was a pitiful little list of her possessions, with the names of those who should have them. She even left me her ladyship's nightdress case, to thank me for my kindness to her!

Kindness! When I'd failed to add up all her little unhappinesses to make the sum of her huge agony.

'I really do not think I can bear to bother with the Hednesfords now,' I said, putting down the brandy glass untouched.

'They won't leave till they get their jewellery,' Matthew pointed out. 'And seeing you pull yourself together will help the others.'

'Is someone looking after Mr Hodge?'

'The professor. And Parker. They are with him in the Family wing. Pounceman is offering to lead prayers in the servants' hall, if you and Thatcher think it a good idea. Meanwhile, he is reading to Samuel. Ah, here is Thatcher now!'

The young man's calm demeanour was at odds with the tear stains on his cheeks. 'Sir, ma'am, Sergeant Burrows requests that we open the safe and take the Hednesfords' jewels to the breakfast room, which I have just had cleared.'

'Thank you, Dick. Dear me, this is such a bad day, is it not?'

'It will be better without the Hednesfords, if you will permit me to say so. But Sergeant Burrows wants us to be with him while his lordship and her ladyship look at the contents. And I agree, if I may make so bold. We do not want rumours and whispers to circulate about our honesty, do we?' It might have been a man of fifty speaking, such was his gravitas.

'Indeed we do not. Equally, one would not want to see any of her late ladyship's treasures on Lady Hednesford's person.' I stood, making an effort to straighten my shoulders. I could deal with my grief when I did not have to support others' spirits.

I rather expected to find Mr Wilson in the breakfast room, but was disconcerted to find Mr Pounceman arriving as I did.

'It seemed to me right to have an independent witness in the case of any disputes,' Sergeant Burrows declared, as Elias stepped from the room as quietly as his boots would let him. 'Mr Wilson will take an inventory to be signed by the relevant parties. I am sorry to ask you to attend, Mrs Rowsley, given the terrible shock you have just had, but I think it's for the best.'

'I'm sure it is,' I heard myself saying.

'Damned sure,' Matthew agreed, breathing, 'George' incomprehensibly into my ear. He continued, 'If I may, Sergeant Burrows, I would like to know what arrangements Lord and Lady Hednesford are making for the return of their friends' servants to Wales.'

Although he was obviously displeased to have his moment of drama postponed, Burrows said, 'It seems a fair enough question, my lord.'

'How did they come? They can return the same way, I presume.'

'Both men are still very unwell, according to Nurse Webb. They may have to remain here until the summer.'

'So let them stay. If our puritanical friends want them back earlier they will have to make arrangements. Now, it is time we left,' his lordship said. 'Enough of this charade. Just give my wife her jewels and load her luggage on to my carriage.'

For some extraordinary reason, Burrows embarked on a comparison between private coach travel on appalling roads and the swifter railway system. Matthew was swift to join in, as was Mr Wilson, a real railway enthusiast. In Lady Hednesford's situation I would have wanted to scream. But at long last, the jewellery casket was opened and its contents spread on the green baize covering the table. The contents were very fine indeed. But there was nothing familiar at all, except the way the diligent lawyer listed each item, asking her ladyship to initial it to show she had received it.

'There! Now we may go!'

'Of course – but Elias seems to be carrying something, your ladyship.'

Then she said, with her tinkling laugh, 'Oh! The little girl with a bird. It hung in the bedchamber, Hednesford – do you recall it?' Her smile implied that her husband was far too preoccupied with other female matters to worry about a picture.

He shrugged. But clearly he recognized it as the work of a master. 'Why have you brought this here?' he asked.

'Because it might have been the last time it appeared in the House,' Elias said. 'It was in one of your trunks, your ladyship.'

'No! No! How could it?' Surely her disbelief was genuine. 'How could it?' she repeated, as the implications dawned on her.

It had taken Lord Hednesford some time to work out his response, but here it came. 'More to the point is why some jackanapes saw fit to open my wife's property. It is an outrage.'

Matthew nodded reasonably. 'Of course. But so is the removal of one of the Family paintings.'

'I swear – why would I do anything like that? Mr Rowsley, you are a fair man – would I be capable of it? Mrs Rowsley?'

'I don't know,' I said as calmly as I could. 'I hope not. Tell me, how did you fare with Florrie? Your acting maid?'

'Why should you ask? A maid is a maid.'

I thought of Olwen and the anger Matthew had seen in her face. I thought of Florrie's admiration of her ladyship – heroine-worship, as Mr Carlyle might have described it. I thought, most of all, of the poor guilty corpse. But now was not the time for a philosophical discussion of the nature of love and hatred. 'Did she behave herself? Obey instructions willingly?'

'Oh! You want a reference for her?'

'Ma'am, I am simply wondering if she . . . liked . . . you, for want of a better way of putting it.' Was it possible that one of her last acts was to implicate a woman she loathed in a crime? Heavens, I loathed her too, but I didn't want her to suffer for something she did not do. 'Lord Hednesford, when you and your wife argued over the contents of your trunks, did you find any pictures or other valuables that you did not recognize? That might have come from your Welsh friends' home?'

'Why should I? She'd put in enough of mine not to worry about—'

'Mine! Inherited from my father! They were part of my marriage settlement, that you, my lord, agreed to!'

Mr Wilson raised a dry index finger. 'As I have said before, the ownership can be discussed between your respective lawyers, should this come to a divorce, which I hope and pray it does not. But for now, you both agree that all the items therein came from your joint homes. Excellent. Pray proceed, Mrs Rowsley – I suspect you are going to do something that must go against the grain.' He smiled ironically.

'I am. Lady Hednesford, I have no reason to like you, and every reason to love the person I believe perpetrated what I will call for a moment this trick. But I will say that I believe that you did not know the Dürer was in your possession. I think an unhappy young woman might have tried to make you look guilty of a crime you did not commit.' I turned to Mr Wilson and then to Sergeant Burrows. 'Would you have any objection, gentlemen, if our guests went on their way?' Every last one of them, I added under my breath.

THIRTY-THREE

Matthew

The thaw brought two inquests and two funerals.
The verdicts of the former were foregone conclusions. The latter could not have been more different.
It was agreed that we should hold Florrie's first: I believed that planning it would help Harriet deal with her almost overwhelming guilt. She believed that had she understood the depths of the girl's grief for her ladyship she might have dealt better with the situation. In vain did Bea and I remind her that as far as we knew her ladyship had done nothing to endear herself to any maid, indeed descending to physical violence towards Florrie herself as her last illness took hold. All the young women had been in dutiful rather than personal mourning, and there was no way of knowing that Florrie was any different.

We had to accept that Florrie would not – could not – be buried in the hallowed ground of the churchyard, and that there could be no formal funeral service. Even that most liberal of clergymen, my dear papa, told us that. So we had to find a site that would not affront society but would not involve her being buried in quicklime: we chose a dell in a remote part of the estate's woodland. The only servant who wanted to be involved in her interment was Fulke-Grosse's man, Hodge, who accepted with reluctance that a rough coffin carried on a farm cart was the best we dared do.

It was a most beautiful spring day, warm and loud with birdsong. George, who had made the coffin, offered to drive. He, Francis, the professor and I walked behind the cart to the open grave, where I knew that Harriet would be waiting.

We lowered the coffin with respect. To my astonishment Francis stepped forward to offer a prayer he said the Romans used in such circumstances. He did not offer to translate it. Hodge threw in the first handful of earth, and then seized one of the shovels to add the rest. Together we relaid the mossy turf.

Harriet said, 'I understand that we must not mark the poor girl's grave, but I thought you might like to plant this.' She handed Hodge a root of snowdrops and a trowel, motioning us all to stand back while he knelt, and then gathering him to her as he sobbed.

At last, Hodge supported by Harriet as if he were her brother, it was time to return to the House. George offered me a lift. 'That coffin,' he said at last, 'was supposed to be rough and crude. But I couldn't do it to her, gaffer. So I lined it with a bit of cloth the missus found for me, and popped some rosemary in too. Struck me you've got to be very troubled in your spirit to do what she did.' He spat, and said no more.

On another beautiful day, Pounceman, still relying on his impressive walking stick, conducted Mary's service, with more gentleness than I could have expected. Of course only male voices were raised in the psalms and hymns. The grave was pitifully small. The estate would pay for a suitable headstone. Until then, only a sad wreath could commemorate her.

But as we turned to walk back to the House, the graveyard suddenly filled – it was as if a flock of black doves descended! All the House womenfolk were there, nurses, cooks, washerwomen and dairymaids. Bea and Harriet hung back until they had all laid the posies they had carried under their shawls or cloaks before laying their own bouquets.

I was grateful that Hodge was not there. He was busy packing the last of the professor's things before their departure after lunch: they would return as soon as possible with a small team of skilled restorers and, assuming the weather made possible work on the Roman remains, by Francis. As for John Timpson, also one of their party, a telegraph to the Cambridge professor with whom he had been corresponding resulted in a post at the Parker Library, where he would, under supervision, work on the manuscripts he so loved. Would he ever come back to us, to complete the work he had started? I did not know. Meanwhile, I had recruited a promising young man who had been working on the Blenheim estate to be my clerk and, with his experience, effectively my deputy. He had the express approval of Wilson, who was returning to Shrewsbury on an early afternoon train.

With the last farewell wave to all the men heading for the station, the servants could hold their wake. If it turned into a party, so be it. Bea had plans for a walk in the grounds – on her own or in company she did not disclose.

Harriet and I had an engagement too. Not perhaps the one I would have chosen, but one we felt we must keep. Mr Pounceman had invited us to take afternoon tea with him – and we ought to grasp the olive branch.

As is the way of these things, we spoke at first of everything and nothing. But then he put down his cup, a clear prelude to a meaningful remark. 'During this morning's service, Harriet, I felt what you must have been feeling at the time, that none of the people who knew poor Mary best could say their fare-wells in an appropriate way.'

Accepting the sudden use of her Christian name, she smiled. 'I was indeed.'

'So I was wondering if you could find in the House an appropriate place to hold what I might term a service of commemoration for the child. An attenuated version of the funeral service. Some accessible readings. The shortest of sermons. Some hymns to rouse the spirits.' He hesitated like a rider about to tackle a big fence. 'We have spoken about opening up the chapel, have we not?' Without enthusiasm on our side, to be truthful, but neither of us spoke. 'Would not this be the ideal moment? Now all your guests have departed, cleaning it would give all your staff something to focus on. And though it would not be hallowed, it would be a suitable place for such a sombre moment.'

And so it was agreed, with smiles and pleasantries all round. Harriet was probably grinding her teeth at the thought of the chaos.

As we left the rectory, we sighed in unison. So much for the period of quiet we both needed, Harriet especially: she had only got through the past days by cleaving absolutely to her duty. And I had made plans how she might, for once, rest and be waited on. This might well scupper the lot.

'You have had so much to worry about, my love,' I began, 'that I too started to have ideas. We have had no time alone since our wedding journey. Now spring is here – yes! Can you hear that skylark? – the moment this damned memorial service is over, we are to have a holiday. We are to travel to France. Or Italy. Or anywhere no one knows us and no one needs us. Where shall we go?'

Like a joyous child, she skipped with pleasure. 'Oh, Matthew – anywhere! Let us have a quiet supper tête-à-tête tonight and discuss it all!'

'Absolutely!'

As I turned to kiss her, I heard the sound of hooves.

'Good day!' It was Ellis Page, bringing his horse to a halt and raising his hat to Harriet. 'Dear me, Matthew, when Marty made that quip about one funeral bringing on another, I never thought it would be so prescient. Not just Mary's . . . I'm afraid the old Welsh coachman may not last the day. Bea has told me that she has plenty left over after your visitors, so I will see you later! Be careful,' he added. 'Some of the lanes are very slippery.'

We waved bravely. I swore under my breath. I believe she did too.

'But he is a dear good friend,' she said. 'We can wait a little longer.'

'Can you? There's something I want to do straightaway.'

'Is there indeed?' Dimpling, she tucked her arm into mine. But then she withdrew it. 'Marty!'

The innkeeper pumped our hands enthusiastically. 'I'm so glad I caught you. I've got some really good news! Now the canals are thawing, the narrowboats are moving again. The Stride family will be coming this way – yes, with little Lizzie, of course. So at last his lordship will be able to meet his daughter. I'll come up tomorrow morning, and we can decide how best to arrange it. How are your plans for putting running water into the House? I have a friend who might just be able to advise you . . .'